PRAISE FOR THE PURPLE

"A.D. Lawrence has built a tantalizing deb⟨u⟩ setting that is devious and sinister at its core. ⟨I⟩ ⟨...⟩ by the romantic elements of the story, and believe readers who ⟨...⟩ mystery that couples superbly with a cup of coffee will be pleased with this latest release!"

–Jaime Jo Wright, author of *The Haunting at Bonaventure Circus* and Christy Award–winning, *The House on Foster Hill*

"*The Purple Nightgown* draws us into a web of misplaced trust, tangled missteps, rolling remembrance and regret, and loyalties old and new in a taut telling of true history of greed satisfied by preying on the vulnerabilities of those who suffer. With convincing presentation of medical conditions and relatable characters who grow through their circumstances, author A. D. Lawrence crafts a well-paced story that takes us to a satisfying ending."

–Olivia Newport, author of the Tree of Life series

"Beware! Once you start reading *The Purple Nightgown*, you won't be able to put it down! Lawrence drew me in from the first page and kept me reading until the very end. If you like true crime fiction, you will love reading the story of Stella and Henry!"

–Kathleen Y'Barbo, author of *The Black Midnight*, *The Chisholm Trail Bride*, and *The Alamo Bride*

"Truth often is stranger than fiction, but the combination in *The Purple Nightgown* is positively compelling. From the get-go, I had a hard time putting this story down. Author A.D. Lawrence spins a heartbreaking tale of desperation and, ultimately, hope. This is one story that will stick with you long after you've read the last page."

–Michelle Griep, Christy Award–winning author of Once Upon a Dickens Christmas series

the PURPLE NIGHTGOWN

A.D. LAWRENCE

BARBOUR
PUBLISHING

The Purple Nightgown
© 2021 by A. D. Lawrence

Print ISBN 978-1-64352-892-2

eBook Editions:
Adobe Digital Edition (.epub) 978-1-64352-894-6
Kindle and MobiPocket Edition (.prc) 978-1-64352-893-9

All scripture quotations, unless otherwise noted, are taken from the King James Version of the Bible.

This book is a work of fiction. Names, characters, places, and incidents are either products of the author's imagination or used fictitiously. Any similarity to actual people, organizations, and/or events is purely coincidental.

Cover Image: Magdalena Russocka / Trevillion Images

Published by Barbour Publishing, Inc., 1810 Barbour Drive, Uhrichsville, Ohio 44683, www.barbourbooks.com

Our mission is to inspire the world with the life-changing message of the Bible.

Member of the
Evangelical Christian
Publishers Association

Printed in the United States of America.

Chapter One

May 1911

H ow's your headache, Miss Stella?"
Stella Burke glanced up at Jane from her position on the blanketed ground and forced a smile. "A little better." Her companion didn't need to know how little. Stella slipped a ribbon between the pages of her book then let her fingers trace the title. *Fasting for the Cure of Disease.* While the author's methods may have been a little unorthodox, Linda Hazzard's patients were lauding her as a miracle worker. And Stella desperately needed a miracle.

The sun's rays reflected off the Pacific Ocean's rippling water, intensifying the pain behind Stella's eyes. Swirling starbursts danced at the corners of her vision. Not again. Tears prickled her throat.

"You're a terrible liar." Jane's Scottish brogue lilted the words. She tucked the lap blanket tighter around Stella's legs with aged hands. "You've got another one starting, don't you?"

Stella nodded, rubbing her temples.

Dr. Wagner had promised the sea air would cure this pain in her head, but she'd spent the past three months on Rodeo Beach in Northern California and nothing had changed. Gulls hopped along the sand, screeching. Children whooped and hollered. Each shout punctuated the throbbing. "I need to lie down."

"That's probably wise. Let's get you home." Jane stowed Stella's book in the wicker picnic basket at her feet then shook the sand from the blanket. An envelope fell to the ground.

Stella reached for it, but a stiff breeze sent it tumbling across the beach. She scrambled for the letter as it blew toward her automobile and waiting driver, but her blurred vision worked against her. Still, she couldn't lose that letter.

"I've got it." The driver ran onto the beach, the bill of his cap catching the sunlight.

The mere sight of Henry coaxed a smile. Though he'd grown up on the outside, he was the same thoughtful mischief-maker he'd been when they were children. Memories of the pranks she and Henry used to play on the cook, Mrs. Priory, sprang to mind. How red the old woman had turned when they'd switched the salt for sugar in her pottery bowl on the counter. And the look on Mama's face when the fish had tasted sweet as taffy. Of course, Stella had to copy the book of Revelation twice as punishment, and Henry had trouble sitting for a week afterward, but it had been worth it.

Henry jogged toward her, envelope extended. "Here you go, Miss Burke."

She took the letter from his gloved hand. "It's Stella. We've been through this, Clayton." She paid him back with the name formality dictated she use.

"That wouldn't be proper."

She met his gaze, catching his lopsided smile with what little vision her eyes afforded. He'd maintain an air of propriety as long as Jane was present, but next time he took her for a drive along the coast, he'd drop the pretense. They'd be Henry and Stella again. Friends.

Tingling started in her left thumb and spread through her palm. Why did these headaches bring such odd symptoms? Dr. Wagner called them migraines, but whatever their proper name, relief seemed like a distant dream.

Stella stepped toward the motorcar. The numbness in her toes and the wind tugging her ankle-length skirt made trekking the beach a challenge. Henry offered his arm. She accepted. His wool jacket provided scratchy comfort beneath her fingers. He opened her door and helped her inside. The concern in his hazel eyes carved a hollow feeling within her. Jane climbed in beside her while Henry walked to the front and cranked the handle. The motor roared to life. When he slid into the driver's seat, he glanced over his shoulder and reached into the back seat, a violet between his fingers. "Saw this in front of the motor and thought you might like it."

Her favorite flower. Warmth spread through her chest, and for a moment the pain above her eyebrow dulled. "Thank you." She held the delicate blossom to her nose. The scent conjured summer memories of a simpler time. Times when she ran to Father for advice, and her only worries were remembering the spelling of *Mississippi* and caring for a litter of abandoned kittens in her bedroom without Mother's knowledge. She sighed. She didn't get headaches back then or have to consider marriage to wealthy men. Afternoons were for exploring the hillsides behind the house with Henry, playing pirates, and hunting for fairies.

When she was a child, all of Stella's plans for the future had included Henry, but after Papa died five years ago, Uncle Weston warned her against marrying a man without money and a title. Marrying beneath her station was out of the question.

Plenty of men with all the attributes her uncle required had requested her hand in marriage without so much as an intelligent conversation beforehand. How could they know they wanted to spend a lifetime with her without knowing the first thing about her? Not even simple things, like her favorite color. Or her favorite flower. No. She'd die an old maid before agreeing to marry some wealthy hobbledehoy who only showed interest to increase his fortune.

Henry drove the automobile onto the main road leading into San Francisco.

Stella closed her eyes, propped her elbow on the door, and rested her head in her hand. The tingling traveled up her arm and settled in her left cheek. When she opened her eyes, she caught Henry's reflection in the windscreen. He flashed her a smile and returned his gaze to the road.

Sinking into the leather seat, Stella let her eyelids droop while Jane prattled on about the fraying lace on her hankie.

The automobile screeched to a stop, and she forced her eyes to focus. Henry opened her door and stood at attention as she stepped onto the sidewalk at the entrance of the Burke estate. The swirling lights no longer blocked her vision, but nausea tickled her stomach. If she didn't get inside soon—

Henry's brow furrowed and he took her hand, breaking protocol. "Let me help you, Stella. You're pale."

Jane hurried ahead, giving orders to the butler and requesting one of the maids to "bring a cup of tea to Miss Stella's room."

Henry walked Stella to the door then patted her hand. "Get better." He leaned down. "I despise seeing you like this," he whispered in her ear. "Maybe we can go on a drive tomorrow."

Stella nodded, stomach in knots. She allowed Jane to usher her upstairs, help her change into her nightgown, and make a fuss tucking her between the cool sheets. The maid entered, teacup in hand. Stella thanked her and sipped the warm brew.

"I don't suppose you feel like eating?" Jane tested Stella's forehead with the back of her hand.

The thought of food swelled the churning inside her. Excerpts from the pages of Linda Hazzard's book sprang to mind. Hazzard believed fasting cured every ailment from toothaches to tuberculosis. Maybe her methods could put an end to these migraine headaches for good.

"No supper tonight, thank you." Stella chewed the inside of her cheek. "And please tell Cook I won't be eating tomorrow."

Jane clucked her tongue. "Are you sure that's wise? You must eat something or you'll waste away. You could stand a little fattening up as it is."

Stella pulled the coverlet to her chin with a sigh. "Dr. Hazzard recommends fasting in her book. It's good for the body, Jane. You should do it with me. Didn't you say your rheumatism has been festering?"

"That it has." Jane kneaded her lower back with a wrinkled hand. "But I like a good pot roast enough to endure it."

Stella cringed at the thought of pot roast and pulled the pillow over her splitting head.

Jane stepped out of the room, closing the door softly behind her.

The pain reached a crescendo, and Stella bit back a sob. The day was only half done, and she was already in bed. Earlier than yesterday. If something didn't change, life would pass her by, and she wouldn't be living. Just existing. The sea air hadn't helped, and she couldn't live like this a day longer. So many people who had followed Linda Hazzard's fasting plan found healing. Could fasting be the answer to her prayers? Besides, even if Dr. Hazzard's methods didn't help, her recommendations couldn't do any harm.

Chapter Two

Stella smoothed her purple skirt then adjusted the pin at her bodice while Jane wrestled her dark curls into a fashion that, if not pretty, was at least presentable.

"Your uncle Weston's invited a young man to dinner this evenin'." Jane lifted a jeweled comb from the dressing table then used it to pin up Stella's hair.

Not another one.

"I don't have to be there, do I?" When would her uncle realize she was destined for solitude and end his search for a husband? But the words from yesterday's letter surfaced, cracking the door of possibility. She might make a concession for a certain someone. If only he didn't insist on keeping his identity a secret.

Clicking her tongue, Jane shook her head. "You know very well you're to be there. He wants me taking extra care to make you pretty."

Stella's reflection in the mirror slumped her shoulders. She'd never been a beauty. Before Papa's death, she was the last girl asked to dance at parties and benefits. Of course, word of her inheritance had changed all that. But her headaches had worsened after losing him and stole what little bloom her cheeks once possessed. She studied her folded hands in her lap.

Why were men so shallow? If looks didn't attract them, money did. And it wasn't as if the men of her acquaintance were prize catches themselves. Not when they droned on about their horse's lineage or some man named Ty Cobb. Did none of them read? The world was changing. The English were building unsinkable ships. Scientists were

10

making great medical discoveries. But it seemed men were more interested in baseball than progress.

With her hair marginally tamed, Stella slipped into her shoes and paused for Jane to fasten the buttons. She'd rather forgo shoes altogether, but the dull edges of her headache would not withstand another of Uncle Weston's admonitions to "act like a lady." Her fingers brushed the silky coverlet on her bed. "Thank you, Jane."

"You're welcome, Miss Stella." Jane closed the buttonhook into a drawer. "Will you be wanting to take another trip to Rodeo Beach today?" She checked the gold timepiece fastened over her heart. The one Stella had given her three Christmases ago. "If we leave within the hour, we can get there before the crowd gets too heavy."

Stella toyed with her fingers, shaking her head. "I'd prefer a drive along the coast. Why don't you take the day off? Give your hip a rest and write your brother. You've talked about it for weeks, and I'm sure he would love to hear from you." A day with Henry would be a welcome relief. He didn't expect her to keep her shoes on or play the perfect lady.

Jane gave a slight nod. "If that's really what you be wanting."

Stella pulled open her bedroom door. The light spilling through the windows overlooking the street resurrected yesterday's throbbing. "Have Clayton bring the car around at ten o'clock sharp." She tightened her jaw. Skipping supper last night was the first step on the path to eradicating her beastly headaches once and for all. And a drive without Jane's incessant reminders of how to carry herself might be the second.

Jane curtsied. A wince pinched her eyes. Stella grasped her arm and helped her right her posture.

"Now, Jane, I remember having this conversation more than once. No more bowing. It makes me uncomfortable." She patted her maid's shoulder. "Besides, you've taken care of me since I was eight. You're family."

The old servant's eyes glistened. "I thank you for saying it, but if your uncle Weston—"

"Leave Uncle Weston to me. And have a wonderful day." Stella descended the curved staircase, hand grazing the balustrade.

The aroma of eggs and bacon sent her salivary glands into a tail-spin. Her stomach grumbled, but she pressed her hand against it, reminding herself that if Dr. Hazzard's claims were true, hunger pangs were a small price to pay.

Hartsell, the butler, pulled out her chair, and she sat opposite her uncle and the wall formed by his morning paper. He lowered the paper then shot her a smile as he turned the page. "Feeling better?"

She spread a napkin in her lap. "I am, thank you." She cleared her throat. "I have some business ideas to discuss. Is now a good time?"

Uncle Weston set his paper beside his breakfast plate. "Stella, darling, there's no need to—"

"I've given this a lot of thought." Stella straightened her shoulders. "And Father did leave the clothing business to me. Besides, I'd like to think I'm more of an authority on ladies' fashion than you are." She lifted a brow.

Her uncle conceded with a tilt of his chin. "I'd love to hear your ideas." He lifted his cup in Hartsell's direction, and the butler strode to his chair with the coffeepot.

Stella leaned forward, elbows on the table. A twitch of Uncle Weston's mustache reminded her to sit up straight, arms at her sides. "The women's clothing styles we manufacture limit our clientele. The dress samples I saw last week were so frivolous. I've never seen middle-class women wear such things, let alone the women in the Mission District."

Uncle Weston's cup clattered against the saucer, and his eyes widened. "And how would you know what women in the slums wear?"

Stella lifted her chin. "You can't shelter me from reality. And getting back to my ideas for the company, I believe we should provide a wider variety of styles at different price points. It feels silly to limit our outreach by catering to only one class."

"Your father named me as your advisor in matters involving Burke Clothiers until you turn twenty-five. The monthly business meeting is scheduled for Monday morning. I'll speak with the board on your behalf." He reached for his paper. "It's a good idea, but we'll need to discuss how beneficial it would be for the bottom line."

A smile tugged Stella's mouth. "I could go." She plucked her skirt's fabric. "I'll be twenty-five in a month, and it would be good practice to present the expansion idea myself. I'm capable of speaking on my own behalf."

"I've no doubt of that." The newspaper crinkled. "But wouldn't you rather spend tomorrow at the beach?"

"Not really."

"The company's in good hands. I'll present your ideas. No need for a young lady to involve herself in matters of business." The black-and-white barrier rose to hide his face.

Stella shook her head. That was the end of it? She trusted Uncle Weston, of course, but the yearning to play an active role in the company her father had built ached in her chest. Surely she could do more than select fabric swatches.

Hartsell stepped beside her with a sterling silver serving dish of scrambled eggs. Steam curled its tempting finger in the air, but Stella shook her head. "Just tea this morning, Hartsell, thank you."

The butler's eyes narrowed, his bushy black brows nearly blocking them from view. "This isn't another one of your wellness endeavors, is it, Miss Burke?" His rich voice wrapped her in an auditory embrace.

"What if it is?" She nudged the china cup painted with violets to the edge of the lace tablecloth.

His gaze softened. "Then I hope it helps." He poured tea into the cup with a smile.

"How's Greta feeling?" Stella waved away the cream and sugar Hartsell offered. His wife suffered from consumption, and the last news Stella received had been bleak.

Hartsell's smile faded. "Nothing to worry you about, miss." He cast a glance at Uncle Weston, who answered with a stern glare over his paper.

Stella's heart sank. An answer like the one Hartsell had given couldn't be the harbinger of good news. She rested her hand on the butler's then gave it a squeeze. "I haven't stopped praying."

His unsteady smile bespoke gratitude.

She pulled her shoulders back, sitting like the proper lady her uncle wished her to be while sipping her tea. The headline of her uncle's paper caught her gaze.

SUFFRAGETTES PUSH GOVERNOR JOHNSON FOR RIGHT TO VOTE

"May I see the front page if you're finished with it?" The right to vote. How wonderful that would be.

Uncle Weston lowered the printed pages full of happenings in parts of the world she might never see. His graying mustache twitched. "You don't want to be bothered with this boring folderol." He jerked his chin, indicating the latest issue of *Vogue*. "That might interest you." He returned to his paper.

Stella flipped through the fashion magazine, blood simmering. Why did he assume the latest styles would be more enticing than California giving women the right to vote? Perhaps she should join the suffragettes. She grinned. That would show him she was more than ribbons and bows. Her gaze caught on a hat modeled by a woman who shared her light complexion and dark eyes. How pretty. Her fingers traced the sweeping brim and the garland of roses. Maybe she didn't despise ribbons as much as she wanted to. She dog-eared the corner of the page for later inspection.

Hartsell cleared his throat, drawing her attention from the magazine. The butler held a silver tray bearing an envelope with familiar handwriting. Her chest fluttered as she took the letter. She checked the time on the grandfather clock in the corner. If she hurried, she could read the letter before meeting Henry for her drive.

"Please excuse me." She sprang out of her chair, tipping her teacup on the table. Her uncle glanced over the paper, his eyes a mixture of irritation and bewilderment. She'd never live up to his expectations. She grabbed her napkin off the floor where it had landed and began mopping up her spilled tea.

"Let Hartsell take care of the mess." Her uncle's voice was firm.

Stella righted her teacup, thankful it hadn't chipped. "It's no trouble."

Uncle Weston cleared his throat and pinned her with an unrelenting gaze that reminded her of her place. "You're a lady, and it's high time you started acting like one. I invited a young man to dinner tonight, and I expect you to be on your best behavior. Don't embarrass me." He shook the paper. "And Hartsell can clean up the tea."

Her cheeks warmed, and tears smarted her eyes.

She cast an apologetic glance at Hartsell, nearly bursting into tears at the sight of his knowing smile. He didn't mind her scattered ways like Uncle Weston did, and he'd never say such crushing words. Though she strived to please her uncle, somehow she always fell short.

Letter in hand, Stella climbed the staircase, the joy of reading its contents dashed. Still, she opened the drapes, flopped on the bed, and tore the envelope's seal. After Papa's funeral, a stranger had sent his condolences. She'd read his letter at her life's lowest point, and the genuine care and encouragement his words had provided left her a little less woebegone. After writing back her thanks, the correspondence between them had continued.

She slid her hand under her pillow and pulled out a crinkled envelope. Every letter he'd sent her since had contained a pressed flower. She shook the packet's contents onto the bed. Cherry blossoms, daisies, pansies, and violas. Their scent had long expired, but the simple, heartfelt gifts stirred longing in Stella's chest. The person who may be her best friend on earth never signed his name to the messages he sent. If his haphazard handwriting was any indication, the writer was a man. But that was all she could make out. She shook her head. What kind of ninny didn't even know the name of such a close friend?

When she pulled the folded paper from the envelope, a pressed violet dropped into her hand, its petals vibrant. God had really created something beautiful when He spoke violets into existence. The intricate purple channels, carved through a creamy center, pointed to the golden-yellow fuzz that held everything in place. She sighed and raised it to her nose. Her imagination provided the delicate scent of the flower Henry had given her yesterday at the beach. How had her unnamed friend known she'd need his words of encouragement today? But he always knew. His replies to her letters never failed to bring relief. How could he know they would coincide with her headaches and frustrations?

With violet in one hand and letter in the other, Stella rested her head on her pillow, reading the pointy, jagged handwriting she'd grown to love.

Henry could wait a few minutes.

Chapter Three

The steering wheel vibrated beneath Henry's fingers, and gravel crunched as he pulled the automobile to the mansion's front door. Relief loosened the muscles in his shoulders at the sight of the empty porch. Thank goodness he hadn't kept Stella waiting. He killed the motor, hopped out, and folded down the leather top of the 1911 Stanley Touring. She'd appreciate the freedom of the wind in her hair. Hopefully a headache wouldn't cut their time short again.

He polished off a smudge on the green paint with his sleeve. Never had he imagined driving a car like this. Although chauffeuring for a family of means hadn't been his dream, his plans would keep until Stella married and no longer needed him. After all the time they'd spent together, he couldn't leave her. Not yet.

But the image of Stella walking down the aisle to meet one of the jack-a-dandies her uncle introduced her to planted a sick feeling in his gut. They wouldn't appreciate her. Not like she deserved. As he tightened his fists, his leather gloves groaned. If only things could be different. But even if he saved for years, he'd never have enough money squirreled away to make her a tempting offer of marriage. Besides, he was nothing more than an employee in her eyes.

He checked his timepiece. It wasn't like her to be late. Perhaps she'd received his letter. A smile pulled at his mouth. She'd needed a friend after her father passed away, so he'd sent her a note, posing as an equal. Guilt stabbed him. He'd never planned on the letter exchange lasting so long. Just one note to assure her she wasn't alone. When she responded, he almost told her the truth, but the smile on her face and

17

the lifting of her spirits spurred him onward. Now the whole situation was like a runaway buggy. He'd tell her. . .one day.

The front door opened, and she stepped onto the porch, a basket in hand. Sunlight gleamed off the dark curls that peeked from beneath her hat. A breeze tugged at the pink roses and gauze adorning the brim. She flashed a brilliant smile.

His confession could wait.

"Feeling better?" He opened the automobile's door.

She paused before climbing in, smile growing. "Much better."

Was her excitement the result of his letter? He swallowed the tingling in his throat as he closed the door behind her.

"I'm so glad you put the top down." She fiddled with the finger of her glove. "It's a perfect day."

"That it is." He cranked the motor then slid behind the wheel. His coat pocket crinkled, and he pulled out the newspaper article he'd saved for her. "Thought you might be interested in this bit of news."

When he reached into the back seat to hand her the newspaper clipping, their gloved fingers brushed. His chest ached, but the lack of emotion on her face proved she didn't share the sensation.

She scanned the headline and bit back an excited grin. "Can you believe women might get the vote here in California? I'll be the first woman at the polls come election day."

"I'm sure you will be." He worked the clutch and accelerator until the motorcar lurched into action. Stella's hand on his shoulder froze him.

"Can we make a stop in the Mission District? Ethel just had a baby, and I have a gift for her."

His gut clenched. "I'm not sure your uncle would approve. If he finds out—"

"He won't." Stella adjusted the basket on the seat beside her.

Henry tipped his hat. "The Mission District it is."

❧

Stella reclined into the leather seat behind Henry, the article in her hands. Her swimming vision lingered, though the worst of her headache had faded. Reading the letter had further weakened her eyes. Maybe Henry would read the article to her when they stopped at the beach. She pulled off her elbow-length gloves and relished the cool May air on her skin. If only she could remove her shoes, but while taking them off posed no problem, the multitude of buttons made putting them on without a buttonhook nearly impossible.

The mansions of Nob Hill gave way to the tenement buildings of the Mission District. Children played hopscotch along the walkways, babies cried, and frazzled mothers did their best to console them. A crew worked on the cable for a trolley scheduled for operation later in the year.

Henry pulled to a stop at the front steps of Ethel's building. "I'll come along." He held open her door. "You shouldn't be alone in this part of town."

She'd been here many times since meeting Ethel at the soup kitchen where she volunteered. The woman had needed help preparing for her child's arrival, and over the last weeks, there hadn't been a hint of danger. Though Stella couldn't tell Uncle Weston for fear he'd make her give up the friendship, Ethel had impressed Stella with her sunny smile in the midst of gloomy circumstances. The woman was truly an inspiration. Pity Ethel's husband didn't value her as such. But it was just like Henry to worry. If something happened to Stella, Uncle Weston would have Henry's job. "If you insist on coming, you can carry the basket." She extended the gift, and he took it by the handle.

A dog yipped from somewhere down the sidewalk and children laughed and shouted. A red-haired boy ran across her path jabbing a rolling hoop with his stick, and she stepped aside to avoid a collision.

Henry grasped her elbow and helped her up the steps. "You're sure this is a good idea?"

Why was he being such a baby? "We're fine. Her door is on the left." Stella gestured with her hand. In the corridor, the mingled scent of sweat and rancid meat brought the familiar swirls at the corners of her eyes. When she glanced at her hand and wiggled her fingers, it was as if she watched someone else take charge of her movements. An infant's wails prodded the dormant ache behind her eyes. *Lord, please, not again.*

Why wasn't the fasting working? Though she'd barely started, shouldn't she notice some difference? The optical light show faded but left anxiety pricking her stomach. Nothing helped. It was only a matter of time before she'd need to curl up in bed with the drapes drawn and a pillow over her head.

Henry rapped on the door, and the screams from inside the apartment intensified. Stella squeezed her eyes closed, breathing deep and praying the pain would remain manageable.

The door swung open, and Ethel, baby crying against her shoulder, answered. The exhaustion in her blue eyes shamed Stella for focusing solely on her own struggles. At least when she was hurting she could go to her room and sleep undisturbed. Poor Ethel looked like she hadn't shut her eyes since the child's birth a week ago.

"Let me take him." Stella reached for the weeping bundle. The scent of sour milk clung to the pitiful little boy, and she swallowed the nausea building inside her.

Smiling, Ethel relinquished the baby, gratitude smoothing the lines under her eyes. "Thank you, Miss Burke. Stanley hasn't been home in two days. Says little Roger keeps him awake." She dabbed her eyes with the corner of her stained apron. "Keeps me awake too, but Stan doesn't care."

"I'm so sorry. I wish there was something I could do."

The baby's cries diminished to sniffles, and he drifted to sleep in Stella's arms.

"It's a blessing just to have you here, and little Roger must like you." Ethel smiled, but exhaustion killed the cheery expression.

Rocking the baby back and forth, Stella caught Henry's eye then glanced at the basket. He held it out to Ethel.

"We brought you a gift." Stella laid Roger in the bassinet in the corner, careful to make no sudden movements.

"You didn't have to do that, Miss B—"

"Stella." She smoothed Roger's downy hair. "Friends don't bother with formalities."

"I suppose not." Ethel wiped her hands on her bodice and took the basket from Henry. "But you really shouldn't have."

"I absolutely should have." Stella grinned as Ethel removed the basket's covering. "You just had a baby, so you should be spoiled."

Ethel pulled out a pair of blue knit baby booties, one remarkably bigger than the other.

"Jane tried teaching me to knit, but I'm not a very apt pupil." Stella eased into the chair beside the bassinet and rocked it with her foot. When she glanced at Henry, she found him gazing at her with an odd expression. A mixture of admiration and amusement reflected in his eyes. Her cheeks caught fire.

"They're perfect." Ethel caressed the uneven stitches as if she held the Holy Grail.

"The rest is for you." Excitement sizzled in Stella's nerves. Ethel worked hard. She deserved something pretty.

As Ethel pulled a pale pink dress with lace trim and a sash of dark pink silk from the basket, she gasped. "This is too much, Miss—Stella."

"Not at all." Stella shook her head. "It's actually part of an idea I had for my father's business. Serviceable, stylish clothes for everyone. But I'm afraid my uncle is a little narrow-minded when it comes to change. Let me know how you like it, or if there are flaws in my design. You're doing me a favor, really."

"You designed this?" Ethel's voice was little more than a croak.

Stella nodded. "But Jane sewed it for me. She's an angel. You'll tell me what changes I should make?"

"Don't change a thing." Ethel held the gown against her wiry frame. The pink brought out the color in her cheeks. "It's beautiful."

"You make it beautiful." Stella willed away the pricking in her eyes. "There's something else in there somewhere. I saved the best for last."

Ethel lifted a Hershey Bar from the basket, and a smile transformed her from a tired mother to a woman filled with delight. "How'd you know I've been wanting this?"

"What woman doesn't want chocolate?" Stella shrugged.

The door burst open and banged against the wall. Stanley stood in the doorway, reeking of spirits, his thin brown hair askew. Angry brows lowered over bloodshot eyes. "This place is a pigsty, woman." He covered the distance to Ethel in two steps. "I work all day. Least you can do is clean up." He shook his finger in his wife's face.

Tears filled Ethel's eyes, and she hung her head.

"You probably ain't cooked nothin' either." Stanley snatched the new dress off her lap and inspected it with a sneer. "This what you've been spending my money on?"

Stella sprang to her feet, head swimming with the sudden movement. "It was a gift from me." She lifted her chin, standing to her full height though she was at least a foot shorter than the burly man.

"What does she need this for?" He crumpled the gown and tossed it across the room.

Insufferable man. Stella balled her hands into fists. "Why are you such a bully? You leave her alone for two days with a crying baby then stomp back in here like an ogre when you get hungry? Do you have so little to control in your life that you feel better about yourself after taking it out on your poor wife?" She should let the matter drop, but frustration spurred her forward. "You know what kind of men treat their wives this way?" She jabbed a finger in his chest. "Small men."

Stanley scrubbed a beefy hand across his mouth. Anger flickered behind his eyes. "You can't talk to me like that." He raised a fist to strike her, and Stella's stomach dropped. "You filthy—"

In half a heartbeat, Henry landed a punch to the drunken man's jaw. Bone cracked and Ethel's husband buckled to the floor. Roger fussed, and his mother hurried to the bassinet and lifted him out, cooing soothing words.

Stella's breathing came in short gasps. That horrible man would have hurt her if Henry hadn't—

She glanced at her chauffeur, who rubbed his fist and drew in a sharp breath.

Stanley stirred, groaning and muttering profanities.

"You'd best leave, Miss Stella." Ethel bounced her wailing child, her eyes glossy with unshed tears.

Guilt weighted Stella's chest. Had she just made an already unpleasant life more difficult for her friend? When would she learn to keep her opinions to herself? "I'm sorry, Ethel, I—"

"The old fool had it coming." The ghost of a smile worked the corners of Ethel's mouth. "He's tipsy. Won't remember a thing. But you'd best not be here when he comes 'round."

Stella nodded and followed Henry to the door. With a final wave to her friend, she stepped into the hall.

Henry adjusted his coat. "And my worries for your safety were unfounded?" Though his tone was stern, the gleam in his eye lightened her concern.

"If only I'd kept my big mouth shut." She stepped into the sunshine, head hammering, then pulled open the automobile's door and climbed in.

Henry groaned, jogging up beside her, gripping the door. "You're putting me out of a job." He closed the door, and Stella rested her hand on his.

"I can't seem to get anything right today." She squeezed his hand. When he winced, her gut twisted. "You're hurt. Let me see." She pulled off his glove. A growing purple lump across his knuckles brought a sting to her eyes. *This is all my fault. I caused this.*

"It's fine." He jerked his hand away, moved to the front of the automobile, then turned the crank.

Gasoline fumes burned Stella's nose as the incident in Ethel's apartment flashed. Henry had defended her, much like the heroes in the novels she read. Her heart warmed.

He rounded the automobile and slid into the driver's seat. When he rested his hands on the wheel, one gloved and the other bare, his jaw hardened.

Stella tapped his shoulder. He turned. Their gazes met, and the familiar ache settled in her chest. What did society or her uncle's opinion matter? Henry was a good man. Always kind and thoughtful. And smart. And weren't those the things that really mattered? No doubt he could go places if he left her family's employ. But the thought of losing him left her hollow.

Henry cleared his throat.

She shook the daydream loose from her brain and held his glove between them. "Would you like your glove back?"

A boyish smile tipped his lips. "Thanks." He slipped on the glove then prompted the auto into motion.

That smile always dispelled her doubts. Made her feel anything was possible.

Stella sighed and slumped against the seat. Her reflection in the windscreen clipped the budding hope in her chest. Henry would never see her as more than a friend, although her money might draw him as it drew Uncle Weston's wealthy acquaintances. How she hated the fortune her father had left. When people viewed her, they saw nothing but a dollar sign.

Had the fact that her uncle signed his paycheck been Henry's inducement to come to her rescue? Oh well, in one month, she would be free to do as she pleased with her inheritance. Even give it away and live a normal life. If the stress Uncle Weston complained of was any indication, money brought nothing but grief. It was a luxury she'd happily relinquish. She'd likely lose many in her circle of friends, but the people who remained would be the sort she needed in her life. True friends.

A flash of blue caught her eye. What on earth? "Stop the car, Henry."

The tires screeched, and Stella scanned the alley where the streak had appeared. She opened the door and stepped onto the sidewalk. "I saw something. I'll be back in a moment."

"I'm not letting you hunt through dark alleys alone. You must know that." Henry climbed out then closed her door.

"I'm not a child." Stella strode into the narrow space. Why did he insist on treating her like an accident looking for a spot to occur?

"I know that." He matched her pace.

The odor of rotting garbage forced Stella to cover her nose. "Well, you don't treat me like it. Sometimes—" She stopped. Three children with dirt-smudged faces leaned against the brick building. Their ragged clothing hung on their shoulders.

Up close, the fear and desperation in those youthful eyes left her ashamed of the comfort she enjoyed. She unclasped her handbag and riffled through its contents. A peppermint and three dollars. Not nearly enough to ease their suffering.

A boy who looked to be around eight eyed her while two younger girls clung to each other. "Whatcha doin' here, lady?" He swiped his blue shirtsleeve across his nose.

Stella held out the dollar bills. "When did you eat last?"

"Ain't none of your business." He crossed his arms. "We don't need your charity."

"Then where are your parents?" Stella peered down the alley, but it appeared empty.

He hung his head, jaw clenched.

"They promised not to leave us, but they're gone," one of the little girls whispered. Tears formed muddy trails down her cheeks.

Henry neared the children and swallowed hard, eyes wearing a sadness Stella had never seen there before. Should she take them home? But what if the boy was telling the truth? If his parents returned to find them missing, they would be beside themselves with worry.

Stella held the money toward the girl. "What's your name?"

"Rose." She accepted the gift. "This is my sister, Daisy. And that's Robby." She jerked her chin in the boy's direction. "He's rude."

Stella suppressed a chuckle, then her stomach twisted. This situation wasn't funny. "I'm sure he doesn't mean to be." A rat scurried from behind a stand of garbage cans. This was no place for children. She should have Cook feed them a hot meal and tuck them into warm beds. "It's very nice to meet all of you." A pallet covered with filthy blankets lay at the end of the alley. Was this where they slept? No. It couldn't be. They must have a home somewhere. "Do you live around here?"

"Our parents are comin' to get us later." Robby thrust his hands into his pockets, his baggy shirt sleeves hanging clownishly at his wrists. "You don't have to worry about us."

How could she not worry? Their frayed clothing shouted neglect. Were their parents really coming for them?

Henry placed a hand on her shoulder. "It's time to go," he whispered, voice hoarse.

Stella blinked back the grief filling her eyes. Why couldn't she do more? "Maybe we'll meet again." She waved to Rose and Daisy, who replied with shy smiles.

Henry helped her into the automobile, and she struggled to hold back her tears.

He met her gaze, resting a hand over hers. "We'll check on them again. Make sure their parents return."

"Do you promise?" Leaving them now didn't sit well. If Robby had lied, they'd spend tonight on that pallet.

"I promise."

Stella determined to hold him to it. She'd read her letter again and think of a way to help. Her friend was right. Her life was nothing more than a show. Well, maybe he hadn't said as much in so many words. He was far too genteel to be harsh, but his letters left her feeling artificial. As if her life hadn't truly begun. And that had to change. More than anything, she wanted to make a difference, but she wasn't doing that now.

As the motor purred, she adjusted the bunched fabric of her skirt and fixed her eyes on the shoreline. The waves lapped at the sand, sunlight sparkling off the water. Then, just as quickly, the tide washed out to sea. Always the same. It mirrored her life. Dress fittings, fashion magazines, visits with friends.

Nothing of consequence. Of course, she helped Ethel, but that was simply the right thing to do. It wasn't grand.

How could she ever hope to make a difference when everything she did—or more accurately was permitted to do—carried no lasting value? She pulled out her hatpin and moved the oversized frippery to her lap.

Would Uncle Weston present her idea to the board, or had he only agreed in an effort to quiet her? After all, he had said more than once that he'd handle the thinking and leave her to pick out fabric. As if giving her a menial task would keep her brain from turning gears.

Sunbursts flashed across her vision, and she closed her eyes to block them out. *Will I ever be free of these headaches?* The lights persisted against her eyelids. Her throat constricted. How could she ever make a difference if pain held her prisoner? *God, please let fasting help. I can't live like this forever.*

Chapter Four

Henry cast a quick glance over his shoulder. Stella hadn't said a word since they'd left the Mission District. And she was seldom at a loss for words. When he caught a glimpse of her pinched features and her fingers kneading her temple, he longed to hold her close.

"You all right back there?" He returned his eyes to the road, keeping his voice low so as not to aggravate her discomfort.

She groaned. "It hurts."

Those two words punched him in the gut. He'd take the pain for her if possible. "Would you like to go back?"

"Could we stop for a moment? Somewhere quiet. The motor jangles my nerves."

He strained to hear her whispered words. A deserted beach hailed him on the right, and he pulled to the side of the road, drawn to the shade of a tree's sweeping branches. "Here we are."

Her eyelids cracked open then quickly closed. A tear escaped the corner of her eye and trailed down her cheek. He'd seen her headaches before, but never tears. Not since she'd gotten her foot caught between the spindles on the staircase when she was six.

Unsure how best to help, he climbed out of the driver's seat, rounded the automobile, and slipped onto the bench seat beside her. She squinted. Pain drew lines under her eyes. When he opened his arms, she leaned against his chest. Sobs jerked her shoulders, and she mumbled syllables that didn't quite form words. During her worst headaches, her words jumbled, leaving him with little idea what she said.

He breathed in her perfume, rubbing circles on her back.

Her crying slowed, and she pulled in a quivering breath.

With her head resting on his chest and her eyes closed, he studied her features. The paleness of her skin magnified her freckles. Long lashes almost touched her cheeks. Her upturned nose reflected the sass he admired.

The way she'd stood up for Ethel and wished to help those poor children with something more heartfelt than money increased his admiration of her. If her uncle didn't force such mundane tasks on her, she could do great things. God had designed her for something better than sifting through fabric samples, of that he was certain.

Deep breaths signaled sleep. Her lips parted. Drool dripped onto his coat. She'd be mortified when she woke, but he didn't have the heart to disturb her slumber. Not when it was the only thing that offered her a modicum of relief.

He leaned back in the seat. Plans whirled in his head. Blueprints for the house he'd build for underprivileged children. A playground in the backyard. A seesaw. Maybe a jungle gym. Their joyful laughter echoed in his ears. After losing both parents before he turned twelve, he held a special place in his heart for the needs of orphaned children. If the Burke family hadn't taken him in, he might be living on the streets. But despite their physical care for him, they hadn't included him in family outings. He'd been their ward and a marked differentiation between himself and Stella had been maintained. The children in *his* home would feel a part of something. They'd be family.

As the plans developed in his mind, Stella's face was never far from his thoughts. He shook her image loose. No doubt she would make a loving caregiver for the children he hoped to help. Watching her with Ethel's baby dispelled all doubts on that score. But Stella was an heiress. What he had to offer her paled in comparison to what she already possessed.

Shadows from the shade tree played across her face while birds warbled from the branches. A gentle breeze toyed with curls that had won the battle against the jeweled comb holding them hostage. He brushed one from her forehead, resisting the temptation to plant a kiss where it had lain. It would be neither proper nor welcome.

Her lashes fluttered, and confusion puckered her brow. She bolted upright, fingers dabbing her mouth. "I'm so sorry." Her eyes widened.

"No need to apologize." He brushed at the moisture on his coat. "I'm glad you were able to sleep. How do you feel?"

"A little better." Pain still shadowed her eyes. Her stomach gurgled, and she pressed her hand against her middle, cheeks blooming three shades of pink.

"You hungry?"

She opened her mouth as if to speak then shook her head, but her protesting belly betrayed her lie.

"Come on, now. There's an ice cream parlor up the road. It's your favorite." He reached for the door.

Stella bit her lip. "I wish I could. It sounds wonderful."

"Why can't you?" Gravel crackled beneath his boot.

She focused on her clasped hands. "Have you heard of Dr. Linda Hazzard?"

"Judging by the name, I'm not sure I want to. Sounds a little dangerous for my taste." He grinned, resting his arms against the automobile's door.

"Well, if you're going to have that attitude, I shan't tell you." She crossed her arms.

He rounded the car to eliminate the distance between them. "I was kidding. You may be the one with the attitude, young lady."

She lifted her chin, clearly attempting to maintain her fake annoyance, but her lips twitched, giving way to a faint smile.

"Tell me about Dr. Hazzard." He leaned against the car. "She is a real doctor?"

"Of course." Stella's arms relaxed at her sides. "I'm reading her book, *Fasting for the Cure of Disease*. She's helped so many people find healing. I started my first fast, and I shouldn't break it for ice cream." Her shoulders drooped. "Although it sounds heavenly."

"So how does it work?" How would starving herself cure Stella of the headaches that had plagued her since her father died? Sounded like adding more discomfort to her already pain-filled days.

"She believes the body is full of toxins, and fasting purges them from a person's system."

"Toxins?" He raised a brow. "What sort of toxins?"

Stella shrugged. "I just started reading her book, so I couldn't tell you. But I know they're not something you want living inside you."

"And ice cream feeds the toxins?" He'd never heard such balderdash.

"Food in general feeds them. That's why she prescribes long-term fasting to her patients."

Concern tickled his insides. Stella's talk of toxins and fasting created more questions than answers. But the hope on her face silenced further tearing down of Dr. Hazzard's theories. Too many months had passed since hope had sparked in her eyes, and he'd do nothing to rob her. She'd tried countless remedies from gypsy tonics to lumbar puncture. Nothing had diminished the intensity or frequency of her headaches. And her doctor's prescription for sea air provided her little more than a vacation to the coast.

Maybe Linda Hazzard's methods would offer the relief Stella craved. But abstaining from food for heaven knew how long could potentially do more harm than good.

❧

Stella's stomach complained.

As Henry cranked the automobile to life, she squinted. The ground tipped beneath her, and she gripped the door to steady herself. Maybe she should eat something. If she didn't, she might faint. Besides, Uncle Weston would expect her to eat dinner with his guest. Maybe it was best to start fasting in increments, beginning with shorter lengths of time then working her way up.

"Henry." She pulled in a steadying breath.

He wiped gloved hands on his pants. "Yes."

"I may have changed my mind about the ice cream."

His smile grew an inch. "I hoped you would." He climbed behind the steering wheel then turned the motorcar onto the road.

At the edge of the San Francisco city limits, Henry parked in front of a small brick shop wedged between a shoemaker and a jewelry store.

"Here we are." Delight lilted his voice.

He helped her out of the car then opened the shop door as a bell above trilled. A couple stepped onto the sidewalk arm in arm, carrying ice cream cones. A woman dressed like a nanny sat with a little boy at a round table, finger wagging as she scolded. Chocolate ice cream stained a ring around his mouth.

Stella's mouth watered.

The shop owner greeted them from behind the counter. "What can I get you?"

"One vanilla and one strawberry." Henry guided Stella to the table farthest from the window. What would she do without him? Not only did he know her favorite flavor, but he understood how the sunlight affected her headaches. He pulled out her chair, and she sat.

The apron-clad proprietor set dishes and spoons on the table. Henry nudged the bowl of strawberry ice cream toward her.

She scooped out a ladylike portion and took her first bite. The cold sweetness danced on her tongue and froze her pain to a dull ache. She sighed. "This was a fabulous idea. Thank you." Her second spoonful better suited a lumberjack, but Henry wouldn't mind.

"No need for thanks, Miss Burke." He winked.

Why did he insist on formalities when he knew they infuriated her? She reached into her handbag and pulled out the article he'd given her. "Would you read this to me? My eyes are—"

"Of course." He took the paper and flattened the creases.

Stella savored her treat as Henry read about the suffragettes' meeting with Governor Hiram Johnson and the solid case they'd presented for women's voting rights. His response left room for hope that women could stand in line next time the polls opened.

An advertisement on the back side of the article froze Stella's spoon midair.

"Wait a minute." She rested a hand on Henry's arm, and he paused reading. "Turn the page over. I hope my eyes aren't playing tricks, but it looks like Linda Hazzard has opened a clinic."

He flipped the article, brows rising. "You're right. The Institute of Natural Therapeutics in Olalla, Washington. 'Personalized care and treatment for the cure of all ailments. Dr. Hazzard's proven fasting regimens will restore health and vitality.' The address is here too, and a picture. Looks brand new."

He handed her the article, and she strained to focus on the white building surrounded by pine trees. "Is Olalla close to the coast?"

"I believe it's right outside Seattle, so yes, very close to the coast."

The sea air would meet Dr. Wagner's requirements, and a fasting plan designed by Linda Hazzard herself with Stella's unique needs in mind would be the best kind of medicine. Surely if she sat under Dr. Hazzard's care, a cure for her headaches could be reached.

This had to be too good to be true.

"I'm not sure I like that look on your face." Henry slurped his melting ice cream. "What are you thinking?"

"How would you feel about a drive to Olalla?" She folded the article and returned it to her handbag.

His shoulders stiffened. "I'm not sure that's wise. Letting someone starve you seems a little extreme."

"She won't starve me." Stella firmed her jaw. "And I just want to get a feel for the place. If I'm not comfortable with her regimen, I won't stay." His eyes didn't show a hint of budging. Why was he so much more difficult than Jane or Hartsell? *They* trusted her judgment, offered support, let her order her own life. But Henry insisted on questioning her at every turn. Wasn't her family paying him to be agreeable?

"Tell you what." He clinked his spoon into the empty dish. "Finish her book and we'll discuss it. If you still want to see the place after knowing her angle—"

"Her angle is healing people, and that's what I need." Stella rubbed the pain over her eyebrow. "Why must you make this harder than it needs to be?"

"Because I care about you." He placed a hand over hers then withdrew it. His gaze dropped to the floor.

Emotion stirred within her, dissolving her agitation. He was such a good friend. And he hadn't read the portions of Dr. Hazzard's book as she had, so it stood to reason he'd be uncomfortable with the woman's unorthodox methods. Maybe if they read the remainder of the book together, he'd be on her side. She desired his support almost as much as she craved relief.

She'd prayed for years to find a cure for her headaches. Maybe the Institute of Natural Therapeutics was her answer.

Chapter Five

Stella rushed through the front doors, not bothering to wait for Hartsell to open them. How had she let time get away from her? Uncle Weston would be furious with her disregard for the dinner he'd planned.

Maybe she should head to the dining room without dressing for dinner. She checked the mirror in the vestibule. Her hat rested at an odd angle and windblown hair puffed from beneath the brim. She removed her hat, determined to smooth the mess, but found the task impossible. No, this would never do.

Her uncle's voice carried from the dining room. "I'm not sure where she is, but I've no doubt she'll arrive shortly." While his guest might not have detected the hint of annoyance steeling Uncle Weston's voice, Stella did.

She dashed up the stairs two at a time and ran to Jane's room at the end of the hall. Three raps brought the matronly woman's answer. When Jane's gaze fell on Stella, her eyes widened. "My, but you could use some help." She checked the timepiece on her bodice. "And you're late." She exited the room, jerking the door shut.

Stella hurried to her bedroom with Jane close behind. She tossed her hat on the bed and settled on the stool before the dressing table. "I'm sorry I'm late. Henry and I stopped for ice cream, and—"

"I'd best come with you next time you ride to the coast." Jane worked at a knot in Stella's hair with a hairbrush. "These outings with Clayton may not be entirely proper."

Clayton? Oh, of course, Henry. She'd failed to use his formal title.

But she'd despise giving up their solitary drives by including Jane's company. As much as she valued the woman, she couldn't be as much herself as when she was alone with Henry. . .Clayton. He understood her, listened to her ideas. Of course, his contrary attitude tormented her at times. Although there was something refreshing in the way he didn't bow to her every whim.

"Oh, Clayton and I are very proper. And you need time off now and again." Stella turned in her seat, earning her a tug to the scalp. *Ouch.* She lifted her hand to the stinging spot.

"Aye. But I worry for Clayton." Jane pinned a curl in place.

What could she possibly mean by that? "Why worry for Clayton?"

"I'm afraid his time with the family may have given him a taste of a life that isn't rightfully his."

That was more confusing still. "I'm not sure I understand."

"Clayton may aspire to—" Jane frowned. "He may feel it possible to make connections that are above his station."

Above his station? Realization dawned, and electricity buzzed across her skin. "You don't mean—"

"I do." Jane secured another section of hair. "And since your uncle would never consider him a proper suitor, he's bound to be disappointed."

"Henry doesn't care for me. Not like that." Stella slid her fingers into a glove then pulled the sleeve up to her elbow. But he'd said as much at the ice cream parlor. Surely he meant his words as a token of friendship, nothing more. "I don't know how he could." Her cheeks ignited. Jane had a keen eye. What if she was right?

"You sell yourself short." Jane finished her hair. "But we shouldn't talk about it anymore." She stilled and glanced at Stella in the mirror. "You care for him too, don't you?"

Stella lowered her gaze to her lap. Did she? She couldn't imagine life without him. But she couldn't fathom living without Jane or ice cream either. "I'm not sure." She shook her head. He knew her better than anyone. Aside from the man who wrote the letters. If only she knew his name.

Jane strode to the closet, retrieved a gauzy purple gown trimmed with gold, and took her place beside Stella once more. "It's best for you both if you keep to what's expected of you." Jane flashed an unsteady smile. "Avoid the heartbreak."

As Jane fastened the buttons at her back, Stella mulled her words. If she took Jane's advice, she'd avoid conversing with Henry except to order the motor. But how would she convince him to take her to Dr. Hazzard's institute? Why couldn't he take orders like normal drivers instead of demanding a list of reasons why she needed the trip? She pulled on her other glove.

She'd have Uncle Weston give Henry a firm talking-to. Guilt pricked. No. Henry didn't deserve trouble. In his way, he was trying to protect her. A smile twitched her mouth. Like he had at Ethel's apartment.

"I caught a peek at the young man your uncle invited." Jane grabbed the amber bottle of Narcisse Noir and dabbed the fragrance behind Stella's ears. The floral aroma filled her senses. "He's very handsome."

Stella's thoughts reverted to Henry. Surely her uncle's guest couldn't rival Henry. Not with his rigid jaw, or the laughter that twinkled in his hazel eyes, or— What was wrong with her? The memory of his lopsided smile when he'd brushed her saliva from his coat left a strange tightness in her heart. He was so patient, so kind, so—

"You're smiling. I'm glad you're pleased to meet this one." Jane ushered her to the door. "It's high time you were settled in a home of your own."

Best to play along. Jane needn't know Stella's mind had been occupied with the very man she'd been warned against.

Stella planted a quick kiss on Jane's cheek. "Thank you for getting me ready." With the hem of her dress in hand, Stella skipped down the stairs.

At the closed dining room door, she braced for another evening of awkwardness and boredom. Silverware clinked against china. They'd started without her. No matter. She squared her shoulders and entered the room, not missing the reprimand in her uncle's eyes as he and his guest stood.

"I'm sorry I'm late." She eased into the chair the footman held for her. "I wasn't feeling well, and time got away from me."

Uncle Weston sat, gaze softening. "I hope you're better, my dear."

"Much." She spread the napkin in her lap.

"I'd like you to meet a friend of mine." Her uncle gestured to the man at the foot of the table. "James Harris, this is my niece, Stella Burke."

The gentleman acknowledged her with a nod. A lock of chestnut hair grazed his forehead. "It's a pleasure to meet you, Miss Burke." His blue eyes twinkled. Jane hadn't been lying when she said he was handsome. Stella's heart stalled. But now that he'd seen her plain features, he'd not give her a second look.

She selected a spoon and dipped it into the cream of chicken soup. Though the ice cream had been delicious, she hadn't realized how famished the fast had left her. In a few bites, she devoured the first course.

When she glanced at her uncle, his brows hung low over his eyes. His gaze darted to their guest, and Stella sat a little straighter. She should say something to him. But what? The thought of asking about his horse's lineage before he had the chance to mention it sent a cringe across her shoulders. No sense opening a conversation that would have no end. Before Mama died, she'd always said to discuss the weather or the condition of the roads if you found yourself at a loss.

"The weather has been very fine." Her hands fidgeted in her lap.

"Very." James smiled. Even his teeth were perfect. "Have you read anything agreeable recently?"

No doubt she'd misheard him. What man asked a woman of books? She leaned forward, lifting a questioning brow.

"Do you not enjoy reading?" He set his spoon in his empty bowl.

"Very much." Had her uncle coached this man on topics of conversation? "I read an article today about the suffragettes working to give California women the right to vote."

Uncle Weston cleared his throat and gave a slight shake of his head as he wiped his mouth.

"And what are your feelings on that matter?" James lifted a wineglass to his lips.

"It would be wonderful. We've made great strides, but so many things still need to change. The thought of voting with my conscience thrills me to my fingertips." Her voice shrank. "What do you think?"

"Oh, I agree. I, for one, would be happy to have a wife cast a ballot.

It would be like having two votes." He set down his glass.

"And if your wife didn't agree with you?" A footman stepped beside her with a tray of quail, and the aroma of roasted fowl made her stomach beg for a taste. She served herself and returned her attention to her uncle's guest.

"Then I would not permit her to vote no matter what the governor of California should say." He shook his head. "How is a woman to decide on her own what is best for the political realm?"

"She could learn." Stella stabbed her quail with a fork, appetite waning.

"That's faulty logic." James jabbed his fork in the air as if emphasizing a point, then took a bite. "Men and women are very different, you see. While men make decisions based on facts, women let their emotions determine their actions. You can't deny it."

"I don't wish to deny it." Stella clenched her jaw. "But don't you think both fact and feeling should be viewed as strengths? Just as a woman's understanding can be broadened by facts, a man's stubbornness can be softened by feeling."

Uncle Weston coughed theatrically, ending their discussion. When Stella dared to meet his gaze, he shot her a warning glare. She lowered her head and took to pushing the food around her plate.

She'd ruined another marriage prospect with her plain face and unpopular opinions. Not a total loss, however. A lifetime with a man who didn't value her point of view didn't appeal in the slightest.

As she lifted a bite to her lips, she counted the days to her twenty-fifth birthday. Thirty-seven days more, and she'd be free to use her money as she willed and have an input in the clothing business. Do something to make a difference. Something more than rattling around in this giant house and breathing sea air. Her father most likely had expected she'd be married by now, allowing her husband to acquire the family fortune in her stead.

The disappointment in Uncle Weston's eyes made something inside her wilt like a dandelion in the heat of summer. If Papa were still alive, would she have disappointed him too?

She shouldn't speak of this with Henry. But he'd understand how she felt. He always did.

Henry opened the cover of *Fasting for the Cure of Disease* and took a seat on the stool beside his workbench in the garage. The scent of motor oil soothed his nerves. Crickets hummed from outside the open door. What sort of crazy blather had Stella read about fasting? He shook off the prejudicial thought. If Linda Burfield Hazzard's treatments could heal her, Henry wouldn't stand in the way. Still, unease gnawed his gut. The whole thing carried a stink he wished Stella would stay far away from, but she'd been indulged and given free rein too often to accept his oppositional stance without a concrete reason. Well, if she required a reason, he'd find it in the pages of Hazzard's own writing.

He scanned a poem printed on the first page.

Some, as thou saws't, by violent stroke shall die,
By fire, flood, famine; by intemperance more
In meats and drinks, which on the Earth shall bring
Diseases dire, of which a monstrous crew
Before thee shall appear, that thou mays't know
What misery the inabstinence of Eve
Shall bring on men.
If thou well observe
The rule of 'Not too much' by temperance taught
In what thou eat'st and drink'st, seeking from thence
Due nourishment, not gluttonous delight.
Till many years over thy head return; So mays't thou live, till,
like ripe fruit, thou drop
Into thy mother's lap, or be with ease
Gathered, not harshly plucked, for death mature.

—John Milton, *Paradise Lost*

Henry rolled his eyes and propped his elbow on the bench beside his toolbox. The woman was a quack if she attributed the fall of man to Eve's inability to fast. But Stella had brains to spare. She'd see though this tomfoolery no doubt.

Unless her wish for healing clouded her judgment.

His brain replayed the events leading to Stella's headache that morning. Ethel's husband and the subsequent altercation then interacting with the ragged children on the street appeared to be the catalyst. He craned his neck until it cracked. What about yesterday's headache? The children at the beach had raised a commotion. Could stress or raised voices be at the heart of her problems instead of overindulgence in food? The thought of Stella fasting for her ailment didn't sit well with him. She was already rail thin, and the nausea that accompanied her migraines often killed her appetite. In some ways she was fasting out of necessity, and it hadn't helped.

But her affinity for Linda Hazzard's regimen would render his logic useless.

He flipped to chapter 1, settling in for a long night of reading. The first sentence presented a study in confusion. He turned the book upside down then back again. Though educated by Stella's tutors, he couldn't make out the meaning of Hazzard's jargon. He knew the meaning of each separate word, but they were indecipherable in the manner she'd tossed them together.

Rustling sounded at the door, and he snapped the book shut. Stella stormed in, hands balled into fists. The gold trim on her dress caught a flicker of light from the oil lamp hanging from the beam, making the beads sparkle. Henry hid the book beneath an oil rag. If Stella discovered his plan to discredit her beloved Linda Hazzard, she'd never forgive him. And he couldn't bear the thought.

She huffed, crossed her arms, and leaned against the workbench. A curl fell free of her pins and fluttered into her line of vision. She rammed it behind her ear, loosening the remaining pins. Curls toppled around her shoulders and down her back.

How could she be so spoiled and still manage to look so adorable in the process? He forced the thought from his head. Her uncle would toss him into the unemployment line if Henry dared speak such a thought aloud. Especially since the man was in pursuit of a perfect husband for his niece. Someone who could meet her needs far better than Henry on his meager salary. Weston's shifty eyes were always in search of his next money-making endeavor. And the men he arranged for Stella to meet tended to possess values that flowed in the same vein. Thankfully, Stella had acquired her mother's attributes, and while she was a trifle on the entitled side, she never failed to offer a generous hand to someone in need. With any luck she'd escape the noose of matrimony a few weeks longer—until her uncle no longer held all her cards. She could do better than those money-grubbing fancy men.

"I guess your gentleman caller wasn't the hero you'd hoped?" He thrust his hands into his pockets.

"Don't you dare call him that." Stella jabbed his chest with an index finger, voice low. "He's not *my* anything. And he never shall be if I have a say in the matter."

Relief coursed through him. Each time one of Weston's men missed the mark, hope sparked. Though Henry had tried to employ logic to squelch the tender flame, it stubbornly flickered. He cleared his throat. "Want to talk about it?" He hopped off the stool and offered it to Stella with a flourish of his hand.

She started toward the seat but halted when she came abreast of him. Her eyes floundered then found his. Wide and soft, they pinned him with an unspoken question.

His breathing stilled as he studied the vulnerability scrawled on her brow. "What's wrong?"

"Do you—" Her cheeks bloomed pink, but her gaze didn't falter. "Do you care for me?" Her tone was low, intimate.

His mouth went dry, and he struggled to swallow past the lump in his throat. How could he answer without losing her friendship or his employment? "Of course." Why had her simple question acted like a punch in the gut? And his answer, though two small words, hovered in the air between them, riddled with complexity. He longed to tell her he cared for her more than anything. To wrap his arms around her and hold her close, eliminating the cavern of class and family that divided them, and remind her that in all the important things, he was her equal. But he had no right to such feelings or claims. "We're friends, right? Friends care about each other."

Her shoulders drooped. The softness in her eyes deepened to sadness. Had his answer disappointed her? She brushed past him and sat on the stool.

"We *are* friends, aren't we?" He rested a hand on her shoulder, but her perfume enticed him closer. If he didn't remember his station, he might kiss her. An act that would cost him his job, his dream, and Stella. He withdrew his hand and took a step back.

"Best friends." Her words came out as rough as the first crank of the automobile's engine.

"Tell me about the disappointing gentleman." Henry rested his elbows on the worktable behind him, listening as Stella related the dinner and her uncle's disapproval.

"I'll never be good enough. He wants me to be a proper lady, to find a husband, and heaven knows what else. But none of the men he brings have the qualities that matter to me. We both know that if it wasn't for my inheritance, none of them would give me so much as a second glance."

Henry shook his head. "We don't know any such thing." He stepped in front of her, capturing her gaze. "If those nincompoops don't have the brains to see you for who you are, they aren't worth all this fuss and bluster. Besides, you said yourself they weren't the type you're looking for. Who cares what they think? You'll know when the right one comes along, and you're too good a person to give your heart to someone who doesn't deserve it." He licked dry lips. He'd already said more than he ought. "You've told me you don't think you're pretty, but I wish you'd stop."

Stella's eyes glistened, and Henry ached to put his arms around her. Like he had in the motorcar when her headache returned. "Do you think I'm pretty?"

His heart throbbed in his throat. "You're beautiful." He tucked an obstinate curl behind her ear, but it sprang out in rebellion. "But it has nothing to do with your dress or your hair or whatever else people put so much value on."

Her smile slipped. "What then? If I'm plain on the outside, none of the men Uncle Weston invites to the house will see me as more than a bank account."

"Stella, when you were holding Ethel's baby today, easing her burden, standing up for her when her brute of a husband spoke ill to her— that was the most beautiful you've ever been. It was as if you found your purpose, something that went far deeper than fabric swatches and posh benefits. You were passionate, and it shone in your eyes. You were stunning."

Stella took his hand and gave it a squeeze. The fog of unspoken words thickened between them. So many things he yearned to say, but propriety kept them imprisoned behind his teeth.

"Thank you." Stella returned her hand to her lap, leaving his with a cold, empty sensation. "Sometimes I think you're the only one who sees any value in me."

"That's not true." He stepped back. "What about your uncle? He must value you after hearing your ideas for expanding the clothing line." The business she would soon control should be a much safer topic.

"I brought it up this morning." Stella reached into his toolbox, pulled out a wrench, and weighed it in her hand.

"How'd it go? I know you were worried the thought of expanding the line wouldn't be well received." He rubbed sweaty palms on his pants. If he didn't find something to do, he'd be tempted to overstep his bounds and say something that wouldn't be well received.

He took the wrench from her then scooted under the motorcar. Looking busy provided a better option than wrapping his arms around her and experiencing the inevitable sting of rejection.

"Uncle Weston said he'd speak with the board on Monday." He heard the eye roll in her tone.

"But you don't believe him?" He tightened an already fastened bolt on the motor.

"He didn't sound too keen on the idea."

"Probably because *he* didn't think of it." Henry scooted from under the automobile to meet her gaze. "I thought you wanted to pitch the idea to the board of directors yourself."

She chewed her lip. "I asked about that, but he said the company needed me to pick fabrics for the fall clothing line." She plucked at the rag covering his copy of Linda Hazzard's book.

Henry's stomach dropped to his toes. *Please, God, don't let her notice.* He scrambled off the floor and slipped beside her, blocking the book with his arm. Surprised by how close to her he stood, he inched backward.

Stella raised a questioning brow, a childlike spark ignited in her eyes. "What are you hiding?" She peeked around his shoulder, but he shoved the cloth-covered book back with his arm.

"It's nothing." Did he sound as guilty as he felt?

A smile turned her lips. "I'm almost certain it's the opposite of nothing." Mischief danced in her smile.

He knew that look.

He tried to step away, but she'd already reached under his arm and worked her fingers into the spot that made him lose control. Just like when they were children and he dared to defy her, she tickled him until he moved away from the workbench. As he writhed out of her reach, laughter doubled him over.

As soon as he left the oil rag unattended, Stella lifted it. Eyes wide, she met his gaze. "Why were you hiding this?" She picked up the book and ran her hand over the spine.

"Well, I was—"

"Thank you." She sent him a warm smile.

Clearly she'd misunderstood his objective, but setting her straight may not work in his favor. "You're welcome? But I'm not sure why you're thanking me."

"You're looking into Linda Hazzard's treatment plan." She stepped toward him and secured her arms around his waist. "You want to understand so you can help me. It means more than you'll ever know."

Her fragrance stole his ability to reason, and he wrapped her in a friendly embrace—they were friends after all. Best friends, to use her words.

She shifted, and the letter in his pocket crinkled. The one he planned to post in the morning bearing her name and address. Thank goodness she'd only found the book.

He should tell her the truth about the letters. It wasn't fair to keep sending them. Not when she believed the man writing her was a member of her economic class.

"Stella." The word exited his mouth as a rasp, so he cleared his throat.

"Yes?" She backed away, smoothing her dress with gloved hands.

How did the fops her uncle paraded through the house as potential husbands not see how beautiful she was? And why did Weston continually set her up with men who, while wealthy, were deficient in the areas that truly counted? He drew in a sharp breath. Telling her the truth about their correspondence could change the dynamic between them.

"Well?" She fiddled with her hairpins, doing more harm than good.

His confession could leave her feeling betrayed. Bile climbed his throat, burning the words he ought to say. "I think we should go through the fasting book and see if Linda Buzzard might be on to something." Why couldn't he muster the courage to get the truth out? Shameful coward.

Stella blocked a laugh. "It's Hazzard."

Henry shrugged. "I don't see the difference."

"You're impossible, Clayton." She shook her head.

"It's taken years of perfecting my craft." He cracked his knuckles. "Glad to know my hard work has paid off and I'm officially impossible."

"When do you want to start?" Stella waved the book.

"How about now, Miss Burke?"

Chapter Six

Stella's pulse pounded in her ears. Why had Jane planted the idea that Henry had feelings for her? And why had the thought transformed her into an awkward schoolgirl? She'd taken leave of her senses, and now he must think her a fool. When she met his gaze, he flashed a crooked grin. The same one he'd beamed after stuffing a frog down her dress one summer day ages ago. Her heart fluttered against her rib cage.

She shouldn't have hugged him. But when he'd wrapped his arms around her. . . Never had she felt so safe. So loved. Not since Papa died. In that moment, memories and longings embraced and the jumbled jigsaw pieces of her life had fallen into place for the first time. But that wasn't right. He wasn't a piece in her puzzle box. He didn't belong to her. Not in that way.

What had he told her when she practically pleaded for a declaration of his feelings? She upturned the graveyard of her mind for those painful words.

Friends care for each other.

Friends. Nothing more. And nothing in his actions indicated he felt any differently for her than whatever other friends he might have. Her heart slowed. What if he was courting someone else? She had little idea what he did on his weekly day off. For all she knew Henry was on the cusp of marrying some lucky girl.

She swallowed hard, but the knot in her throat remained. Uncle Weston would never give his blessing to her and Henry. It was best he found a girl who could make him happy.

She ran her hand over the book's cloth cover.

Her uncle might approve of the man she'd been corresponding with since Papa died. Judging by his eloquence, he was educated. And the way he spoke denoted his presence in the same circles she traveled. He could be anyone really. Maybe she'd met him before. But if she had, they hadn't spoken at length. None of the young men of her acquaintance inquired about her ideas or dreams. Their concerns rested in trivial pursuits. Unlike her mystery correspondent.

What if he was old? She cringed. What a cruel trick that would be. Or he could be married, which would be worse still. She should ask in her next letter.

Nevertheless, something about the turns of phrase he used struck a chord. As if she knew the man who penned the words and had for a long time. Should she ask his name? If she did, the spell might be broken. He might prefer to remain a mystery, and she ought to respect his wishes.

"What are you thinking about?" Henry wiped his wrench with a grease rag.

She shook her head. "Nothing." *And everything.* Thank heaven he couldn't read her thoughts.

"Would you rather wait until morning to start reading?" He grinned. "Dr. Buzzard's book can wait."

He'd offered to study the book with her, and if she didn't capitalize on his generosity, he may change his mind. "Let me read you Dr. *Hazzard's* definition of fasting." Stella leaned against the worktable and flipped to the first chapter of Linda Hazzard's book. Henry slipped back under the automobile, wrench in hand. "You're not listening." Her chest twinged. How would she persuade him to take her to Olalla if he hid under the motorcar and didn't try to understand?

"I read the first page. The one with Milton's work." He poked his head into the open, lips pursed and brows raised. "She's taking his words completely out of context. Using that line in *Paradise Lost* to push her crazy theory." He dramatically rested the back of his hand on his brow. "If only Eve had fasted instead of eating the apple, the human race wouldn't have plunged into sin." His voice carried the lilt of mockery.

Stella bit back a giggle, but it escaped in a fitful burst. "Maybe that wasn't *exactly* what Milton meant."

He chuckled. "Maybe? The thought never crossed his mind." Henry returned to his job beneath the auto. "But go ahead and read her definition of fasting. I promised I'd help you decide if the Therapeutical Institute would be a good fit for you."

"Institute of Natural Therapeutics." Stella shot him a mock scowl then found the paragraph she sought. "Here it is." Her finger guided her across the line. "Fasting is defined as follows: 'The voluntary denial of food to a system which is diseased, and which, because of disease, does not require nourishment until rested, cleansed, and eager again to take up the labor of digestion. Then, and not till then, is food supplied; then, and not till then, does starvation begin.' "

She glanced at Henry, whose face was hidden under the motorcar.

"Well?" She slipped her finger between the pages.

He crawled from the ground then brushed off his pants and shirt. "So who gets to decide when your system is ready for food?" He shook his head, eyes clouded. "Where is the threshold between fasting and starvation?"

She shrugged a shoulder. "I guess when my headaches are gone, I'll know I'm ready to eat again."

"I've noticed a pattern with your headaches." He reached into his toolbox and pulled out something Stella couldn't identify.

"What sort of pattern?"

His brow creased as if he'd thought the matter over at length. "It seems after you've been stressed, headaches follow. Like today. After you stood up to Ethel's husband and dealt with the heartbreak of those needy children, your symptoms set in. While you were speaking with Ethel and holding the baby, you seemed more your old self than I've seen since—"

"Since Papa died?" Tears blurred his face from view.

He nodded.

"I did have the initial symptoms of the headache just before Ethel invited us in." She traced the title of the book with an index finger. "But they went away for about an hour."

"Can you pinpoint what brought them on and describe what you felt?"

He would never understand. Unless he experienced one of her headaches, the usual course of symptoms would sound like she'd swallowed too much laudanum.

"I smelled something vile in the hallway, and little bursts of light started at the corners of my eyes, then I felt like I was watching myself from somewhere outside my body." She shuddered. "I hate thinking about it for fear another headache will strike."

"Perhaps you should keep a journal and write down the circumstances surrounding each headache. Maybe there's a common thread we're missing."

Did that mean he wouldn't help her get to Dr. Buzzard's clinic? Her jaw clenched. Now he had *her* thinking the woman's name was Buzzard.

"I'll still see you safely to the clinic if you feel it's the best option." He took a step closer, and her breathing faltered.

She shouldn't have come out here to whine about her terrible dinner companion. Taking a giant step backward toward the door, she chewed the inside of her cheek. "What do I have to say to prove I really need to talk to Dr. Buzz—Hazzard for myself?"

An aggravating smirk quirked his lips, and a breeze blew through the open door, ruffling his nutmeg hair. Despite the good looks of her uncle's guest, James paled in comparison to Henry. How had she never noticed the dimple in his cheek before? "I'll take you to see the old Buzzard once you finish her book and journal for a week. We can review the journal together if you like." He crossed his arms. "If we can find a way to help you without going to her extremes, it would be best. Besides, do you think you could go without ice cream until she starves your headaches away?"

"She wouldn't starve me." Stella flipped to the first page of the book. "Clearly, you weren't listening when I read her definition of fasting." She cleared her throat. " 'The voluntary denial of—' "

Henry slipped the book out of her grasp and held it above his head. "I heard you the first time."

She reached for the book, jumping for momentum. Why did

he have to be so tall?

He dangled it within reach then jerked it away when she grabbed for it.

"I'll name my next headache 'Henry.' " She wiggled her fingers in the traditional tickling gesture.

Henry's eyes widened, and he handed her the book. "You play dirty."

Stella lifted her chin, biting her lip to hide a grin. "I learned from the best."

Moths fluttered around the lantern, and lights on the main floor of the mansion flickered off. "You should probably go." Henry rubbed the back of his neck. "Jane will be looking for you."

Jane. Stella's heart seized. She'd think Stella had acted in direct defiance, talking to Henry. "I'll see you tomorrow." She handed Henry his copy of the book then ran for the door.

"You'll work on that journal?" Henry leaned against the doorframe.

Stella nodded. "I'll start keeping record in the morning."

Sunlight streamed through Stella's bedroom windows. She rolled over in bed, reaching for the letter from her anonymous friend. One more perusal couldn't hurt. Especially after Jane's scolding last night.

Stella's throat prickled as regret washed over her. Once her week of journaling ended and Henry took her to the institute, she'd cut ties with him.

She shouldn't wait that long. The sooner she stopped speaking to him the better. She could make him take her to Olalla now. After all, she was the master and he the servant. But the thought of pulling rank made her chest ache.

Why was life so unfair? If fortune didn't tether her to a life of duty, she and Henry could remain friends, or maybe more if he was keen. Nothing would have to change.

But Jane was right. Her uncle would never give his blessing to someone of Henry's station, not even for something as simple as friendship. Would any of that matter once she turned twenty-five? Though she wouldn't live under Uncle Weston's guardianship, she had no other family. Could she disrespect him so?

Doubt fogged her mind. If she wasn't certain of her feelings for Henry, it wasn't fair to string him along. He might truly care for her. Best to let him go now, rather than wait and inflict additional pain. Tears trailed hot down her cheeks. That meant no more drives to the coast. How she'd miss those times spent with the person who knew her best.

The letter crinkled between her fingers. Well, whoever wrote these letters understood her too. Maybe now was the time to devote herself fully to this friendship. Though she may never know the man's name, there was something romantic and tragic about writing letters and sharing bits of her heart with someone she'd never see face-to-face.

Unless he was old or married, of course. But she may never receive answers to those questions either.

She unfolded the page then scanned the sharp, slanted words.

My dearest Stella,

I pray this letter finds you well. In fact, you're in my prayers and not far from my thoughts every day. Have your headaches improved with the sea air?

In your last letter, you mentioned your idea for expanding your father's clothing business, and I must admit, it's brilliant. How the stuffed shirts on the board didn't think of it sooner is a mystery. Offering goods to a wider client base could only grow the business. Have you considered a clothing line for children? That may be another avenue that would increase the company's profits while providing jobs to the working class. Just a thought which you're free to ignore.

You asked in your last letter about my hopes for the future. I could talk forever about that, but I would not wish to bore you. Suffice it to say, past experience has formed me into the man I am today. Though I lost my parents earlier than I would have liked, I was cared for by benevolent people. I've visited the poor neigh-borhoods here in San Francisco, and see so many children who lack the care I received when I was orphaned. That's something I'd like to change.

*During our correspondence, I've found we share similar
ambitions. We both wish to make a difference. To leave something
of value when our time on Earth is through. Providing a family
for children who have none is how I hope to leave my mark, much
like your desire to make your father proud with your plans for the
inheritance he left you.*

*I pray my dream of building a children's home is attain-
able. As for the other, the one I hold too close to share, it is a mere
fantasy.*

*Your letters always bring a smile to my face. I await the next
with anticipation.*

Yours very truly

Stella clasped the letter to her chest, lungs evicting a sigh. What
was the unattainable dream he referred to? Though she didn't know
the details, she understood the sentiment. They were so much alike,
although his dreams traveled the moral high ground. His desire to do
good, to impact the lives of others, left her longing for the same. More
than fashionable clothes, people needed food, shelter, and the hope
she'd found in the Lord.

But Papa had left the business to her, and duty bound her to it.
What if she offered to provide clothes and shoes to the children in his
home? It seemed a small contribution, but it may be a means to help
a worthy cause.

The adorable, dirty faces of Robby, Rose, and Daisy sprang to
mind. Her arms longed to gather them into an embrace. To let them
know they were cared for. And how she'd love to put them in contact
with this man once he built his children's home.

Was he close to reaching his goal? These children couldn't wait
much longer. She plucked at her lip. There had to be a way to speed
the process.

If they formed a partnership, the home could be built so much
sooner. She kicked off the bedclothes then padded to her writing desk,
plans swimming through her brain. With their combined resources, so
many children would find a sense of belonging. A family.

She eased onto the chair then grabbed a fresh sheet of paper and her fountain pen. Anticipation tingled her fingers. Finally, a way to leave her mark, to invest her life in something bigger than herself.

Her pen hovered over the paper. Would he see her suggestion as an imposition on his dream? She pinched the bridge of her nose. If she couldn't speak with Henry any longer, she didn't dare jeopardize this friendship.

What should I do? She breathed the prayer out of habit. But the urge to join his endeavor forbade her from waiting on an answer. It couldn't hurt to ask. If she asserted that the orphanage would remain his project and he was free to refuse her offer, there should be no harm in the proposal.

She pulled in a breath then touched pen to paper.

My dearest friend,

Your dreams are contagious. As I read your plans for a children's home, my heart melted. I've visited poor areas in the city, seen the hunger in children's eyes, and wished for a way to help. To make a difference. Despite my desire to make Father proud, my tasks at Burke Clothiers are shallow and unfulfilling. For years, I've believed there must be more to life than fabrics and fripperies, but this is the only life I've known and I'm unsure how to break free of it.

I realize it's asking a lot, but would there be room in your plans for a partner? An investment into the lives of unloved children would be far greater than any profits the clothing business will provide, and my uncle Weston was less than enthused about my ideas for growth. I fear the business world will make no room for me. Even if you should decide the orphanage would run more smoothly under your sole care, allow me to donate clothing for your "family" when the project is running.

Speaking of children's clothing, your idea to branch the business into that market is perfect. I'll mention it to my uncle after his anger has cooled. (I'm afraid I've spoiled his plans to marry me off to a wealthy man yet again.) If he is as indifferent to this idea as the last, the expansion will simply wait until I'm of age and may speak with the board members myself.

Thank you for your prayers. Though I haven't noticed a dif-
ference in my headaches, I hope to have progress to share in the
near future. Dr. Linda Hazzard has written a book on fasting.
I'm reading it now, and just yesterday I learned that she operates
a health clinic in Washington. I've asked our chauffeur to take me
for a visit, but he's formed a childish prejudice against her meth-
ods. Don't worry, though, he'll come around to my way of think-
ing. He always does. And he means well. If he was convinced Dr.
Hazzard could help, he'd never stand in my way. It is simply my
job to convince him.

Yours ever truly,
Stella

As she reached for an envelope, a faint knock stopped her hands. "Who is it?"

"Jane." A pause.

After last night, Stella would prefer readying herself for the day. She steeled her nerves. "Come in."

The door creaked open, and Jane poked her nose inside. "I need to apologize." She closed the door for privacy. "I shouldn't have spoken to you the way I did. Though what I said was true, my tone was unkind."

"You were right." Stella's throat constricted. "And it took a harsh scolding to get my attention." She wiped her eyes. "If Henry feels as you believe he does, it's not fair of me to allow our relationship to go beyond that of a master and servant. Though I hate the thought of it."

Jane wrapped an arm around Stella's shoulder, and she leaned into the old woman's embrace. "Aye. It won't be easy. You've been friends so long. But by and by, you'll see it was for the best. Better a little heartache now than a broken heart later."

"Why does life have to be this way?" Stella opened her desk drawer, withdrew a handkerchief, and dabbed her eyes. "If I did love Henry and he loved me, why shouldn't we be together?"

"In your position, you have more to think of than yourself." Jane motioned toward the dressing table, and Stella obediently took her place, slipping the letter she'd written into her nightgown's sleeve. "Your decisions impact the lives of others. The people who work for you depend on you to make wise financial decisions so they can continue feeding their families."

"But didn't Father leave me more than enough money? And I don't see what harm marrying someone like Henry would do." Stella toyed with the lace on her nightgown. "Wouldn't I have enough money for both of us?"

"Why must you be so contrary?" Jane ran a comb through Stella's hair, taking care not to yank through the knots. "Why not find a man your uncle would approve of and settle down?"

"Because I have met the men my uncle approves of." Stella puffed out a sigh. "Honestly, being a spinster would be a blessing in comparison."

"Hush." Jane nudged her with the comb. "God might take you seriously." A gleam settled in her eyes. "You're still writing your mystery man, aren't you?"

Heat crept into Stella's cheeks. "Yes."

"Maybe it's time you ask for his name." Jane sectioned her hair then began plaiting it into a loose braid.

Stella swallowed hard. Each time she considered asking the question, the idea left her uneasy. Asking his name might lead to other things. What if he wanted to meet her? He might be disappointed by what he saw. She studied her reflection in the mirror then looked away. Not knowing his identity postponed rejection. But if he agreed to partner with her in his plans for the children's home, they'd have to meet in person. Her heart stuttered. Maybe she shouldn't post the letter.

But should helping poor orphaned children be scrapped simply because the romance angle would be lacking? Thoughts of the lives she could touch quelled her regret at remaining an old maid. "Maybe soon I will know his name."

Splotches rimmed with light blocked most of her reflection in the mirror while a tingle settled in her left thumb. How could she hope to help him or anyone else when headaches continued to cripple her? Beastly things. She massaged her temples.

Resolved, she squared her shoulders. No more games, and no journal. A trip to Dr. Hazzard's clinic could wait no longer.

"Jane." Stella tilted her head while Jane fastened her earring. The teardrop-shaped amethysts that fanned to form a violet caught the light beaming through the window. Stella closed her eyes to block the sharp pain the reflection caused.

"Yes, miss?"

"Pack my bags. I'm going on a trip." No matter what Henry thought of Linda Hazzard and the Institute for Natural Therapeutics, he'd take her there. Like it or not.

Chapter Seven

Henry closed the book on fasting then tossed it onto the workbench. How anyone could publish such rubbish left him concerned for the verity of the other books he'd read. Skipping a meal was one thing, but Hazzard's techniques required long periods of abstaining from food. How could going days or weeks without eating be the answer to anyone's problems?

He slouched onto the stool, arms crossed. How would he break the news to Stella he wouldn't take her anywhere near that so-called clinic in Washington State?

The garage door's hinges creaked, and Stella peeked in, dark braid resting on her shoulder. The sunlight streaming in behind her gave her a haloed appearance.

Straightening, Henry took a deep breath. Better to tell her now than wait until she'd completed her week's journal. "Stella, I—"

She raised a hand, silencing him. Last night's playfulness gone, she narrowed her eyes. The pain behind them weighted his shoulders. "You will take me to Dr. Hazzard's clinic tomorrow. I'll pay for your lodging there and back. I can't go any longer without relief."

"But—"

"No arguments." She lifted her chin. "I've allowed you too many liberties, and I apologize. But the family doesn't pay you to form opinions." She dropped her gaze to the ground. "Linda Hazzard is the only licensed fasting professional in the world, and I will see her." The last phrase left her lips barely above a whisper.

The words were a blow to Henry's middle. How could she speak so coldly? As if they hadn't been best friends for years. He struggled to swallow past the knot in his throat.

She didn't know what she was asking. Even if she'd read that crazy book in its entirety, desperation rather than logic must be fueling her decision. Under no circumstances would he take her. Whether she considered him a friend or not, he'd look out for her best interests.

"Looks like you'll be taking the train." He grabbed a wrench from the toolbox then stepped beside the auto.

"What?" She arched a brow. "I thought friends took care of each other."

Why had she chosen that tack? If she'd continued acting like a spoiled child, her pleading would have been easier to ignore. But her reference to their friendship made refusal all the more difficult. Couldn't she see that his care for her made taking her on such a journey impossible?

"I want to take care of you." He moved to the door where she stood. "But I don't think the old Buzzard's clinic is the best way to accomplish that."

"You don't get to choose." She took a step closer until mere inches separated them. "You'll take me tomorrow, and it's not open for discussion."

She'd never understand. After years of every whim being granted, she couldn't see past her selfishness. Yesterday, at Ethel's apartment and in the alley with the orphaned children, a spark of empathy had shone in her eyes. She had transformed into a woman who didn't acknowledge economic standing. But that ember had died sometime during the night. Maybe with the onset of today's headache. Somewhere deep down, the little girl who didn't bother with social class still existed, and a woman who yearned to care for others struggled for freedom. Her letters had revealed her heart's deepest longings. Why had she buried that part of her being?

Although she stood to inherit vast sums of money on her next birthday, enough to buy him a thousand times over, he'd never kowtow to her wishes when they might hurt her in the end. He'd do what was best for her, because he loved her.

His heart slapped his ribs, and her perfume distracted him from her harsh words. Admitting his true feelings, if only to himself, evoked a smile.

"Does that grin mean you'll take me?" Stella's voice lifted, hope alight in her eyes.

He shook his head. "Not at all." As the joy on her face gave way to pain, his heart withered. "I wish I could make you understand. But I can't take you."

"Why?" Her eyes misted.

He couldn't tell her. Not the real reason anyway. "I read her book." He rested a hand on her shoulder. "She'll starve you."

"She'll help me fast until my headaches are gone." Stella shrugged out of his reach. "I would never let anyone starve me. And I found another advertisement for the clinic in Uncle Weston's study. She's helped so many people. My eyes got tired while reading all the wonderful things they said about her. Don't you want that for me? How can you claim to be my friend but deny me the one thing that might truly make a difference?"

His gut churned. "I don't have a good feeling about it. Something doesn't sit right."

"Take me." She grasped his arm. "Jane will come along. Look at the place. If you still feel uneasy after seeing the patients and talking with Dr. Buzz—Hazzard, we can turn around and come home."

"And you'll listen to me? Even if you don't like my opinion?" This might be the only way to cure her of her desire to check in at the Institute of Natural Therapeutics.

Stella hesitated then nodded.

"Even though I'm not paid to think?" He lifted a brow, the sting of her words still fresh.

"I didn't mean it." Stella rubbed his arm, then drew her hand away as if his skin was covered in thorns. She stepped back and raised her chin. "You'll take me tomorrow?"

Why the sudden coldness? Especially now that she figured she'd get her way? "I'll take you."

A smile parted her lips, and she threw her arms around him. "Oh, thank you. I can't—"

"But if I'm still uncomfortable with the place, you won't stay." He gripped her shoulders, meeting her effervescent gaze.

She froze, and her expression softened. The open door let in a breeze that ruffled the hair escaping her braid.

He should tell her.

About the letters. That he loved her. So many things.

But after the way she'd ordered him to drive her despite his distaste for the idea and then demeaned his ability to form a coherent thought, it was clear she knew he wasn't good enough for her. And he never would be.

In a perfect world, their differences wouldn't matter. But there was no such thing as a perfect world.

She blinked then shook her head as if to dislodge a wayward thought. "Henry, I—"

"I need to get back to work." He stepped to the motorcar. "Got to have this beauty in working order for our trip. You do realize it's a two-day drive one way."

Stella nodded, a line forming between her brows. Her cheeks turned a sickly shade of gray.

"Are you all right?" He cupped her elbow.

She shook her head. "I can't see my way to the house." A tear whispered down her cheek. "The lights are blocking everything. I can't see." She slumped against him, clinging to his shirt front.

"I'll get you inside." He drew her close. "I'm sorry if our conversation sapped your strength and left you feeling so poorly."

Stella shook her head against his chest. "I was hurting before. But you certainly didn't help."

There was that spunk. As long as she held on to her mettle, the migraines might wage battles, but they wouldn't win the war.

If only Linda Buzzard's clinic would prove to be the medical miracle Stella believed it to be.

Please, God. Let me be wrong.

Chapter Eight

Stella squirmed on the automobile's leather seat. Rain hammered the windows; the steady drum in her ears enraged the pain that hadn't loosened its hold in three days. She covered her eyes with a gloved hand.

"There, there, dear." Jane fiddled with the blanket on Stella's lap. "Dr. Hazzard will fix you up good as new."

Even if she could see past the stabbing in her forehead, Stella didn't dare meet Henry's eye in the windscreen's reflection. If he didn't approve of the health institute, she'd be compelled to break her promise, though she detested the thought of abandoning her word. Linda Hazzard offered her a glimmer of hope—something she hadn't felt in far too long. If she didn't chase this solitary spark of optimism, she might as well give in and let the headaches win.

What was the worst that could happen?

It wasn't as if her health could deteriorate further. She'd not experienced a pain-free day since Christmas. Since things couldn't possibly get worse, she'd remain the same if Dr. Hazzard's treatment failed.

Tall pines guarded the road on both sides, and their scent of sap and evergreen twisted Stella's stomach. She moved her hand from her eyes to cover her mouth. Though she hadn't eaten a bite since yesterday, the few contents of her stomach formed an angry coup.

By sheer force of will, she swallowed the bile climbing her throat.

The forest gave way to city buildings. Why Linda Hazzard kept her office in the Northern Bank and Trust building in Seattle instead of on the grounds of the Institute for Natural Therapeutics seemed odd, but who could argue with genius?

Stella toyed with her coat's mink collar.

"Here we are." Henry turned down a busy street and stopped in front of a three-story masonry building. The snowcapped Olympic Mountains provided a majestic backdrop.

Stella's skin prickled and a chill snaked down her spine, but she straightened. Why this uneasy feeling? Dr. Hazzard had helped so many. Surely Stella had mistaken the thrill of anticipation for apprehension.

Henry pulled open her door, and Stella stepped onto the pavement.

Jane glanced with furrowed brow at the imposing building. "You never told me Washington was such a dreary place."

Stella cut a sidelong glance to Henry, but he appeared occupied with his own assessment. His lowered brows told her he didn't approve. He turned to Stella, lips pursed. "You sure you want to go through with this? We can still leave."

Shoving her concerns aside, Stella clenched her jaw. "I don't intend to leave." She lifted her skirt out of a puddle then strode to the front door. Each step compounded the agony behind her eyes.

Why was he so judgmental? Just as one shouldn't judge books by their covers, Linda Hazzard's skill should not be measured by the dripping, foggy Pacific Northwest. She may be a medical miracle worker, but the weather remained far from her control.

Henry rushed ahead and held the door for Stella and Jane. As Stella passed over the threshold, she shot him a determined glare, but the concern in his eyes strangled her triumph. She let Jane walk before her into the white-paneled foyer. The sharp odor of fresh paint hung like fog in the air. The polished marble floors carried a sheen Stella used as a mirror until the hopeless state of her flyaway hair forced her gaze to her childhood friend.

"Don't fret, Henry." Stella stepped closer for a remnant of privacy. "This is temporary. I'll follow her instructions as best I can so I can return home all the sooner."

"But what if it's not safe?" The muscles in his jaw bounced.

She placed a hand on his arm, touched by the worry written on his countenance. Clearly, his care for her went deeper than the salary

Uncle Weston paid him, and shame warmed her cheeks for letting notions of his mercenary spirit enter her head. "It must be safe. I've read accounts of the patients she's cured."

"I read *Fasting for the Cure of Disease*, and the premise is bunkum. She believes digestion is the underlying cause of every ailment. But how does digestive distress have any bearing on the pain in your head?"

A woman carrying a reticule squeezed past them out the door.

"Why don't you ask Dr. Hazzard when we meet? I'd hate for you to worry about me while I'm here." Stella forced a smile. The thought of spending time away from him ripped a hole in her chest. How would she cope without Henry's support? He knew her better than anyone. She lowered her hand to her side. Perhaps Jane was right. This separation was for the best. For both of them.

"How do you expect me not to worry?" His hazel eyes grew earnest, and his Adam's apple bobbed as he swallowed. "Stella, I have to tell you something."

Her gut tightened. Dread and ecstasy surged through her veins while her heart thumped like a Navajo drum. The soft yet fervent passion in his eyes told her that what she both hoped and feared was true. But confessions wouldn't do either of them service. "Please don't." Her gaze darted to Jane, who talked with a man in wire-rimmed spectacles, hopefully making arrangements for a meeting with Dr. Hazzard.

"But—"

"You're my best friend." Stella's eyes burned with tears she couldn't shed. "Let's not spoil that now."

He tightened his jaw, letting out a breath through his nose.

What could she say to smooth this over? He probably thought she didn't share his feelings, but a part of her did. A large part. Larger than she could speak aloud. Emotion thickened her throat.

"Dr. Hazzard will see you now." The man adjusted the garters on his shirtsleeves and led them up a staircase. At the top, the clap of their shoes against the hallway's slick tile echoed as if they journeyed through the catacombs. Their guide stopped at a door with a placard bearing the name LINDA BURFIELD HAZZARD.

Stella stepped closer to Jane near the doorway and linked her arm in the crook of the older woman's elbow.

If she didn't maintain a proper distance from Henry, the thread of unspoken words hanging between them would choke her. How fortunate that Jane had come along. Stella's feelings would never carry her away as long as her companion's influence steadied her. As Jane had said, many people were counting on her to make wise decisions. Loving Henry would only let them down.

"You ready, dearie?" Jane patted Stella's hand with cold fingers.

Was she ready? Henry's worry had dampened her former optimism. With a firm nod, Stella stepped into the office. A woman in an ivory blouse sat behind the desk, her bearing as erect as that of a drill sergeant. She motioned to the two chairs at her desk, and Stella took one while Jane eased into the other, joints snapping. Henry stood behind Stella, the strength of his presence calming her frayed nerves. How could he be equal parts impossible and indispensable?

"So good to have you here." The woman glanced up, wearing a smile that seemed rehearsed. Her hair, which had been gathered into a knot at the top of her head, didn't dare move. "I'm Dr. Linda Hazzard. You've come to check into my sanatorium?" She held an ink pen poised over a stack of official-looking papers.

"No, she hasn't." Steel edged Henry's voice. "We've come to learn more about your treatments and see if they'd help Miss Burke."

Dr. Hazzard's eyes narrowed. "Depending on her maladies, my regime could make all the difference. Most of my patients are returned to perfect health before leaving the facility."

Perfect health. The weight in Stella's chest lightened. It sounded far too wonderful to be realistic, but even a slight improvement would change her life. If the man who had written the letters agreed to a partnership, she might have the strength to make a true contribution—something beyond clothes and shoes. "It sounds wonderful." Her voice was barely a whisper.

The doctor nodded. "Seems your friend has no faith in alternative medicine. Are you a meat eater?" She spat the last two words as if they tasted like castor oil.

Stella nodded. At Linda Hazzard's condemning glare, she lowered her gaze to her lap. Never had one look conveyed so much disdain.

"That must change. Meals at my clinic are strictly vegetarian." Hazzard sighed through clenched teeth. "Meat eaters are foolish, disgusting, suicidal."

"Is that so?" Jane grasped Stella's hand then gave it a reassuring squeeze.

"Indeed." Dr. Hazzard gave a curt nod. "Let me tell you about one of my patients—a former meat eater. Mrs. J. B. Barnett suffered many ailments before we crossed paths. Nausea, vomiting, constipation. . ."

Stella cringed. How could Dr. Hazzard speak openly about such personal matters?

The woman continued. "Along with her physical issues, she experienced bouts of melancholia. She even mentioned thoughts of suicide. For years she burdened her family. Always sick, in need of care. Nothing traditional doctors administered cured her body or her mind."

"But then she met you." False deference dripped from Henry's voice.

"And it's fortunate for her she did." Dr. Hazzard rested clasped hands on her desk. Her eyes, as dark as tar pits, glinted with her fervor. "I started her on two vegetarian meals per day. After a week, it dropped to one. Daily internal baths produced old fecal matter—"

"Internal baths?" Stella cocked her head. Wasn't bathing an external practice?

Dr. Hazzard offered a tight smile. "Enemas."

Stella's mouth went dry. "Daily?"

"It sounds much worse than it is." Though the doctor's voice still carried an air of disengaged candor, her tone softened a degree. "But it's a necessary practice. It helps flush the toxins from your digestive tract and leads to ultimate health."

With a heightened consciousness of Henry's presence behind her, Stella shifted in her chair, deigning to meet his gaze. That he should hear such intimate details of the treatments she would undergo suffused her with crawling heat.

Jane patted her hand then addressed Henry. "Clayton. Why don't you go check on the motorcar?" The dear woman always understood.

"The auto's fine." He crossed his arms.

"Then find something useful to do." Jane's brogue thickened with her annoyance.

He leaned closer to Stella's ear and whispered, "You promised that if I felt uneasy, you'd come home and forget this foolishness. How can I get an honest assessment if I'm not allowed to listen to the treatment plan?"

At the determined set of his jaw, Stella met his unyielding gaze. Who did he think he was that he could order her life? As if all decisions surrounding her health rested solely on his shoulders. He wasn't the one living with pain, so he deserved no say in the matter. "No matter what the treatments entail, I'm staying."

He stared at her in disbelief. "But you promised."

Her gut twisted, but after the little she'd heard from Dr. Hazzard, she couldn't be certain if the sensation was guilt or the toxins that had set up housekeeping in her digestive tract. The dull ache behind her eyes grew to a jagged pain. "Clayton, please go. I can't bear for you to hear all this." She kneaded her temples with her fingertips. Why must he make this difficult? Though the treatment sounded rigorous and unpleasant, perfect health was the goal.

Henry stomped toward the door, stopping short of the threshold. He spun and pinned Dr. Hazzard with a hard glare. "Can you end Miss Burke's headaches? Will all this be worth it?"

The woman behind the desk rose. Though she didn't match Henry in height, her frame was large and rather masculine. Muscles rippled in the backs of her hands as she smoothed her skirt. "I can make no promises. But I guarantee that Miss Burke will receive the best of care. I'll offer her my most beautiful treatment and oversee all her affairs personally. My methods are proven. Consider the place as a spa rather than a clinic, because I provide a spa experience."

Hands thrust in his pockets, Henry stepped into the hall.

Dr. Hazzard resumed her seat. "Where were we?"

"You were telling us of a Mrs. Barnett," Jane said, casting Stella a hopeful smile.

"Ah, yes." The doctor rested her elbows on the desk. "During the next phase of her fast, she ate a little fruit, then we started the total fast."

"How long did it last?" Stella asked. And why the sudden longing for strawberry ice cream?

"Forty-eight days." Dr. Hazzard's flat tone made the outrageous number sound slightly less shocking.

"But she must have been starving." Stella rested a hand on her middle.

Linda Hazzard shook her head. "She kept busy. Gluttony and boredom often hold hands. With her hours occupied by useful tasks, she didn't even think of food until the forty-fifth day of her fast. At that time, her body had expelled the toxins that were poisoning it and for the first time in years, Mrs. Barnett experienced true hunger. Not the craving most men and women give in to."

Stella let the words sink in. She was given to cravings, eating whatever suited her fancy. Strawberry ice cream topped the list, but how many times had she eaten simply because it was dinnertime? More often than she cared to admit. "And what were Mrs. Barnett's results?"

"Complete healing." Dr. Hazzard beamed. "We slowly returned her to solid foods. Her digestive issues as well as her melancholy were things of memory. She returned home with a purpose and a vivacity she'd never known before."

"And you think you could do the same for me?" Stella gripped the chair's wooden arms.

Dr. Hazzard traced a cursory glance over Stella and gave a brusque nod. "I see no reason you shouldn't regain your health. You don't appear too infirm. Why, I rescued a boy in Minnesota from death's front door. Your case is nowhere near as severe as his."

Her assurances fanned the embers of hope in Stella's chest, igniting them into a flame. Had Dr. Hazzard's treatment really saved a child from dying? If it was so, no doubt the migraines could be chased away along with the toxic matter keeping health out of reach.

Jane nodded, approval gleaming in her eyes. "It all sounds so wonderful." She squeezed Stella's hands. "Just think, Miss Stella, in a short while you'll be enjoying life again."

Enjoying life.

Stella's vision blurred. Perfect health was finally attainable.

Henry paced the pavement beside the motorcar. Though Stella's rejection still stung, concern, rather than disappointment, carved a hollow in his gut. "Something's not right." He raked splayed fingers through his hair then affixed his eyes on Jane. "Why are we not allowed to see the old Buzzard's precious clinic?"

Jane pinned him with an admonishing gaze. "It's just her way. Her husband will take Miss Stella to Wilderness Heights as soon as we leave."

"Wilderness Heights?"

"That's what she calls it." Jane untied the cord securing one of Stella's bags to the back of the automobile. "And she's promised to oversee every aspect of Miss Stella's care. Now are you going to help me or not?" She motioned to a trunk.

"I don't want to." Henry crossed his arms.

The old woman settled her gnarled hand on his forearm. "You've got to let her go. It's for the best. Surely you must see there's no future for the two of you."

Henry opened his mouth to speak then closed it and cleared his throat. "You misunderstand."

"I misunderstand nothing." She shook her head, eyes soft. "She thinks about you more than she ought to. The separation will help you forget her, and it may remind Stella of her duty to her family and those under her employ. They depend upon her, you know."

Did Stella really think of him as Jane said? Henry forced back a smile. He shouldn't be happy, but a bit of the tightness in his chest eased. As he hefted the trunk and followed Jane to the loading dock behind the building, he rehearsed the fragments of the treatment the Buzzard had prescribed for Stella. He shouldn't have listened at the door, but if he didn't have the details, worry for her would chew him into swiss cheese while she was away.

Fasting.

Daily internal baths.

Osteopathic massage.

Even though none of it struck him as appealing or even sensible given Stella's current condition, the flicker of promise in her voice compelled him to hope with her. If nothing else, the positivity might take her mind off the headaches, thus reducing their frequency and severity. And after Dr. Buzzard regaled both Jane and Stella with stories of people she'd cured and lives she'd saved, the chances of Stella going home before receiving treatment had died a miserable death.

Maybe Stella was right. The treatments, while far from the norms of traditional medicine, hadn't caused harm. If they had, the state of Washington wouldn't permit Linda Burfield Hazzard to continue practicing.

"Set the trunk there." Jane indicated an automobile parked in the alley behind the bank.

He followed her instruction then returned for another load.

His biceps complained under the weight of her trunk. These bags must contain everything Stella owned. How long did she plan to stay at Wilderness Heights? A dog yipped from somewhere down the street.

A little boy in a blue cap barreled into him, followed by a scrawny puppy. Henry gripped the child by his shoulders and crouched to meet his eyes.

"You all right, little chap?"

The boy's breathing was ragged. His gaze darted to the bank then fixed on Henry. He shook his head. "Let me go. I can't stay here." He wrenched his arms free.

Fear lurked behind the innocent blue eyes, inspiring protectiveness in Henry. "Are you in trouble? I can help. What's your name?" And where were this boy's parents?

Again the child glanced at the bank. "Jack."

Henry followed his line of sight to a second-story window. Linda Hazzard's silhouette swayed behind the glass. A drill sergeant if ever there was one.

"She might see me and take me to her graveyard." Jack gulped while the dog licked his hand as if sensing his master's distress. "That's what'll happen if I don't run straight home."

Dread curled in Henry's stomach. Surely the child's imagination had gotten the better of him. But most children wanted nothing more than to be heard. "Tell me about this graveyard. Where is it?"

"Not here." Jack ran the back of a dirt-smudged hand across his nose. "My aunt owns a bakery close to her graveyard in Olalla." He pointed to the doctor's shadow in the window. "Aunt Betsy's seen the skeletons." His voice quavered. "They come to her shop begging for bread."

The hair on Henry's neck rose. Skeletons? "Tell me more."

Jack shook his head, eyes wide. "If she finds out I didn't go home, I'll be next." He called to his puppy and darted down the sidewalk, the dog at his side.

The tale was too fantastic to be true. Probably just a local fable used to frighten little boys around a campfire during scout meetings. Or something parents told their children to inspire obedience. But surely someone had seen something out of the ordinary to invent such a story. Skeletons? Just how little did the Old Buzzard feed her patients? Was she starving them until they looked like corpses? But if that was the case, the authorities would step in. Wouldn't they?

Henry massaged the back of his neck. He'd warn Stella before she left. Tell her to keep watch for strange happenings, anything that might be out of place or worrisome. If she felt the slightest prick of concern, she could send him a telegram, and he'd drive up straightaway.

When he'd piled the remainder of Stella's bags in the alley, Jane handed him an envelope. "Miss Stella asked that I have you post this letter."

His mouth dried. "But I want to see her off."

"She thought it best you see her after her course of treatments."

"But that could be months." And how could he warn her of the young boy's frightening story?

Jane nodded, pity in her smile. "Aye. And no doubt you'll both have moved on by then."

But he didn't want to move on. "I have something to tell her." The story may be the overworked delusions of childhood, but what if it wasn't?

"I'd be happy to pass on your message."

As Henry shared Jack's strange talk of skeletons begging for food, Jane's brows arched. "Seems like the boy believes a ghost story." Her voice was light, but the way she wrung her hands said otherwise.

"I'm sure you're right." It really was too wild to believe. He stilled the old woman's anxious fidgeting. "But tell her to be on her guard. And if she needs to leave, all she has to do is send a wire."

"I will." Jane's eyes glistened. "I'm sorry things couldn't be different. You care for her, and sometimes I wonder if that isn't more important than all the details the wealthy put stock in."

Henry studied his shoelaces. "And you think she cares for me?"

"What good would it do if she did?" Jane lifted a shoulder. "Now, be off with you. Post that letter, and we'll head home."

Henry kicked a pebble across the pavement then strode from the alley to the sidewalk. He could drive, but a walk would clear his head and perhaps dispel the gloom Jack's fears had invited. He lifted the envelope and scanned the address.

His post office box in San Francisco. Maybe his inability to tell Stella he'd been writing her for the past five years was a blessing, for it had given him the chance to peer into her heart once more. He settled on a bench outside a barber shop.

After unfolding the letter, he scanned the text. Some of her usually well-formed letters swayed as if they'd been written while he was driving.

My dearest friend,

I mentioned Dr. Linda Hazzard in my last letter, which I doubt you've had a chance to receive.

I shall arrive at her clinic this morning. Though I haven't received your answer regarding my suggestion, it became apparent to me that in my state of health, I'm of no use to anyone. For years my headaches have crippled me, sending me to bed early and making a normal, fulfilled life something I can only dream about.

No more.

With Dr. Hazzard's help, I shall conquer this. Even if you aren't amenable to my ideas, my life can't continue on this path.

Please, pray for me. That the treatments will be successful and I will return home whole.

Though I'm many miles from home, I would like to continue

our correspondence for the duration of my stay at Wilderness
Heights. I hope to hear from you soon. I am enclosing my tempo-
rary address.

> *Yours ever truly,*
> *Stella*

Henry fished a scrap of paper bearing an address on Orchard Avenue in Olalla from the envelope. He slid the information into his pocket with a sigh.

What suggestion had she made? He ran a hand over his face. With any luck, the letter would be in his box when he arrived home, dispelling the mystery. One thing was certain, whatever her idea, he'd be amenable. Other than this confinement in Buzzard's sanatorium, he'd never begrudge her anything she wished.

His throat constricted. She wanted nothing more to do with him. Didn't even want to see him before her admittance to Wilderness Heights. Yet she wanted to converse with a character he had fabricated when she needed a friend of her own social standing. It wasn't fair to keep it secret any longer. To continue feeding her hopes, knowing the truth would dash them to splinters.

He sprang off the bench and checked his timepiece. If he ran, he might catch her. The time apart would give her the opportunity to forgive him for leading her on, or at the very least turn her angry boil into a simmer.

As he ran toward the Northern Bank and Trust, dodging women in wide-brimmed hats and boys on bicycles, he stuffed Stella's letter into his pocket. His stomach churned, and the sensation had little to do with toxins or poor digestion. He should have told her months ago. Years ago.

With each letter written in secrecy, he'd driven a larger wedge between them. How could he expect forgiveness?

As he rounded the bank, his steps slowed. He couldn't hope she'd forgive him, but she deserved the truth.

Clouds of exhaust billowed from the tailpipe of Hazzard's automobile.

Was he too late?

"Stella!" He choked the word past the fumes filling his lungs and stopped beside Jane.

As the car pulled away, Stella turned. Their eyes met, hers filled with a cocktail of hope and sadness. She pressed gloved fingers to her lips and blew him a kiss.

The man behind the wheel turned the motorcar down the alley and out of sight.

So many things left unsaid. He'd been a fool to write her in the first place.

Jane gave his arm a pat. "Next time we see her she'll be a different person."

The sinking sensation in his chest affirmed her words. Stella would be a changed person, and as her letter requested, he would pray for her. For her health. For her safety. But most of all that she would find a way to forgive him.

Chapter Nine

As the car dipped into a pothole, Stella braced in her seat. Tears surfaced, but she swallowed hard against them. Jane's advice to leave without saying goodbye to Henry may have been wise, but she'd wanted to apologize for her harsh words in Dr. Hazzard's office. When she had seen him dashing toward her in the alley, she'd nearly lost her resolve and begged the driver, Dr. Hazzard's husband, Sam, to stop the motorcar and give her a moment to clear the cobwebs she'd allowed to form between them.

Jane's recounting of a little boy's story of skeletons walking the Wilderness Heights grounds had wound her nerves into knots. Stella had almost reconsidered her journey onward, but Jane had assured her she'd only relayed the tale to keep a promise to Henry and she saw no need to give credence to such a far-fetched story. Stella had erased the thought, justifying her disregard as a little boy's propensity to believe unearthly things. But when she'd seen the expression on Henry's face, something more powerful than fear had expanded within her. How she'd miss him. She choked on a sob. But he might not give her a second thought after her last words to him.

She cut her gaze to Sam Hazzard. He had a handsome face and his dark hair fell in a wave over his forehead. When the sun peeked from behind a cloud, its rays glinted off his gold wire-framed glasses. "Do you work at Wilderness Heights?" A silly question, but the silence between them had crossed the line from companionable into awkward.

"I do what Linda asks." His words were clipped, uninviting. When he shifted, the scent of vanilla wafted through the air.

Stella leaned back and sighed. *This will be a jolly ride.* The sarcastic thought made her bite her lip. Her head rested on the seat, and her stomach growled. Was it hunger, or just unnecessary cravings as Dr. Hazzard had said? For the first time since she could recall, she hushed her thoughts to listen to her body. A vast pit yawned in her stomach, begging for food, not caring whether it be filled with strawberry ice cream or plain brown bread. She was hungry.

But the patient Dr. Hazzard had mentioned, Mrs. Barnett, hadn't been hungry for a full forty-five days after her fast commenced. Did keeping busy as the doctor purported really silence hunger long enough for the body to heal and allow the toxins to make their escape through the internal baths? The thought of daily enemas sent a cringe coiling down her spine. Since true hunger was already so close, maybe her treatments would be of short duration.

She pressed a hand against her complaining belly. Hopefully her stay wouldn't last long, and she'd be well.

Mist hung in the air as a remnant of the morning rain. Evergreens stood sentinel along the road, and the mountains boasted God's handiwork. Such a lovely scene. She breathed in the mountain breeze perfumed with pine and salt from the ocean a mile to the west as it blew through the cab.

Perfect health. Whenever she doubted, she'd remind herself why she'd come. Replay the details of Mrs. Barnett. And perhaps Dr. Hazzard would tell her the full story of the little boy who lived as a testament to her miraculous treatments.

The trees on her right parted, revealing a crisp white building. Rather primitive and nothing like the grand picture her mind had painted. But just as she'd come close to chiding Henry for judging Linda Hazzard before they met, she would postpone forming an opinion of Wilderness Heights a while longer.

Little cabins dotted the hillside behind the main building, each connected to the larger structure by a dirt path like tributaries. Sam stopped on a pebbled drive in front of the main house, and Stella stepped out, surveying the landscape. A cabin door opened, and a woman stepped into the sunshine. As she strolled the lane toward them, her dress, which hung loosely on her gaunt frame, tangled between her legs. She stumbled then fell to her knees.

Stella glanced at Sam who watched, lifting a small brown bottle labeled "Vanilla Extract" to his lips. Why wasn't he moving to help her? Couldn't he see the woman needed assistance?

With her skirt's hem gathered in her hand, Stella dashed to the woman who seemed too weak to stand. When she gripped the woman's arm, the feel of skin stretched over bone made Stella recoil. What had happened to make her so painfully thin?

Regaining her bearings, Stella steeled her nerves. If she could help, no amount of aversion would stop her. "Are you quite all right?" The answer was plain, but nothing more original came to mind.

The woman fixed dull gray eyes on Stella.

Stella's heart broke at the sight of her face. Sunken cheeks, thin lips that didn't boast enough flesh to cover her teeth, no spark. Was this one of the skeletons the boy had talked about?

"What is your name?" The words struggled past the knot in Stella's throat.

A macabre smile stretched paper-thin skin. "Dorothea Williamson." Her voice was as frail as her grip on Stella's hand. "But you can call me Dora. Everyone does." The more she spoke, the more pronounced the cadence of her British accent became.

"How long have you been here?" Stella swallowed once then again, but the lump in her throat grew.

Dora shook her head, her brown hair limp against her shoulders. "I've not finished my treatment yet. But I'm getting better."

If this was better, what had been her condition upon arrival?

Stella guided Dora over the knobby path to the white building.

"Let me rest here a moment." Dora pointed a trembling finger toward a chair on the veranda.

"I can sit with you." Stella helped her into a seat.

Sam clomped onto the porch, shoving the vanilla bottle into his jacket pocket. "You'll come inside, Miss Burke. I'll show you to your room and get you settled."

"But—"

"Dr. Hazzard's orders." He hefted her trunk and pushed through the front door.

"You'd better go." Dora offered a faint smile. "Dr. Hazzard knows best."

As Stella followed Sam Hazzard into the sanatorium, her knees turned to mush, and the familiar pain behind her eyes took on new life. What had she gotten herself into?

❧

Stella pulled her purple nightgown from her trunk and laid it in the dresser drawer. Thoughts of Dora's weakened condition distracted her from the headache that hadn't completely let her go. What maladies had the woman endured to bring her to this point? If she'd consulted as many physicians as Stella had, Wilderness Heights must have been a last resort. Maybe if Dora had come sooner, she wouldn't have gotten so very sick. And why was she housed in a cabin instead of the main house? Dr. Hazzard must know Dora was far too weak to trek to the house for her treatments. If there wasn't enough room in the main house, Dora could take her room, and Stella the cabin.

A knock at the door halted her unpacking.

"Come in." She closed the drawer.

The door swung open, and Linda Hazzard strode inside, a white robe draped over her shoulder. "Glad to see you're getting settled." She planted her hands on her hips. "I'd like to start your treatments right away."

Stella eased onto the bed. The metal frame squeaked beneath her weight. "I'd like to discuss two things before we begin."

Dr. Hazzard crossed muscular arms and lifted a brow. "Very well."

"I met Dora Williamson today, and she was looking very poorly. Is there some—"

"Sometimes a person must get worse before they can get better. The process of eliminating toxins from the body is strenuous, but I assure you she's on her way to recovery." The doctor's tone carried not the slightest hint of patience. "When she first arrived, she suffered from both physical and mental ailments. Healing takes time. The toxins didn't develop overnight, and one can't expect to rid the body in a few days."

The words wrestled in Stella's brain. Dora had seemed perfectly lucid. Dr. Hazzard's treatments must be healing her mind at least. Her body was sure to follow.

"And what was your other concern?" The doctor's jaw muscles jumped.

"We haven't had a chance to discuss my ailments, and I'm sure you need to know my medical history before we proceed with the regime." Stella rested her hand on the cool cast-iron bed head.

"I need to know nothing of the kind." Dr. Hazzard took a step closer to the open door. Hushed voices filtered in from the hallway while feet shuffled across the floor. "You may think you know the full extent of your problems, but modern medicine has lied to you. Whatever your symptoms, they are not your true concern. They merely point to the root of the problem. Digestion. You've overeaten and indulged, eaten meat, filled your digestive tract with toxins. And those toxins are like poison in your system. What you really suffer from is a slow form of suicide. But when we treat your sickness at its source, the outward manifestations of an unclean digestive system will cease."

"So my headaches are just a symptom of the larger problem?" Stella wrapped her arms around her middle. How many doctors had she consulted in her quest for health? But none had ever told her digestion was to blame for her migraines. Perhaps that was the reason none of their methods had worked. They'd never eliminated the root problem.

A genuine smile softened Dr. Hazzard's stoic features. "Now you're catching on, my dear." She handed Stella the stiff robe. "Strip down and put this on. I'll be waiting just outside the door. It's time for your first massage."

Stella held the skimpy covering against her chest, cheeks hot. What if Sam was in the corridor? He couldn't see her in such a state of undress.

Dr. Hazzard stepped out of the room, securing the door behind her. If the doctor wasn't concerned about her husband, she must have sent him on an errand.

Stella removed her clothing, letting it fall in a pile on the plank floor. Though she was capable of caring for herself, homesickness settled near her heart at the absence of the gossip and laughter she shared with dear Jane.

Robe snug around her shoulders, she stepped into the hall on bare feet. No signs of life in the corridor. Silence thick enough to feel against her skin pervaded the space. What now? Where was Dr. Hazzard? Stella rubbed a chill from her arm. Should she wait here or search for her?

Dr. Hazzard's voice echoed from somewhere down the hall, and Stella jumped at the sudden break in quiet. She followed the sounds, though she could not make out the words. She peeked in an open door to her left. Dr. Hazzard stood inside, hands on hips, blocking most of the room from view. A commode stood in one corner and a sink in the other.

When the doctor stepped to the right, a human form—even frailer than Dora's—appeared on an ironing board suspended over the bathtub. Blue lips, glassy eyes. Brown hair matted around her head. A nose the same shape as Dora's. Was the woman dead?

"No, I don't need the saw, Sarah. I haven't a big enough kettle no matter how I piece her apart." Dr. Hazzard lowered her voice. "We'll call Butterworth's to take care of her after dinner. It'll be a burial, not a cremation in this case, since we can't prepare her for the crematorium. Just be sure to preserve her organs." The doctor shook her head. "Did you see the condition of her liver? No amount of fasting would have saved her. She was too sick already."

The dark-haired woman in the nurse's uniform nodded and placed a handsaw on the washstand.

Stella covered a gasp. The woman hovering over the bathtub lay completely exposed. The spaces between her ribs gaped beneath a membrane of blue-veined skin while her shoulder blades protruded. Bruises in various states of healing speckled her arms and legs. Some a sickly yellow-green, others nearly black. And her face—what little Stella could see of it—was nothing more than a skull with pale skin clinging to the hills and valleys like wallpaper gripping water-damaged plaster. Whoever this woman had been, she made poor Dora look like the picture of health.

Heart thwacking against her ribs, Stella blinked back tears. She'd never seen a dead body in this condition before. Of course, she'd held Father's hand as he passed, but while sad, the moment was peaceful.

This woman had suffered much. Had she been alone when she passed? Why would Dr. Hazzard want to saw her to pieces? To prepare her for cremation if that were an option? And why wait until after dinner to call for help? If she was concerned about postponing Stella's osteopathic massage, Stella would willingly wait to start treatments out of respect for the dead. But should she make her presence known and release the doctor to deal with the tragedy?

Despite the grisly scene, she couldn't tear her gaze away. Like an accident she'd seen in the clothing factory when she was a girl. A man had caught his arm in some piece of machinery. The sight of blood and his hand lying dead on the floor, severed from his arm, had sickened her, yet at the same time held her transfixed.

Wait. Surely her eyes deceived her.

She squinted. Deep purple bruises on the woman's neck made Stella's heart stand still. What if the woman hadn't died of natural causes? Perhaps something—or someone—had helped her along. Instead of an undertaker, Dr. Hazzard ought to send for the police.

The nurse, Sarah. Had she done this? Or was it Sam? Stella chided herself. While Sam lacked much in the way of personality, suspecting him of murder was a leap.

Stella stepped away from the door. If her suspicions were correct and the woman had been strangled, Dr. Hazzard would report the crime.

She padded down the corridor, slipped into her bedroom, and pulled the robe tight around her neck. Henry had been right to worry. The little boy's story of the skeletons had been more fact than fable. If only Henry were here. She'd cable him in the morning. Ask him to take her home. After all she'd seen, she couldn't stay. It may not be safe. Besides, if Dr. Hazzard cured patients as sick as Dora Williamson, perhaps Stella wasn't ill enough to seek the kind of treatment others viewed as a last resort.

But Linda Hazzard had seemed so certain her treatments would answer all Stella's prayers. Should she call for Henry or remain here for treatment?

At the thought of Henry and home, peace embraced her. Yes. She'd swallow her pride, admit her wrong, and go home. Since Henry had read Dr. Hazzard's book, he could help her fast in familiar sur-roundings. Thank heaven he had read the cursed thing. Though how he made sense of it was a mystery. When Stella tried, confusion had set in after fifteen pages, and she'd struggled to make heads or tails of the medical jargon.

A chill settled in her bones. First thing in the morning, she'd send the telegram. She pulled the pillow off the bed and hugged it tight. The longer she stayed in this place, the more danger she may find herself in.

But why had Dr. Hazzard and Sarah seemed so unfazed by the presence of the saw in the death chamber? Such things were far from ordinary. Bile rose in Stella's throat, but she forced it down. If the nurse or whoever killed that poor woman had any inkling the crime had been discovered, Stella's life may be the next snuffed out.

Chapter Ten

A knock on Stella's door jolted her awake. Her eyelids cracked. At the sight of her room at Wilderness Heights, she groaned. It hadn't been a dream. This wasn't home, and Jane wasn't waking her to prepare her for breakfast with Uncle Weston. Her throat ached.

Another knock, this one more insistent. "Miss Burke. Breakfast in twenty minutes."

"Coming." She rolled over in bed, clasping the pillow to her middle. Last night's osteopathic massage had been postponed for obvious reasons, though Dr. Hazzard hadn't mentioned the woman's murder.

Footsteps in the hallway had kept her awake long into the night. Probably the police. No doubt Nurse Sarah would be at the sheriff's office for questioning.

Her stomach gnawed at her ribs. After the scare of seeing the skeleton over the bathtub, she had skipped dinner, overcome with another headache. Maybe Henry was right. Stress must play a part. She'd promised to journal her symptoms, and when he brought her home he might suggest it again. Her toes peeked from beneath the covers to touch the cold floor. She moved to the writing desk in the corner and sat on the uncomfortable wooden chair. Might as well start keeping records.

As she jotted the circumstances and feelings surrounding her migraine, her stomach gurgled, reminding her that her notes could wait. Breakfast trumped all else.

She pulled a blue-and-white-striped linen dress from the closet, slipped out of her nightgown, and pulled the dress over her head. One glance in the mirror showed snarled hair, and she puffed out a sigh. If only Dr. Buzzard hadn't denied her request to keep Jane. How would she ever manage alone? Stella bit back a smile. Henry's nickname for the doctor might get her in trouble if it should ever slip out in conversation.

After plaiting her hair as well as her fumbling fingers allowed, she ran her hands over the skirt of her dress to smooth the wrinkles. She checked the clock on the wall. Three minutes to spare.

In the dining room, she scanned the round tables, each covered with a white cloth. Only eleven patients waited for the morning meal. One woman wore a blank expression, her hazy eyes staring into the void, and spittle dripped down her chin. She must have come looking for mental healing. And her cheeks were sunken, though not as badly as Dora's.

Where was Dora? As thin and frail as she was, food would be a lifeline. But her face was nowhere among the others. What if she had to sit with a stranger? Stella swallowed against the dryness in her mouth. She should have stayed in her room and ordered breakfast on a tray.

A middle-aged gentleman with graying hair motioned to her. His smile warmed the lonely chill in Stella's soul. "If you're looking for a place to sit, there's a chair here." He patted the seat beside him.

Stella returned his smile and settled into the offered chair. A young man set a short glass about a quarter full of orange juice in front of Stella without so much as a nod of acknowledgment. The sweet, tangy aroma poked her empty stomach, and she snatched the glass off the table.

"Slow down." The man who'd invited her to dine with him placed a hand on her arm. "You'll want to make it last." He lifted a spoon off the tablecloth, dipped it into his cup, and took a sip fit for an infant.

Make it last? Was this breakfast? All of it?

Stella pulled in a breath, testing the air for eggs, toast, even porridge. Nothing. Hadn't Dr. Hazzard promised the regime would begin with two meals a day? Certainly this didn't constitute a meal.

"What is your name, sir?" She picked up her spoon and followed his example. Never had orange juice tasted more like sweet nectar. Pity there wasn't more to be had.

"Wendell Church at your service." He tipped an imaginary hat. His amiable smile seemed to be a permanent fixture beneath his mustache.

"What brings you here? You look to be in excellent health." Apart from a bright red tinge to his skin, Mr. Church appeared to be a testament to Dr. Hazzard's skill.

He spooned another sip of juice into his mouth, mustache twitching. "I've suffered bouts of indigestion since I was a boy. When I saw an advertisement for Wilderness Heights, I came straightaway. This is my second week, and I've already seen some improvements."

Maybe this place wasn't so very frightening. A woman a few years older than Stella with black hair pulled into the Gibson-girl fashion claimed the chair beside Mr. Church. Though thin, she didn't appear emaciated like the photographs Stella had seen of the children in India—or like Dora or the murdered woman.

"Tilda." He patted her shoulder. "Let me introduce you to a new friend." He cast Stella a questioning glance. "What was your name, my dear?"

"Stella Burke." She savored a sip of orange juice.

"Very well, very well, Tilda Jennings, meet Stella Burke."

Tilda smiled, reaching for her spoon. She already knew about stretching breakfast. How long had she been here?

"It's a pleasure to meet you." Stella forced down the fluttering in her chest brought on by talking with strangers. Lights, sharp and swirling, crept across her vision. She dropped her spoon and rested her head in her hand. Time and consistency would chase the toxins from her body along with the pain, but unfamiliar surroundings made the throbbing worse. Oh, to curl up in her own bed with the drapes closed and a pillow over her head.

"I'm guessing you get migraines." Tilda's voice was barely above a whisper, as if she understood the additional pain a sentence spoken aloud inflicted.

Stella nodded, keeping her eyes closed tight. "Do you suffer from them as well?"

"I do—I did." Tilda's spoon clinked against her glass. The low murmurs of other patients landed like shouts on Stella's ears, each syllable delivering staccato pain.

"You did?"

"I've been fasting for ten days. And in the last two, I've had no attacks. It's a miracle, really." She paused, likely sipping from her spoon. "Before I started Dr. Hazzard's regime, my head ached constantly. There were good days and bad, of course, but I was never without pain to some degree."

"Tell me about the treatments." Stella rubbed the spot above her eyebrow where the throb had settled. "I've been told about massages and"—she glanced at Mr. Church and lowered her voice—"internal baths."

Mr. Church chuckled as he discarded his spoon in his empty glass. "Stella, my dear, we have no secrets big or small among us. Our treatments are similar, so no need to hide behind a cloak of decorum." Chair legs scraped as he shifted in his seat. "And to answer your question, 'internal bath' is just another name for Chinese water torture. I'm sure of it."

Tilda snorted a laugh, and Stella cracked her eyelids to meet the woman's gaze. "Is it really that bad?"

With a reluctant smile, Tilda nodded. "The first time is very unpleasant, but the body grows accustomed to the discomfort." She lifted the glass to her lips, holding it upside down to catch the final drop. "Truth be told, I prefer the internal baths to Dr. Hazzard's massages."

Stella shuddered, pushing her half-finished breakfast away.

"You're not going to finish that?" Mr. Church eyed her juice like a cat does a mouse.

She gestured to the glass. "It's yours if you like, Mr. Church."

With the reflexes of a shell game artist, he switched her partial cup for his empty one. "Much obliged. And you can call me Wendell. Just as there are no secrets, there are no formalities." He scooped juice into his mouth then sighed as if he'd tasted ice cream.

"What are the massages like?" Stella rested her arms on the table. "I'm to have my first later this morning."

An empty look settled in Tilda's eyes, and her brow puckered. "The first time is rather painful. Though I've never enjoyed the kneading and pounding, it helps to know the pain stems from toxins leaving the body. If not for that, I'd never permit it."

Kneading and pounding? Could it be as bad as all that? If Tilda's assessment was true, the sooner Stella sent word to Henry, the better.

"If I wanted to send a telegram to a friend, who would I speak with?" Though Wendell and Tilda had found healing, the fear inspired by last night's discovery still clawed her brain. She needed a plan in case something went awry.

"Rollie Burfield." Wendell drained the last dribble of juice, scraped his finger along the inside of the cup, and licked it.

"Who's Rollie Burfield?" She scanned the room. Several patients stood, their clothes too large for their bodies.

"Dr. Hazzard's son." Tilda pointed to a man at the doorway. He had inherited his mother's dark eyes and firm jaw. "He does the fetching and carrying around here. Give your message to him, and he'll see it's sent."

A tap on Stella's shoulder drew her attention from Rollie. When her gaze met that of the woman she'd seen with Dr. Hazzard and the dead lady, her blood froze. Nurse Sarah. Why was she here? Shouldn't she be at the police station, answering questions about the woman's murder? Unless someone else bore the blame for the woman's death.

"Miss Burke." Sarah's voice dripped with artificial honey. "Time for your osteopathic massage. Put on your robe and meet Dr. Hazzard in the upstairs hall. She'll be with you shortly."

Stella rose, laying her napkin on the place mat where a plate should have been.

In daylight, Sarah appeared young, even pleasant. Her rosy lips parted in a tight smile. "Very good." She squeezed Stella's arm. "I'll let the doctor know you'll be ready in a moment."

"You're Sarah?" Stella bit the inside of her cheek.

"Sarah Anderson." The nurse nodded, white cap bobbing. "If you need anything, just ask. I want to see you feeling much better by the time you leave."

How could this soft-spoken woman be a murderer? The pieces didn't fit. Something was missing. "I do need to send a telegram."

Nurse Anderson guided her to Rollie and the doorway. "Miss

Burke would like to send a cable."

Rollie Burfield shoved his hands into his pockets and fixed Stella with a roguish stare. "Is that so?"

"Don't be impossible, Rollie. I'd hate to tell your mother you were misbehaving."

Though he was a grown man, Rollie's face blanched. "Don't go to extremes." He forced a smile. "Bring me the message once you've written it, and I'll take it to the telegraph office in Olalla."

"Thank you." Stella strode to the staircase. That mother-son relationship must be fraught with dysfunction. If a man who appeared to be in his late twenties harbored such fear, why didn't he move away? Start his own life?

In her room, Stella replaced her dress with the robe then waited outside her door for Dr. Hazzard, fingers clasping the robe's collar at her throat.

Footsteps in the hall signaled the doctor's approach. "Right this way, Miss Burke." Dr. Hazzard ushered her into a room closed in by stark white walls. A table with a thin layer of padding sat at the room's center. "Remove the robe and lie facedown on the cot." The doctor's tone proved that seeing her patients in compromising positions didn't faze her.

No one but Jane had ever seen Stella in such a state. She tightened her grip on the collar.

"Off with it." Patience drained from Dr. Hazzard's voice. "If you ever hope to be well, you must learn to follow instructions. The toxins are killing you, but it seems like you want that to happen."

Stella let the robe drop to the floor and avoided meeting the doctor's stern eye as she scrambled onto the table.

"Now lie still." Dr. Hazzard kneaded Stella's thighs like bread dough. "Your body is full of poison, and while you may experience discomfort, this part of the process eliminates the toxins from the body. It's very important for your health."

Stella closed her eyes tight, fighting the tears that prickled as Dr. Hazzard's kneading gave way to heavy thumps on the back of Stella's head. The discomfort the doctor mentioned far surpassed the pain of any headache Stella had suffered. Maybe that was the good thing about this part of the regime. It took her mind off the migraine.

Dr. Hazzard's hands balled into fists, and she punched and pounded Stella's back, legs, and head. "Eliminate! Eliminate!" At the sound of the battle cry, Stella's heart leaped into her throat. It was as if a demon had taken possession of the doctor's body and was bent on taking out his rage on Stella's back and shoulders.

A tear escaped Stella's eye and trickled down her nose, hanging on at the tip for a moment then dripping onto the padding. This went far beyond fasting—far beyond what her mind had pictured.

But this was only the half of it. The internal baths still stared her down, and Wendell had likened them to Chinese water torture. She bit her lip to hold back the sob building in her throat.

Her mind drifted to flying kites in the meadow with Henry when they were children. As happy memories blocked her current situation, the pain faded. That was the day they'd found that awful man with a gunny sack of kittens. He was taking them to the lake. But Henry had saved them, and they'd bottle-fed the litter together, keeping the mewing darlings in her room. Jane had known their secret, but she hadn't given it away to Mama.

"Eliminate!" Dr. Hazzard's savage shriek and war against the toxins in Stella's body snatched her back to reality.

Another tear fell onto the padding. She needed Henry. *Lord, please, let him forgive my unkindness and come for me.*

Chapter Eleven

Henry carried Jane's bags to the door then drove the motorcar into the shed. Sorrow nagged him, and Stella's face sprang to mind. She'd played him for a fool. Conned him into driving her to Wilderness Heights with promises to return home if the course of treatments made him uneasy. But she'd never planned on getting back in the automobile. From the start, she had known she would break her promise.

But the skeletons little Jack spoke of. The aching dread in the pit of his stomach warned Henry the story was more than a frightening yarn to make children behave. But if Wilderness Heights stood at the heart of some sinister plot, and the rumor mill had reached a little boy in Seattle, why hadn't the police done anything?

He rolled his neck until it popped. If Jack's story held an ounce of truth, the sanatorium would have been boarded up long ago. Stella was fine. This was precisely why one didn't put stock in children's stories.

Footsteps at the door called his mind away from the mountains of Olalla, Washington. A footman, William, approached, mouth in a grim line. "Mr. Weston would like to speak with you."

What use did Weston have with him? If he needed to order the motor, his valet would make the request. "Did he say what it's about?"

"Mr. Weston never discusses his private business with me." William rolled his eyes. "I'm just the help. But he looked none too pleased."

As he followed behind William, a lump formed in Henry's throat, making it impossible to swallow. As they stepped into the foyer, William motioned to the library. Henry nodded. The click of his heels on the tile ripped through the silence holding the house in an iron grip. Without Stella, the place seemed lifeless. Like a ballroom after the lights had been snuffed out and the music hushed.

As he pressed on the mahogany door, the hinges groaned.

"Is that you, Clayton?" Weston's booming voice carried an edge that left Henry grasping for possible reasons his employer would summon him.

"Yes, sir." He snatched off his hat and rotated it in his hands. Weston sat behind his desk, pen in hand. Books lined all four walls, and the aroma of dust, leather, and pipe tobacco hung thick. Henry moved to the chair opposite Mr. Weston.

"Don't bother sitting." The man waved him off as if shooing a fly. "This won't take long." He picked an envelope off his desk and held it for Henry to see.

Henry licked cracked lips, pulse thumping in his temple. The letter he'd sent Stella before he'd known she wouldn't be in San Francisco to receive it. The flap was torn. Clearly it had been read. A rock settled in his gut.

"You've been writing my niece under false pretenses." It wasn't a question. The conclusion had already been drawn with surprising accuracy.

But Henry hadn't signed his name. How had Weston traced the letter to him?

"Surely you knew your scheme would be uncovered." Weston tossed the letter at him, and Henry caught it. "I recognized your handwriting from last week's gasoline receipt. I keep a close eye on expenditures, and it's lucky for Miss Burke that I do." He rose, fingers splayed across the gleaming wood desktop.

Henry found his voice. "It wasn't a scheme. I love—"

"Don't drown me in sentimentality. You no more love her than a cat loves a canary." Weston's hands fisted. "You know she's worth a fortune and you hoped to advance your station. Well, I truly love Stella, and her father charged me with her care. That's not a task I take lightly."

Did Weston honestly believe he was caring for Stella's welfare by providing a parade of clowns disguised as potential suitors? This man's only goal was to form an alliance, and his niece was little more than a pawn in his schemes. "You know nothing of love, nothing of me, and certainly nothing of Stella."

"Excuse me?" Weston's mustache tipped downward.

Henry's job would be terminated. That fact was as evident as a snout on a sow. He clenched his teeth. Stella deserved better than the hand she'd been dealt, and her uncle needed to know his disregard for her had been noticed. "You act as if mundane fabric selections are a contribution to her father's business, but she sees past the nonsense. She's an innovator. Her ideas would grow profit, but you're either too proud or too stubborn to see what an asset she is."

"Are you through?"

"Not hardly." Henry flexed his jaw. "I never meant to deceive her. She needed a friend, an equal after her father died. You were too busy. I'd planned to tell her the truth, but the opportunity never came up."

"Because you saw a chance to make millions." Weston's eyes narrowed. "You're nothing but a fortune hunter."

"Not everyone is like you." Had his mouth ever been so dry? "Money doesn't fuel my fire, and if Stella were poor as a gypsy and living in a hovel, I'd still love her with every breath I take. She's special. She's kind. And those things have nothing to do with her fortune."

"Enough." Weston's voice lowered an octave. "Pack your things. Your services are no longer needed. And don't expect a reference."

Oxygen gushed from Henry's lungs along with the bravado he had possessed moments earlier. No job. No reference. No way to salvage his dream of building an orphanage.

He strode from the library, shoulders heavy.

Jane stood at the door, her brow puckered.

At her pitying look he asked, "How much did you hear?"

"Enough." She chewed her lip. "And I heard why."

Henry grasped the door handle.

"Miss Stella needed someone to talk to so badly after her father died." Jane's words froze him in place. "You gave her back the spark she'd lost. But it's all in the past now. And you'll both be better off for it." Her voice no longer held the certainty it had in Washington. "Why didn't you tell her the truth long ago?"

"I wanted to." But he'd been foolish to nearly bare his heart to her in Seattle. She had known what he planned to say but cut him off before the words spilled out.

"What'll you do now? Do you have a place to stay?" Jane's motherly tone brought burning tears to his eyes.

"I'll find someplace." He blinked until the haze in his vision dissipated. "But it will be difficult to find work without a reference."

Jane pulled a key ring from her pocket and removed a key, then jotted something on a scrap of paper. "I've got a place, and you're welcome to stay as long as you need it."

Henry tilted his head. Why would Jane possess a house when she lived at the Burke estate?

The old woman smiled as if reading his thoughts. "My father died seventeen years back. He left the place to me along with a tidy inheritance."

"Why did you stay if you didn't need the money?"

"I'd just started working here, caring for Miss Stella. She was always such a bright little thing. But her mother was sick and wasn't long for this world. Miss Stella needed me. An upheaval during that time wouldn't have been good for her. And the longer I stayed, the less I wanted to leave. I love her as if she were my own child."

Stella Burke had that effect on people, it seemed. A prickly knot welled in Henry's throat. He'd ruined everything, even their friendship. He scrubbed a hand over his face. How could he make things right between them?

"Don't despair." Jane pressed the key into his palm and closed his fingers around it. "You've got a place to live. And you're a smart young man. Work shouldn't be too difficult to come by."

"Thank you." The words weren't enough.

"It's no trouble." She handed him the paper scribbled with an address then swiped at her eyes. "Everything will work out as it should. Life has a way of shaking us up, but God can settle us again."

Henry swallowed hard. Easy words to say when it wasn't your life coming apart. "When I find work, I'll repay you."

Jane shook her head. "No need."

The library door groaned.

"You'd best be off." Jane's eyes glistened.

The full weight of loss punched his middle. "You won't tell Stella that I was let go? Or why?" The thought of her hearing of his deception from Jane rankled. He would send Stella a letter. Tell her the truth.

"It's not my secret to tell." Jane pulled open the door. "I'll stop by to check on you. Make sure you're eating your vegetables."

Henry forced a smile then hustled to the room above the garage to collect his things. He glanced at the house over his shoulder, and his heart wilted. How would Stella react when she discovered his lie?

With saggy carpetbag in hand, Henry strode toward the post office. Best to cancel his box. He no longer had the means to pay for it. Though he fought the urge to check the box one last time, he slipped the key from his pocket, stepped to the wall of brass squares, inserted the key into number 277, and opened it. An envelope. A smile pulled at his lips, but reality tightened a noose around his throat. This was the last time he'd hear from her. He retrieved the letter. Stella's sweet perfume clung to the paper. After writing one more letter to confess his deception, their correspondence would end. Forever.

There was no way around it. He couldn't go on lying to her, and she wouldn't have given him another thought while he was a chauffeur. Now that he was unemployed, living on Jane's charity, how could he expect anything more? The little he'd once had to offer had blown away like exhaust fumes. He slipped the letter into his breast pocket to savor later. No use torturing himself with her words before he reached Jane's house.

He relinquished the box with the postal worker, returned his key, then stepped onto the sidewalk. Birds sang in the tree branches overhead, mocking his pain. The vexing sunlight beat down on his back. The seams of his shirt chafed against his skin. He slipped off his jacket and slung it over his shoulder, eyes on the pavement.

He stopped. A single violet had sprouted though a crack in the concrete. Stella would love this. For all her hoity-toity ways, the simple things in life gave her the most pleasure. He shoved aside the ache in his chest as he bent and plucked it. While he breathed in the aroma, concern for Stella scratched his brain. What were the treatments like? Was she hungry? Homesick?

"Stop that thief!" Shouts caught his attention, and he glanced up in time to see a boy around ten years old dart past.

A man wearing an apron over his rotund gut huffed behind him. He bent over, hands on his knees, coughing and sucking in air. "That rapscallion. . ." His sentence died in a gasp.

The boy dashed into an alley a few hundred feet ahead.

"I'll go after him." Henry shoved the flower into his pocket and made chase. In a few long strides, he caught up to the shoplifter and reached for his shoulder. The boy dodged his grasp.

A sense of déjà vu halted him beside a row of garbage barrels. This alley. He'd been here before.

Henry's running slowed to a jog. Wasn't this the alley where Stella had found the three children? Their familiar pallet lay along the wall. Two malnourished little girls huddled on a filthy blanket.

The boy stopped and glanced back at Henry, eyes wide. "I was only trying to feed my sisters."

"Robby?" Henry held up his hands.

The boy clasped a loaf of bread to his chest and narrowed his eyes. "Who's asking?"

"It is Robby, isn't it?" Henry's voice softened. He motioned to the girls. "And Rose and Daisy?"

Nodding, Robby wiped his nose with his sleeve. "How'd you know our names? You been spying on us?"

Henry chuckled. "Stel—my friend—a lady spoke with you. I think she gave your sisters a gift."

"Robby, stop being rude." The older girl, Rose, climbed off the mattress. "I 'member her. She gave me a peppermint, but I let Daisy have it 'cause she was crying."

Henry smiled. "That was kind of you."

Rose beamed then turned to Robby and stuck out her tongue. "Ya hear that? I'm kind."

Robby rolled his eyes. "Better knock it off with the ugly faces, or you'll freeze that way. Oh, wait, you already did."

Daisy popped her thumb in her mouth and wiped shaggy blond

hair out of her eyes. A ratty stuffed cat dangled from the crook of her arm. Rose crammed her thumbs in her ears and wiggled her fingers at Robby.

Henry scanned the alley. Where were these children's parents? He crouched beside Daisy and held out his arms. She leaned against his shoulder, sucking her thumb.

He leveled his gaze on Robby. "Your parents aren't coming back, are they?" The hurt in the boy's eyes struck a familiar chord in Henry's chest.

Robby's shoulders slumped, and the sleeves of his oversized shirt covered his hands. He trudged closer to Henry and whispered in his ear, "The girls don't know." Tears choked his voice.

Did Jane's house have room for all of them? Would she be upset if he filled her home with orphans without asking permission? One look in Daisy's blue eyes turned him to mush. He'd risk Jane's displeasure.

"Come with me." He lifted Daisy. She weighed little more than a leaf. Would he have the money to feed them?

"We have to stay here, so we're ready when Ma and Pa come back." Rose tugged on his sleeve, eyes brimming with concern.

This wasn't the time or place to enlighten the poor girl to life's harsh realities. Especially since he didn't know if the children's parents had died or simply couldn't afford to care for them. Hopefully Robby would be forthcoming after a hot meal. "We'll leave a note so they know where to find you." He fished Stella's envelope from his pocket with his free hand. Daisy rested her head on his shoulder. Her warm breath tickled his neck.

"Can I write the note?" Rose bounced on battered shoes.

"You can write?" Henry tore off the envelope's flap and handed it to her then dug for the pencil he kept in his pocket.

Rose nodded. "I'm seven." Her tone informed him that her answer was explanation enough of her scholastic abilities.

Robby fixed understanding eyes on Henry and nodded as if to thank him for sparing his sister heartache a while longer.

Rose scribbled with childlike penmanship, the tip of her tongue peeking from her mouth. Henry moved Daisy to his other hip. "We have to pay for the bread." He cocked a brow at Robby. "You were trying to help, but stealing is wrong. If you ever need anything, ask me. I'll do my best to get it for you."

The boy fiddled with his suspenders. "Yeah. Okay." He clamped the loaf snug under his arm.

"And you'll tell the shopkeeper you're sorry." He returned Stella's letter to his pocket. He had taken more from her than a loaf of bread. He'd stolen her trust. The sooner he wrote her and apologized, the better. But no apology could begin to right the wrong he'd done her. That situation couldn't be rectified as easily as the one between Robby and the baker.

"But I'm not sorry." Robby jutted his chin. "I only done it to feed Rose and Daisy, and I'd do it again."

And how should Henry handle that attitude? Rose placed her note beneath the blanket on their pallet and grinned at him. Aside from the unmistakable joy she found in terrorizing her brother, she seemed compliant. Daisy had fallen asleep on his shoulder like an angel and turned to lead in his arms. But Robby's outright defiance in refusing to apologize? Henry shook his head.

Was false contrition worse than none at all? His conscience pricked. Why did he plan to ask Stella's forgiveness? Was he truly sorry for what he'd done?

He ushered the children out of the alley and toward the bakery. The stern-faced man waited at the door with hands on hips.

Henry mulled the words he'd pen to Stella. While the thought of hurting her left him with a sick ache, remorse over his actions failed to swell in his chest. She had needed a friend, and he'd stepped into the gap. True, he should have been open with her from the start. But if Stella had known the truth, would she have written him or simply continued grieving, alone and friendless?

Robby's eyes narrowed as they approached the angry shop owner.

Henry clenched his jaw. The boy was more like him than Henry cared to admit. Maybe they could both learn a thing or two.

Chapter Twelve

Stella traced the bruises on her arm with her finger. Though she didn't wish to endure another internal bath, Tilda was right. The massages were somehow worse.

Between the darkened patches, her skin was red as an apple peel and hot to the touch. When Stella had been called to bath time, she'd told Nurse Sarah the water was too hot, but her protests were gently stifled with the reminder that these were Dr. Hazzard's orders. The scalding water must offer something by way of healing, but the heat that enveloped Stella's body had made her grit her teeth and swallow the prickling in her throat until either her skin went numb or the water cooled. It had been impossible to tell which came first.

She covered her arm with her sleeve then glanced around the small chamber. White walls. White door. White bedding. White, white, white. The whole place was sterile and uninviting, though Sam and Linda Hazzard used it for a personal home. The sameness of it all rolled a weight onto Stella's chest. This was no home. If she had known how drab her room would be, she would have had Jane pack her purple blanket. Mama's favorite color. She used to bury her nose in the violets Stella brought from the garden much to the gardener's chagrin. Mama had said the color reminded her of home and family. Now, purple reminded Stella of Mama. Why had God taken her so early? She blinked back the tears that marred her vision.

Home and family.

This place offered nothing of the kind. A simple letter from home might ease the ache in her chest. But Jane likely hadn't arrived at the estate until earlier that morning, so it was too soon to receive news from her. And Uncle Weston's business ventures always took first place. Though she'd told him her plans and he'd kissed her goodbye, he might never truly feel her absence. After her rejection of his last prospective husband, she'd fallen from grace in his eyes.

And although logic told her days or even weeks might pass before a letter from her secret friend reached her, her heart yearned for that lifeline as well. Something to remind her that this stint at Wilderness Heights was not only temporary, but needful. That someone—even if she didn't know his name—stood in her corner, cheering her on. If he agreed to her offer of a partnership, she'd have a goal to work toward. Some meaningful reason to keep sipping orange juice. Because the children she'd help in the future would need her to be healthy and strong.

Perfect health. Those words must be stuck to her brain with glue, as often as she conjured them. All the hunger, exhaustion, and loneliness would be worth it when her headaches ceased to burden her.

A muscle in her leg throbbed, and she kneaded it. Dr. Hazzard prodded all her patients to walk the grounds during daylight hours. Even though Stella's legs grew tired, the exercise offered welcome relief from the enemas and the massages that mirrored a beating by a gang of street toughs. She rubbed the back of her neck, but the ache lingered. Dr. Hazzard's heavy fists and her talent for inflicting pain could translate easily into the boxing ring.

What would Henry think of these beatings? A wave of homesickness crashed over her, threatening to drown her.

Had he received her telegram?

Tears prickled, and she clasped a hand over her mouth. He'd been right, but she'd been so stubborn. She choked on a sob. Nevertheless, he would come for her. He had to. Since childhood, they'd grown so close, their souls were practically knit together. When he read her message, though she'd had to limit her word count, he'd understand her true meaning. He would know she was sorrier than she could say in such a stilted form of communication.

She'd given the message to Rollie yesterday, and he had assured her he would see it safely to the telegraph office. She bit the inside of her cheek. How soon until she could reasonably expect Henry? It was a two-day drive to Olalla. Surely when he received the telegram, he'd jump in the automobile straightaway. Come to rescue her like the hero in a love story.

Three days at the most. Within three days she'd start her journey home and put this nightmare behind her.

A knock at her door brought her head up. "Yes." She forced a semblance of composure into her voice.

"Supper's ready, Miss Burke." A nurse peeked into the room.

Stella pressed her hand against her stomach. She'd eaten nothing more than spoonfuls of orange juice and tomato broth since yesterday. The hollow sensation expanded within her. The liquid diet didn't touch the discomfort or take the edge off her growing appetite. This went far beyond craving and gluttony. Hunger. True hunger screamed with every gurgle in her middle. Perhaps her fasting regime was close to completion. That woman Dr. Hazzard had spoken of—Mrs. Barnett—had been given food once real hunger set in. Of course, that hadn't happened until she'd fasted more than forty days. But from the doctor's description, Mrs. Barnett had been much sicker than Stella. Perhaps there were more toxins in her body to eliminate. Stella cringed, the bruises on her back pulsing. That word—eliminate—still rang in her ears from last night's massage.

After only two days, the ravenous beast in Stella's abdomen was threatening to eat her from the inside out. She'd speak with Dr. Hazzard before her next internal bath. With a little luck, tomorrow's breakfast might consist of solid food. Something she could chew. Her teeth had been on sabbatical long enough.

She descended the stairs to the dining room. Her knees buckled, and she gripped the balustrade. Although she hadn't hiked since yesterday evening, her knees still felt like jelly and her feet had stiffened.

Dr. Hazzard stood in the dining room doorway, speaking with her son, who wore his characteristic smirk.

Though Stella didn't strain to listen, their voices carried.

"You need more money?" Dr. Hazzard perched her hands on her hips. "What did you do with the twenty dollars I gave you yesterday?"

The corners of Rollie Burfield's mouth quirked. "Never mind that." He crossed his arms and leaned against the doorframe. "I could shut this place down if I wanted. One word to the police and—"

"Hush!" Dr. Hazzard thwacked him with a closed fist. "I'll get you the money. But if you tell anyone about Claire. . ." Her voice lowered, and Stella slunk into the shadows. Thank goodness the stairs were new enough not to creak too loudly. If Dr. Hazzard knew she'd overheard this private conversation, who knew what horrors she'd inflict.

And who was Claire? Stella bit her fingernail.

Could that be the name of the woman she'd seen the day she arrived? The emaciated creature with bruises at her throat? More than once, Stella had observed Nurse Sarah passing through the corridor or serving patient meals. Was Dr. Hazzard covering up a murder that had occurred under her roof?

Stella's nerves jangled.

Was Rollie involved somehow, or was he blackmailing his mother?

"Enough idle chatter." A sigh escaped Dr. Hazzard's clenched teeth. "Go take Sue her broth. I'll get the money to you this afternoon."

Rollie stomped into the dining room, and Dr. Hazzard massaged her temples.

Stella continued down the stairs, hoping her countenance didn't betray that she'd overheard. As she strode to the dining room, the doctor's impassive gaze met hers.

"Miss Burke." Dr. Hazzard pinched the bridge of her nose. "How are you feeling today?"

"No headaches since yesterday." Maybe the treatments were working in spite of their unpleasant nature. She clasped her hands behind her back. "I am really hungry. It's not just a craving. I'd like a slice of bread or some cheese for dinner tonight if I may."

The doctor's lips curved into a smile that told Stella just how silly her request sounded. "My dear, you've barely begun. You start your full fast tomorrow. Now go get something to eat. This meal is of the utmost importance. The nourishment it will provide will last you until your fast is complete."

How foolish she'd been to think perfect health could be gained in two days. Stella entered the dining room and scanned the tables for

Tilda and Wendell. Where were they? No sign of them since supper yesterday.

Rollie stepped beside her, a bowl of greenish broth in hand. "Looking for somebody?"

"Tilda and Wendell. Have they gone home?"

He shook his head. "Tilda was moved to her cabin this morning. Yours will be ready sometime next week, so you'll see more of her then. Wendell started his total fast today, so he's keeping to his room during meals. It would be cruel to have food near at this stage of treatment."

"Would it?" Stella glanced at the bowl he held and wrinkled her nose. "Nothing in this room smells like food, and if yesterday is any indication, the taste would get one star out of five."

"Don't knock healthy food. It's your meat-eating that brought you here in the first place." Did he believe those things? Or was he parroting his mother's jargon? He stepped beside a table occupied by a gaunt woman, pulled out a chair, and motioned for her to sit. She eased into the seat, and he set the half-filled dish before her. The way his eyes studied her face prickled the hair on Stella's arms. Had he seen her on the stairway?

He had not so much as glanced her direction during his conversation with Dr. Hazzard. He couldn't possibly know what she'd heard. Stella hoped.

What part did he play in this crime? She should do something, but what? Go to the police. How could she get to them while living in the wilderness? She couldn't very well ask Rollie to take her. But the woman—Claire. Her murder couldn't go unpunished.

As soon as Henry came for her, Stella would ask him to take her to the authorities. But until then, she'd give none of the staff reason to wrap their hands around her neck as they had poor Claire's.

Stella met Rollie's gaze with a stern eye. He wouldn't make her cower for all his posturing and smirking. "Has the post come yet?"

"Sure has." He handed her a spoon. "But nothing for you."

Why did he take so much pleasure in disappointing her? Insufferable man. But she'd been a ninny to ask. It was too soon. "But you sent my telegram?"

"I said I would, didn't I?" He thrust his hands into his pockets.

Not much of an answer, but she wasn't getting anything else. She ladled a spoonful from her bowl to her nose, breathed in, and dropped the spoon. It smelled like a pile of something found in the stables. "What is this foul concoction?"

"Lima bean broth." Rollie tugged a cloth from his back pocket and wiped away the splatter on the table. "Most nutritious food on earth."

Why did the most nutritious foods on earth seem to be the vilest? Stella crossed her arms. How low did Dr. Hazzard expect her to stoop? "I won't eat this—" She shoved the bowl away, but it wasn't full enough to slosh over the edge. "There really are no words for this pond scum. I'm paying a great deal of money for these treatments, and this is the last day before I begin fasting in earnest. Bring me something edible."

Rollie pushed the bowl toward her. "This is the dinner Dr. Hazzard prescribed, and you will eat it. Everything she does is for your own good. You came here because you are sick, and if you ever hope to be well, to live, you'll do as you're told without fussing."

"I'm not sick enough to eat this swill." Stella lifted her chin.

"Eat, Your Highness." Rollie's voice hardened. "If you don't, there'll be consequences."

Stella clasped a hand to her neck. Consequences. Had Claire refused to follow orders? She retrieved her spoon then sipped the foul broth, imagining strawberry ice cream. But no amount of mental gymnastics could atone for the flavor.

Rollie stalked away, rag dangling from his back pocket.

"This stuff's awful, isn't it?" The woman across the table dabbed her mouth with a napkin. Her fingers were as thin and frail as her voice.

Stella nodded.

"You haven't been here long, I take it." Dark circles ringed the woman's eyes, and hunger carved hollows in her cheeks. She brushed a lock of auburn hair off her forehead.

"How can you tell?" Stella choked down another swallow of broth.

"Well, you're not thin as a twig for one thing." A smile parted the woman's lips. "And you're still finicky enough to refuse food when it's offered. I'm Sue Chandler." She lifted the bowl to her lips with trembling hands, draining it of the final drops.

"A pleasure." Stella pushed the bowl away, unable to stomach another bite. "I'm Stella Burke."

"You'll want to finish that." Sue eyed Stella's bowl as if she would dive over the table and fight Stella for it if her arms weren't so spindly. "You mentioned starting your fast tomorrow. On my first day, I regretted every piece of cake I had ever turned down, every chicken sandwich." She tucked a thin curl behind her ear. "What I wouldn't give for some meat."

Stomach begging for food, Stella tipped the bowl at her mouth, swallowed the broth in one gulp, then shot Sue a half smile, half grimace.

"Good girl." Sue pushed away from the table and rose on unsteady legs. "No regrets."

When Sue stumbled, Stella sprang from her chair and held her up. Ribs and vertebrae rippled beneath the thin fabric of Sue's dress.

"Let me help you to your room. You ought to lie down." Stella cupped Sue's elbow. More bones thinly veiled by skin.

Walking skeletons. Just like the boy had told Henry.

"I'll be fine." Sue shooed her away. "I always make it to my cabin on my own."

How did Dr. Hazzard expect this woman who was thinner even than Dora Williamson to walk to a cabin and back? The woman looked like walking death. "You can have my room. I'll take the cabin. You shouldn't walk that far."

"Dr. Hazzard assured me walking is good for the constitution." Sue braced her hand on the table.

The doctor also thought lima bean broth teemed with nutritive benefits, but Stella's stomach mutinied against that idea. "Let me speak to her for you. Or let me walk with you."

"No. Stay here. The doctor wouldn't like it."

What kind of woman was Linda Burfield Hazzard that she should encourage the denial of help to a woman in need? Tears clouded Stella's eyes accompanied by swirling flashes of light. She snapped her eyelids closed. Would the cycle of pain never cease? She rubbed her temples.

"Don't be upset, sweet girl." Sue rested a hand on her shoulder. "Maybe I'll see you tomorrow when I come in for my massage."

Heavy prickles radiated up Stella's left arm, and when she glanced up to watch Sue stumble toward the front door, the light in her eyes transformed to wiggling gray blobs. The poor woman needed her help, but even if she would allow it, Stella was in no condition to be of use to anyone.

What if these harsh treatments really were the answer to these recurring headaches? Perhaps one needed to fight unpleasantness with unpleasantness to see results.

She grabbed her bowl off the table and held it upside down over her open mouth. If she didn't throw herself into the treatments whole-heartedly, Stella would become more a burden than a blessing— just as Mrs. Barnett had drained her family's emotional resources.

The numbness crept up her neck and settled in her lip. She would enter this migraine in her journal once her eyesight cleared. When Henry arrived, she'd have close to a week of entries. Maybe her belated compliance with his wishes would induce him to forgiveness.

God, please bring him here quickly. And please take these headaches away. I'm not so sure fasting will help, but I'm willing to try until I have a way home.

Chapter Thirteen

Stella draped a pillow over her head. Even the strip of light that shone under the door compounded the agony. As pain stabbed her forehead, she stifled a sob. Hot tears sprang to her eyes and soaked the pillowcase. If only Jane were there. She'd place a cool cloth over Stella's eyes and tell her everything would be all right in her Scottish brogue.

Home. How she missed it. Even Uncle Weston's relentless matchmaking would be preferable to lying in a strange bed with her head at the threshold of splitting apart.

Nausea tangled her stomach, and the lima bean broth from supper climbed her throat. Stella threw off the quilt, tossed the pillow to the floor, and yanked open the door. The light flickering from the oil lamps acted like a hammer blow to her head, but she ignored the pain and dashed for the water closet with a hand clamped over her mouth.

She knelt at the commode, the tile cold against her flaming skin. The bile rose, and a sharp pain in her middle signaled that the ascent would not be stopped. While she held her hair back, her stomach retched. With each heave, the ache in her head ratcheted to new heights. The few tablespoons of broth had done her no good. She pulled the cord and wiped her mouth as the tainted water swirled downward.

How could Jane's absence sting more than this miserable headache? But it did. Stella was alone. Her vision misted, and she swiped her eyes with her palms. Sweat trickled down her brow. The breeze from an open window dried the moisture and sent a wave of chill bumps skimming her skin. Her teeth chattered.

She wrapped her arms around herself. If she didn't get back to bed, she might catch cold. As she stepped across the corridor, the hall clock chimed three times. Why did Dr. Hazzard insist on keeping the hall lights burning all night? She'd knocked on Stella's door twice her first night at Wilderness Heights to make sure she didn't prefer sleeping with her lamp lit.

Was Dr. Hazzard afraid of the dark?

Stella's fingers gripped the doorknob at her bedroom, but a thump down the hall froze her in place. Low voices filtered toward her, too muffled to decipher. Had someone fallen? Maybe they needed help.

As she padded toward the source of the sounds, something within warned her to go back. To pretend all was well in this house until Henry arrived to drive her home. But curiosity propelled her forward. The slick wood cooled her bare feet with each step.

"It's just as I thought." Dr. Hazzard's voice grew louder. The bathing chamber door stood open at the far end of the hall, and light spilled onto the polished floor. "Her doctors must have prescribed medication when she was a child and it stunted her growth and development."

Stella pressed against the wall. She shouldn't be here. Whatever was transpiring did not concern her. Despite the swelling unease, she peeked around the doorjamb.

The sight stilled her heart. She pressed her hand over her mouth to capture a scream.

Blood pooled on the white tile, and the stench of death, mingled with antiseptic, hung in the air. Both Dr. Hazzard and Nurse Sarah stood with their backs to the door. Sarah held a metal dish, while the doctor lifted a trailing bit of flesh between her thumb and forefinger. Blood dripped from the object she studied. It landed on the rim of the tub then dribbled onto the floor.

A fresh flood of nausea swept through Stella's middle. Dear heavens, not now. She swallowed once, then again.

"Look how shriveled her small intestine is." Dr. Hazzard held it higher. "A sure sign she ingested medication. It's no wonder the fasting regime didn't help her. She was too far gone by the time she arrived." She dropped the small intestine into the dish.

Sarah nodded. "It is very sad. To be so sick that no treatment can offer sufficient remedy." She set the dish in the sink.

The blood on the floor channeled through the grout, staining everything it touched with death and horror. Headache forgotten, Stella fought to avoid sight of the figure in the bathtub. Surely seeing a human corpse would taint her dreams forever. But like a moth to a candle, her gaze wandered to the scene at the room's center.

Thin auburn curls spilled over the rim. Pale cheeks hollowed by starvation.

Sue.

Stella's throat constricted. What had happened to her? The poor woman barely possessed the strength to walk to her cabin after supper. Her lifeless form left Stella scrambling to make sense of the suddenness of her demise.

Could it be as Dr. Hazzard said? Had Sue been too sick to find perfect health at Wilderness Heights? Stella's hand gripped her stomach. If medications taken in childhood had done so much damage to Sue's organs, Stella had no hope of healing. More than once, the family physician had given her vile-tasting tonics. What if she was too far gone? *Oh, Henry. Please hurry.*

"Cause of death is an inflammation of the digestive tract." Dr. Hazzard wiped bloody hands on her apron. "Call Butterworth's in the morning and have them take care of her. I've got a kettle big enough. Let's prepare her body for cremation." She extended a hand, and Nurse Sarah placed the handsaw in her open palm.

Stella's pulse thundered in her ears. She would not be present for the gruesome sight to come. Tears warmed her cheeks, then her chest tightened. What would the doctor do if she found her watching at the door? That could not happen. Silently, Stella retraced her steps. With her bedroom door closed behind her, Stella crawled into bed and pulled the covers over her shoulders.

The weight of what she'd seen pressed on her chest until her breathing grew ragged.

Poor Sue. Sobs racked her body.

Could Stella have done something to prevent the woman's death? Why hadn't she helped her to her cabin? Though her vision was faulty, she could have stumbled along beside Sue despite the splotches in her eyes. Had she died alone? Afraid? What if she'd called out for help and no one heard?

Grief and loneliness grappled in Stella's chest. Did Sue's family know she'd passed? Since Stella had taken more than her share of medication as a child, could she expect the same fate? She wiped her cheeks with the stiff bedsheet.

A floorboard in the hall creaked, and her muscles tensed. Movement interrupted the light under the door. Who stood on the other side? She held her breath, frozen in place, heart pulsing in her ears.

The door hinges groaned.

Stella's heart and stomach switched places. She pulled the covers tight about her chin.

Dr. Hazzard's form stood backlit in the doorway, making it impossible to see the details of her face or notice any blood that might streak her skin and clothing. "Are you well, Miss Burke? I heard sounds coming from your room."

Stella sniffed, willing her voice not to betray her frayed emotions. "I'm not feeling well. My stomach. . .and my head." A sob choked her words. "I want to go home."

Dr. Hazzard rested a chilly hand on Stella's forehead. The same hand that had held Sue's intestine up for inspection moments earlier. "You're burning up. This is a good sign. Your body is waking up. Fighting the toxins." She removed her hand and wiped it against her apron then went to the door and pushed it a bit wider to let in more light. The metallic odor of blood swirled in the air around her. "You're on the way to perfect health. Don't give that up over a little bout of homesickness."

Stella shifted on the bed.

"I've got news." Dr. Hazzard leaned against the doorframe. "A cabin has just become available. You'll be transferred in a few days, once it's cleaned."

A cabin. Sue's cabin. Stella nodded, unable to form a sentence past the knot in her throat.

"Would you like me to light the lamp? It might make you more comfortable." Dr. Hazzard started for the bed table, but Stella shook her head. "Very well. Tomorrow we'll start your full fast, and I'll see you bright and early for your massage."

An involuntary sigh escaped Stella's lungs.

"Don't lose faith." The doctor stepped into the hall. "During your massage, I'll tell you the story of a little boy whose life was saved by fasting. That should bolster your spirits."

The door squeaked closed.

Stella pulled the sheet over her head. The story would never lift the gloom strangling her. Even if it ended with a choir of singing cherubs and world peace. And it wouldn't bring Sue back. She was the second person who'd died since Stella's arrival. That she knew about, anyway. Could there be more?

She shifted to lie on her back, and tears slipped across her temples into her hair, tickling her scalp.

Images of Sue Chandler taking her last breath in a deserted cabin in the wilderness played havoc with Stella's nerves.

What if Henry didn't come for her? She might die alone as well. A stone settled in her stomach.

No. He wouldn't leave her here. Why, he was probably on his way to Washington this minute. Every rotation of the wheels bringing him a little closer.

But when she'd asked Rollie if he'd sent her message, he hadn't answered her question. Not really. For all she knew, her telegram had never been sent.

She squeezed her eyes shut and willed her tears to stop. She had to believe Henry was driving toward her. If she let go of that thin cord of hope, she might not have the strength to soldier on.

Just two more days. Then he'd take her home.

Chapter Fourteen

As Henry sealed the envelope bearing his confession, his chest tightened. The taste of the glue turned his stomach, but not to the degree knowingly killing his friendship with Stella did. Once she read what he'd done, how he'd deceived her for five years, the final page of their friendship would turn and their story would be shelved forever.

He yawned, exhaustion stiffening his muscles. If only he'd been able to sleep last night.

Daisy tottered toward him, dragging her blanket behind her. She held up her arms, and he lifted her onto his knee and kissed her golden curls. Her chubby arms circled his neck and she planted a sloppy kiss on his cheek.

His heart melted. Although Rose had told him that her sister was four years old and talked "all the time," she hadn't breathed a word since he'd brought them home yesterday. The same couldn't be said for her siblings. Shouts echoed from upstairs, and the chandelier at the center of the room swayed, its glass prisms tinkling and casting dancing rainbows on the Persian rug.

Perhaps he'd taken on more than he could handle, but what other choice did he have? Leaving them in the alley was out of the question. Daisy leaned her head against his shoulder and popped her thumb into her mouth. Other than feeding them and making sure they were clean, how did one care for children?

At least Jane's father had left her the perfect house for a ready-made family. Three bedrooms upstairs, all fit with serviceable furnishings. A large fenced yard behind the house would be the perfect place to send Robby, Rose, and their clamor if it reached new heights.

Once the school year began, he'd need to enroll them. But that was months away.

Who would mind them while he looked for work? *Lord, a little help would be nice.* He rested his hand over the letter marked with Stella's Washington address. He didn't deserve help after his deceit. But the Bible stated more than once that God cared for the fatherless. Maybe He'd work a miracle for the children's sake, if not for Henry's.

Though Robby and Rose stomped overhead, a rap at the door cut through the din. Henry stood and adjusted Daisy on his hip. "Quiet up there," he called up the staircase to the two rabble-rousers. "We have company." Though who it could be remained a mystery.

The racket continued without the slightest hint of diminishing. Henry rolled his eyes as he pulled open the door. "Good after—" Oh no.

Jane stood on the porch, a paper grocery bag in one arm. When her gaze landed on Daisy, her jaw slacked.

At the time, it had seemed more prudent to ask forgiveness than permission for the children to stay with him. Maybe that hadn't been such a good idea.

"My, my." Jane stroked the little girl's cheek. "What a darling wee thing."

"I found them in an alley."

"Them?" Jane stepped inside, soft eyes fixed on little Daisy.

"She has a brother and sister." Though how Jane could raise her brows in surprise was a puzzle. The clatter emanating from the upstairs bedroom better suited a herd of pachyderms, not two small children.

"And their parents?"

Henry shook his head. Robby had confided in him last night after the girls fell asleep. Both their mother and father had perished.

Jane's eyes softened further. "Poor little dears." She set the grocery bag beside the front door then extended her hands to Daisy.

The girl burrowed into Henry's shoulder.

"Do you know what happened to their mum and dad?"

"From Robby's description it sounded like cholera." He propped his chin atop Daisy's curly head.

"And were they not taken to a children's home?"

"They were, but both Rose and Robby begged me not to take them back. Said the woman—I'm guessing the proprietor—was, to use Robby's words, a 'real witch.' That's why they ran away."

A smile lit Jane's face. "Then I'd say you did the right thing."

The weight on Henry's shoulders lifted. Jane wouldn't turn them out on the street.

"But next time you bring children into this house, tell me." She retrieved the shopping bag. "So I know to bring more groceries."

How had he ever doubted her? As generous as she'd been to give him a place to stay, the thought of her condemning children to life in an alley was absurd.

"Now, what have they eaten?" Jane bustled past him to the kitchen, and he trailed behind.

"We had bread and cheese for supper last night, then again for breakfast this morning."

Robby and Rose slid down the banister, and Henry shot them a warning look. When they noticed Jane, they stilled. Robby gulped and wrapped an arm around Rose's shoulders.

"Don't look so frightened." Jane set the bag on the kitchen table. "I don't bite. And rails were made for sliding."

A grin split Robby's face. "I didn't know you'd be such a nice old lady, because you've got a mean face, but you know what?"

Did Jane want to know? *Please, Lord, don't let him say something more offensive than the mean face comment.*

"What's that?" Jane's smile never faltered.

"You're all right." The boy puffed out his chest as if he'd given her a glowing testimonial and not the barest minimum of praise.

"Thank you kindly." Jane received the compliment with a wink as she tied an apron around her waist. "Now how about you and your sister help me get lunch?"

Rose clapped her hands. "Oh, goody! I'm tired of bread and cheese." She darted a narrowed glance at Henry and her smile faded. "Sorry."

"It's all right." He eased onto a chair with Daisy. "I'm not much of a cook."

"Never you mind." Jane pulled a parcel wrapped in butcher paper from her shopping bag. "I'm here now and happy to take on the responsibility. I planned to come cook for you anyway, so it's no bother to make a bit more." She handed Rose a potato for each hand and passed a few carrots to Robby. "Now go wash those at the sink."

She'd intended to feed him as well as house him? More than he expected or deserved from a woman who had discouraged a relationship with Stella. "Have your duties changed since Stel—Miss Burke left?"

"Aye. Weston keeps me on for mending, but that's not nearly enough to occupy my time." She sent a wink his way. "But I have a suspicion that my time will be claimed before too long."

Was Stella retuning home? He buried his face in Daisy's hair to mask his smile. But her return to San Francisco would change nothing. They'd be as far apart as ever.

"Miss Stella is still in Washington, and I daresay will be for some time." Jane sliced beef into cubes.

How could she read his mind?

"What I meant was, you'll need someone to mind the children while you look for work." She tousled Robby's hair. "They can't very well be left to their own devices."

"You'd do that for me? For the children?" Gratitude swelled in his chest. Though he'd prayed for a little help, he'd not expected the windows of heaven to open so wide.

"We mean-faced old ladies must have something to do, or we'll cease to feel useful."

"You don't have a very mean face." Robby set the dripping carrots on the cutting board.

"That makes me feel much better." Jane cut them then tossed the pieces into a pot on the stove. She wiped her hands on her apron.

Robby whispered something in Rose's ear.

"Get it away from me!" Rose shrieked as her brother chased her around the kitchen table with his hand extended.

"I'm gonna get you!" Robby closed in on her, but Jane grabbed his arm.

"The very idea." She huffed. "Why are you tormenting your sister?"

"He has a spider." Rose swiped tear-streaked cheeks with the back of her hand.

"Let me see." Jane pried open his curled fingers. Nothing. She lowered her brows at Robby. "I may be all right, but when little boys terrorize their sisters, I turn into a scary old woman pretty quick."

Robby lowered his head.

"You'd best apologize." Jane turned the boy to face Rose, who wore a triumphant smirk.

"I'm sorry," Robby mumbled.

"Now get back to work, both of you." Jane shook her head, clicking her tongue. Then she settled concerned eyes on Henry. "You look exhausted. Did you sleep last night?"

How could he sleep? Worry for Stella had prodded his mind until the sun peeked through the window. Then the added burden of finding a job and caring for three children. What did a bachelor know of nurturing three young lives? Though he'd wanted to open a children's home before Weston terminated him and put his dream on hold, he'd planned to hire a housemother to help with day-to-day operations.

His shoulders sagged, and he glanced at Daisy. She'd fallen asleep in his arms, and her even breaths tugged at his eyelids.

"Go up to bed." Jane lifted Daisy off his lap. After supporting her weight so long, his arms felt like stretched rubber bands.

"Maybe I should. For a few minutes." He hesitated, scrubbing a hand over his face. Rose stirred the vegetables and meat in the pot. Robby reached for the spoon, but she pulled it out of his reach and stuck out her tongue. "Rose—"

"Never you mind." Jane patted Henry's hand. "They may listen better to someone with a slightly mean face than a handsome one." She walked to the stove. "Now, Rose, is that any way for a young lady to behave? Plenty of stirring to go around."

As Henry trekked the stairs, the floorboards groaned. What would he do without Jane? He slipped off his suit coat. When he went to drape it over the chair, paper in the breast pocket rumpled beneath his fingers.

Stella's letter.

He pulled it from the pocket. He'd yet to read it. How had he managed to forget something so precious? These would be the last words she'd write to him.

He opened the envelope and pulled out the paper. Her perfume clung to the page. Eyes closed, he breathed it in. The aroma awakened memories of her embrace in the garage. A perfect moment that could never be duplicated.

Lost in Stella's flawless penmanship, he eased onto the bed. Her words washed over him and drowned him with the desire to see her one last time. To explain in person why he'd acted as he had. His pulse slowed as he read her proposal.

Just a business proposal, of course. Still, the thought of working alongside her. . .

An image of Stella rocking Daisy to sleep, of whispering good-night prayers with Rose and Robby, tore a hole in his chest. Yes, Stella was spoiled, but as she'd so adeptly noted, the life she lived was all she had ever known. But she longed for more. Would she really want to build a life with him? Care for children? Put their needs before her own?

Reality landed a merciless blow to his gut. She hadn't made this offer to Henry, the unemployed chauffeur. Stella believed her correspondent to be some wealthy social equal. He tossed her letter, but instead of sailing across the room, it landed at his feet. Why hadn't he come clean long ago? Or better yet, why hadn't he been the friend she had needed without cowering behind pen and ink?

For the same reason he hadn't asked Jane if he could shelter the children in her home. The same reason he hadn't already chased his dreams. And for the same reason he hadn't told Stella the true depth of his feelings for her.

He was a coward. He had been so concerned with losing his job and risking Stella's rejection that he'd lost courage. Fear ruled his life, made his decisions, stole his respectability. He lay back on the bed.

If only he possessed an ounce of Stella's courage. The way she'd stood up to Ethel's bully of a husband—

Shame pricked Henry's chest. Stella could do better, and she'd always known that. Even if he'd told her the truth about the letters after sending the first one, he'd never had a chance with her.

He kicked his shoes beside the bed and planted a hand over his eyes. If only there was a way to muster up some courage. Even if he never saw Stella again, those children downstairs needed an advocate, someone strong enough to stand in their corner.

Instead, they'd been brought home by an utter failure.

Chapter Fifteen

Stella crawled onto the massage table, legs trembling beneath her. Dr. Hazzard had administered a two-hour internal bath earlier that morning. Each treatment lasted longer than the last. As she lay facedown, the sensation of water swirling through her middle lingered and drowned the hunger pangs.

"I promised to tell you the story of my youngest patient." Dr. Hazzard kneaded Stella's thigh then beat it with a rock-hard fist.

Stella's clenched teeth prevented a response. Why must the doctor be so rough?

"Before you can fully appreciate the triumph of saving the Anderson boy, you should first understand the history of my medical practice. The story I'm about to tell you transpired while I was practicing in Minnesota many years ago. The doctors in those parts despised the idea of fasting. They derided me behind my back and opposed me to my face. But their main problem with me had little to do with the fasting cure. They hated that a woman had the ability to bring healing to their patients when they could not." Dr. Hazzard drove her fist into Stella's lower back as if she'd been guilty of ruining the woman's medical reputation single-handedly, and Stella swallowed a cry. "The little boy who lived, thanks to my fasting regime, was named Edward Anderson. By the time his mother called me, the poor child lay at death's door. She'd heard the negative comments and gossip surrounding my beliefs, but when a mother stands on the brink of losing her child, perhaps it's easier to overlook public opinion and step out in faith."

Dr. Hazzard pummeled Stella's neck. "Mrs. Anderson called me in as a last resort. When I saw little Eddie, I wasn't sure anything could save him. He was so sick. Traditional doctors had tried every medicine in their little black bags, but nothing helped. They were simply keeping him comfortable for his final hours on earth. They administered opioids and forced food and brandy on his rebellious stomach." Another aggravated blow punctuated the doctor's sentence. Hopefully the poor child hadn't been forced to endure such a beating, or he surely would have given up the ghost.

Grinding the words through her teeth, Dr. Hazzard continued. "As soon as I saw him, I put him on an immediate, total fast. I stopped all medication and started regular massages and internal baths."

Pity the poor little boy. Stella bit down on her tongue and squeezed her eyes tight as the doctor's clenched hands awakened old bruises and formed new ones.

"Within an hour, little Edward improved. His temperature and pulse returned to normal, and he rested comfortably." Dr. Hazzard's hands slowed, and Stella released the breath she'd been holding. "Over the next several hours, his mother fretted over him, thinking her growing boy needed to eat, but I held my ground. It was far too soon. By the next day, his pain and swelling had diminished. When he finally broke his fast, his body was returned to perfect working order."

Stella lay still, soaking in Dr. Hazzard's words. They didn't make sense. "If the child was so very sick, how could fasting for one hour bring him around so quickly?" She turned her head to glimpse the doctor.

Hazzard's black eyes narrowed. "Are you questioning me?"

"No." Stella's heart jerked. "I just— If he improved so quickly, might I be through fasting soon?"

Dr. Hazzard bent until she and Stella were separated by mere inches. "What happened last night?"

"Well—" Had she found out Stella had witnessed the frightful scene in the bathroom? Stella's stomach twisted. *Please, Lord, don't let her know my secret.*

"When I came in to check on you, you'd been sick. Complained of pain in your stomach and head. You were eaten up with fever. What makes you think your digestive system is sufficiently rested to take on the work of processing food?"

The doctor's tone proved she didn't expect an answer to her question. Her hands set to work on Stella's back once again.

As the doctor's fingers wreaked havoc on her tender skin, Stella gripped the padded cot, channeling the pain through her fingertips and trying to imagine her times on the beach with Jane. Why hadn't inhaling sea air as Dr. Wagner prescribed eased her headaches? If only something so simple would have produced the desired results.

The blows to Stella's back and head grew more violent. Dr. Hazzard began her tribal cry. "Eliminate! Eliminate!"

With eyes squinched shut, Stella begged her mind to take her away from reality to someplace filled with pleasant memories. To Henry. But the recollection her brain resurrected included the harsh words she'd spat the last time they were together. Not that memory. Tears escaped through closed eyelids. Next, her mind replayed the moment she'd pulled rank and insisted he bring her to this godforsaken place. The cruelty and condescension in her words smote her afresh. He'd deserved none of her ugliness, yet she'd rained it on him like a storm cloud. She swallowed a sob as the end of their argument played out. It had left her with a blinding headache.

Her breathing slowed. He had helped her inside with the same tenderness he'd always shown despite her shameful treatment of him. The grace he had heaped upon her snatched her away from the agony of Dr. Hazzard's fists. Henry truly was the best kind of man. And he had been right all along. She shouldn't have come here. Of all the treatments on earth, why had she fixed her heart on Dr. Hazzard's barbaric methods?

If she ever saw Henry again, if he forgave her selfishness and arrogance, she would abandon Jane's counsel to avoid him. Though Uncle Weston would disagree, love held much more weight than alliances and wealth. Truth spilled its light, as if her eyes had been opened after a long spell of darkness. Uncle Weston's interest in her marriage had nothing to do with her comfort or happiness. The men to whom he had introduced her were spineless, spoiled prigs. Just the type he could manipulate. Papa had left Uncle Weston a handful of shares in the company, so even when Stella took possession of her fifty-one shares, her uncle would have a seat on the board. If she wedded a man whom Uncle Weston could control, he'd have more sway than ever.

She gripped the cot tighter, and tears trailed hot down her cheeks. She'd been foolish and blind to believe his matchmaking attempts were born out of concern for her happiness. Her happiness was the furthest thing from his mind.

Despite Jane's advice, Stella ought to marry for love. And she loved Henry. Really loved him, though her haughty treatment of him showed how little she deserved the reciprocation of such feelings. He'd even saved her life once when they were young, though she hadn't thought about that day in ages. Her chest warmed.

Yes, families depended on her wise choices for their living, but why should loving Henry change that? If her plans to expand the business succeeded, they would benefit more than herself. The boon would trickle like a fountain, filling the cups of her employees too.

Her heart lightened in spite of the fists hammering her back. She'd make notes. Think of ways to expand the business, provide for her employees, and evade the need to marry a wealthy man as opposed to one she admired.

She'd have to let down her mystery correspondent gently. He'd been a faithful friend at the lowest time in her life, and she'd always appreciate his care and concern, but she didn't love him, and forcing feelings to sprout between them wouldn't do either of them any good. After all, didn't everyone deserve to find a partner who loved them wholly and completely? Someone with a heart for only them? They might still partner together for the good of the children, but their relationship must remain businesslike, because her heart belonged to Henry. Perhaps it always had.

Dr. Hazzard dealt a fierce blow to her shoulder, and Stella gritted her teeth against the pain.

If only Henry would hurry. The longing to tell him everything in her heart swelled like a balloon, but the pin of truth jabbed her happy daydream, deflating it. What if she told him and he didn't feel the same? All her life her wishes had been granted, but this was different. Henry had free will, and he might exercise it to reject her. In this situation she may not get what she wanted. Her gut roiled, but this time it had nothing to do with the internal bath.

"All done, Miss Burke." Dr. Hazzard covered her with a sheet. The fabric skimmed Stella's skin, antagonizing the bruises. "Lie still for a minute then get dressed."

"Is it helping?" Stella slowly opened her eyes. "Are the toxins leaving my body?"

"Time will tell." Dr. Hazzard planted her hands on her hips. "You expect results too quickly. This is only the first day of your total fast, and I'll remind you again how sick you were last night. Don't get overeager." She stepped toward the door and gripped the knob. "Once you're dressed, walk the trails. We'll get those toxins out of you one way or another." She stepped into the hall and closed the door behind her.

Stella gingerly touched her fingers to a spot on her neck. The raised flesh felt hot, and pain radiated down her back and legs.

She moved to sit, but the welts that lined her legs screamed in protest. As she pushed up on her hands and knees, pain rocketed through her body, blurring her vision. Why? What good would adding bruises to bruises do? She remained motionless, waves of anguish threatening to topple her, but she willed her limbs to hold her upright.

With the slow movements of an elderly woman, she stood and braced against the massage table. She pulled the robe over her shoulders but stiffened when she caught sight of her reflection in the mirror. Deep purple and greenish welts speckled her arms. Grey smudges nestled beneath her eyes, and her cheeks looked hollow. She ran a hand over her face. How awful she looked. Henry usually despised such self-deprecating comments, but surely he'd agree if he saw her.

Shouting from somewhere in the house postponed her perusal of her haggard features. She padded to the door, cinched the robe at her waist, and stepped into the corridor. The voices grew louder.

"I'm Margaret Conway, and I've come to take Dora Williamson home before you kill her too," said a voice with an Australian accent and no humor. "I spoke with your husband on the way to this death trap. He told me Claire was dead."

Chapter Sixteen

S tella knelt in the darkness, her ear pressed to her bedroom door. Margaret Conway had insisted upon seeing Dora, but she'd returned for a war of words with Dr. Hazzard. A scrap of moonlight cast lacy shadows through the curtain, and an owl hooted from somewhere in the tree branches outside her window.

Voices filtered from downstairs. The Australian woman raised hers enough for Stella to catch her words. "That was not my darling Claire I saw at the funeral parlor. The mortician said it was, but I've cared for her for so many years, I know her as if she were my own flesh and blood. Her hair has never been that color. And the shape of her face—" The poor woman's voice cracked. "That wasn't her. I'd swear to it."

Dr. Hazzard's reply didn't carry up the stairs.

Stella let Margaret Conway's words sink in. If the woman at the funeral home wasn't Claire, who was it? Her stomach growled, but she ignored the gaping hole in her middle. Why would the man at the mortuary claim the woman's body was Claire's if it wasn't?

Stella chewed the inside of her cheek. The bruises on the woman's neck. If she'd been murdered as Stella suspected, Dr. Hazzard might wish to hide the truth. Cleanse herself from legal implications that were sure to follow a murder on her property. But if the undertaker showed Ms. Conway a body he claimed belonged to Claire Williamson, didn't that mean he was involved in the cover-up too?

Margaret Conway seemed to believe Dr. Hazzard was involved in something sinister at Wilderness Heights. Would she have her way and take Dora home?

The two women continued talking, but Stella couldn't pick out anything of substance.

A chilly breeze blew through the open window, and she wrapped her arms around herself. When her fingers pressed the welts on her arms, she loosened her grip to stave off the ache that Dr. Hazzard had assured her would subside. Then she slipped into bed. With her back crying in pain, she lay on her stomach. Not her favorite position, but it took pressure off her aching muscles.

Her fingers trailed to her rib cage. Through the thin fabric of her nightgown, she felt her chest. Though not as pronounced as Sue's, her ribs formed a ripple beneath her skin. As Stella traced the hills and valleys, her throat tightened. Would she end up like Sue? A walking skeleton. What if she too dropped dead as a result of medications she'd had no choice but to take as a child?

She pulled the covers to her chin. No. Sue had been older, probably sicker. Stella would fight and return home healed.

Perfect health.

Why did the mantra fall flat this time instead of bolstering her sagging hopes?

Perfect health.

Still nothing but the waxing dread in her chest.

She closed her eyes and swallowed hard. Henry would come for her tomorrow and find her pride lying like shards of broken glass at her feet. She'd leave and never look back. Maybe Dr. Wagner would—

A faint rap at the door halted her thoughts. Was someone really knocking? She strained for another sound, and a knock, this time a bit stronger, sounded. Stella threw off the coverlet and padded to the door. She cracked it open, and her jaw slacked.

"Wendell? What on earth?" Fear sharpened his eyes, and his face had thinned since they'd last met. The hall lay silent as a tomb. No more voices rose from below. Margaret Conway and Dr. Hazzard must have gone to bed. But what brought Wendell so late?

He pushed past her into her bedroom, and she reached for a blanket to cover her shoulders.

"I must speak with you." The urgency in his voice sent a tremor down her spine.

She hastened to the bed table, lit a match, and touched it to the lamp wick, bathing the room in a jaundiced glow. The light magnified Wendell's altered features. His face had grown gaunt and pale, and his dark blue robe hung limp off his shoulders. "Are you ill?" She motioned for him to sit on the desk chair, and she eased onto the bed, pulling the blanket tighter around herself.

He shook his head. "Something's not right with Dr. Hazzard."

Stella lowered her brows and tilted her head. "Why do you say that? What happened?" She rested a hand on her chest, though it did little to quell the fluttering. Did Wendell know about Claire? About Margaret Conway's attempts to take Dora Williamson away from Wilderness Heights?

"She asked me the strangest questions." He scrubbed a hand across his stubbled jaw as he slumped into the chair.

"What sort of questions?" Stella clasped her throat. How could this night get any stranger? First Margaret claimed the undertaker had shown her a body that didn't belong to Claire, and now Wendell spoke of strange questions.

"She wanted to know details about my fortune. Asked if I had any valuables she could keep in her safe for me. I told her no." He shook his head, forehead puckered. "Why would she ask such a thing?"

"I couldn't say." It did seem odd. What business of Dr. Hazzard's were Wendell's money and belongings?

"Her queries made me uneasy."

"That's understandable."

"I asked to be discharged." He massaged the back of his neck. "She flatly refused. Said I'm not finished with my treatment, and she can't allow it." He leaned forward. "The look in her eye, Stella. Not many things have frightened me since I fought in the Battle of San Juan Hill. But the way she looked at me—like I was fruit ripe for plucking. I'm leaving. And I want to take you with me." His earnest gaze met Stella's, and she bit her lip.

Perhaps Wendell was reading too much into the situation. Dr. Hazzard wouldn't keep any of her patients against their will. No doubt she'd reminded him that his regime wasn't complete, that he hadn't attained perfect health as yet. But she couldn't keep him here. All of them were free to come and go as they pleased.

Besides, it would be foolhardy to leave tonight. Where would she go, and how would she get there? And Henry was coming for her. He'd arrive tomorrow, her knight in shining armor.

While Dr. Hazzard's medical practices didn't suit Stella, she wasn't a dangerous woman. She was a businesswoman, and no doubt knew that the future of her clinic rested on positive word-of-mouth recommendations. She'd never act in a way to jeopardize Wilderness Heights. Which also explained her secrecy in matters of Claire Williamson. And poor Margaret, overwrought at the news of Claire's death, imagined seeing the body of a stranger. It was the only logical explanation.

Dr. Hazzard had said both Claire and Sue arrived at the sanatorium ill beyond the reach of fasting.

Dread wriggled like a living thing in Stella's chest. Did she believe her own justifications? She planted her hands on her knees and drew a weighted breath. If she didn't cling to the doctor's assertions, there was only one other conclusion to draw. Dr. Hazzard was a monster.

It couldn't be true.

"Thank you for thinking of me." Stella rested her hand on his bony one and gave it a squeeze. He'd grown so thin over the last three days. It seemed almost impossible he'd lost so much weight so quickly.

"Come away with me while you can. I'll see you returned safely home." He placed his other hand atop hers and held it in a death grip. "Please."

His urgency whispered fear into her mind. Wendell was truly afraid. Something in the doctor's eye, in her manner, had left the war hero fearing for his life. She swallowed past the thorny knot in her throat. She opened her mouth to consent, but Henry's image stopped her. When he arrived, she must be here to greet him. "I won't be here long." She adjusted the blanket around herself. "Hen—a friend is coming to take me home. He'll be here tomorrow."

"And you'll leave with him?"

Stella nodded.

"Promise me." His knuckles whitened as his grip on her hand firmed.

Why was he so afraid? She'd read the paperwork before signing the dotted line and being admitted to the program. Patients were free to leave anytime they chose whether they'd finished the regime or not. This wasn't a prison. "I promise."

As his pressure on her fingers eased, he breathed a trembling sigh. "Very well, my dear. But mark my words, something is not right with that woman. She tried to get me to sign some paperwork, but when I asked to read it first, she snatched it away." Sweat beaded on his brow and glittered in the lamplight. He swiped it away with the sleeve of his robe.

What could Dr. Hazzard have wished him to sign? "Do you have any idea what the papers were?"

He shook his head. "Didn't see much. But they looked like legal documents of some kind." He chewed the ends of his mustache then rose. "I'd hoped you'd come with me, but since I have your word you'll not stay another night, I must be off."

"How do you plan on leaving? It's too dark now. Did you send for a motorcar?" Stella stood and peered out the window into the deserted yard. Light beamed from the window in Dora's cabin. Was Margaret Conway packing her things? She'd seemed to sense a need to get off the grounds with her charge as soon as she was able. Could both Margaret and Wendell be overreacting? Or was Stella underreacting?

"I must leave while it's still dark. Since the good doctor didn't take kindly to my request for release, I don't see another way." He wrapped her in a fatherly embrace. Her bruised back protested the weight of his arms, and she sucked a sharp breath through clenched teeth. He let go. "I didn't mean to hurt you."

"Think nothing of it." Stella stood still, allowing the pain to ease into an ache.

"We may not see each other again," Wendell said as he stepped toward the door. "But I wish you all the best."

"Thank you. And I hope to see you again one day. . .under better circumstances." Stella held open the door, and he stepped into the hall, making a sharp turn to the right. He paused at the head of the staircase and sent her a tight smile, then crept down the stairs with the prowess of a cat.

The poor man's stressed and starving brain must be playing games with his reason. Dr. Hazzard would never hold a patient against their will. Why, the very idea was ludicrous. But Wendell had been so convinced. Doubt niggled at the corners of her mind. The terror in his countenance had curdled the blood in her veins. What if he wasn't exaggerating? She shook the thought loose. He had to be seeing goblins where none existed. He'd read too much into Dr. Hazzard's inquiries, and in his famished delirium had constructed a horror story in the midst of mundane sanatorium procedures.

Still, concern clamped its gnarled teeth into her brain. What if he was right to be afraid?

She crept to the open window as a gentle breeze filtered in and toyed with the curtains. Should she have left with him? The lamp's flame flickered, sending her narrow shadow jumping across the wall. A door from somewhere down the hall creaked on its hinges. The clock gonged once. Who would be up at such an hour, and why?

Foolish question. She was awake, and sleep had fled her eyes altogether after her visit with Wendell. At least he'd picked a beautiful night to beat a retreat. Silence prevailed—even the crickets had ceased their chirping and gone to sleep.

Cupping her hands on the windowpane, Stella peered into the side yard. Wendell would have to sneak out through the back door. Since Rollie's bedroom adjoined the foyer, he wouldn't risk waking him with the front door's rusty hinges. Why was it so dark? Hadn't the moon been glowing earlier? She glanced at the sky. Clouds rimmed by a silver glow shrouded the moon. How would Wendell see his way into town, even to the road, with no moonlight to guide him?

He could be jumping from an imagined danger into one that put his life in jeopardy.

The clouds drifted, and the moon hovered overhead like a milky pearl. Movement near a rosebush drew Stella's attention. Wendell. He dashed from behind the shrub to a tree on his way to the main road.

Footsteps thunked on the stairs outside Stella's door, and her breath hitched. Did Dr. Hazzard know Wendell was making his escape? But how could she? He'd been so quiet.

Wendell crossed the yard, gaining ground. In a few minutes he'd reach the road. Then what? Where would he go and how did he intend to get there?

The kitchen door opened, and light spilled onto the grass. Wendell froze behind a berry bush. "Wendell, get back here." Dr. Hazzard's unmistakable voice sliced the stillness. She must have known the poor man's mind was uneasy. But if she wanted to call him back so he could leave in the morning in an automobile instead of creeping through the wilderness alone, her tone would do more to frighten him away than to allay his fears. She set a lantern on the step, and the flame illuminated the yard.

A metallic click set Stella's nerves buzzing. She'd heard that sound before. . .but where?

"I'm not asking again." The doctor's whisper may as well have been a shout.

A gun. She remembered that sound from when Papa took her to shoot clay pigeons at his club. Her heart plummeted into her stomach. No. She opened her mouth to scream. To warn Wendell that his life was in danger—

Crack!

The gun's report killed the words in her throat.

Wendell crumpled to the ground. Stinging tears rushed to Stella's eyes. Thoughts fled away as she gaped at the scene on the lawn. The glass fogged with every breath that sawed from her lungs. It hadn't really happened. Had it?

Dr. Hazzard strode to Wendell's contorted body. She nudged him with the stock of her shotgun then with the toe of her boot. She turned to the kitchen door and motioned with her hand. Rollie jogged toward her.

A whispered conversation passed between them, but the breeze changed courses and carried it out of Stella's earshot.

The doctor's head whipped around, almost as if her animal instinct told her someone was watching. Stella took a quick step to extinguish her lamp on the desk. She blew, but her first attempt was too weak and trembling to do much good. With her second breath, the flame died. Dead. Like Wendell. Like Claire. Like Sue.

So much death within these walls. She returned to the window.

Rollie dragged Wendell's limp frame toward a stand of trees. Would the poor man get a proper burial? They wouldn't simply dig a hole in the woods for him, would they? He'd been a kind man, friendly and warm. Tears trickled, leaving warm trails on her cheeks. He deserved so much better.

She glanced at Dr. Hazzard, who stood in the yard with her hands on her hips. The moon shone fully upon her. Who was this woman? What sort of monster was she that human life mattered so little to her? She had acted so pious when speaking of little Edward Anderson and the health he'd found through fasting. Was her seeming care for the boy nothing more than a charade?

The doctor spun to face the house, and she peered up to the window where Stella stood.

A gasp ripped through Stella's lips, sounding more like a scream in the silent room. Her heart thwacked her ribs, and her breath stood still. Had Dr. Hazzard seen her? If she would shoot a man like an animal for daring to leave, what would she do to a witness to her crime?

Stella crept into bed and pulled the covers over her head.

Wendell had invited her to leave with him. If she'd taken his advice, she would—

Bursts of light like Fourth of July fireworks erupted before her eyes. A mixture of guilt, relief, grief, and aggravation swirled in her chest. It wasn't fair she was alive when Wendell was not. It could just as easily be her body Rollie was dragging through the woods. She squeezed her eyes closed, but the sparks and flashes shone bright against her eyelids. Numbness prickled her left thumb then climbed like ivy up her arm as it reached for her cheeks.

Floorboards creaked in the corridor. With each step the groaning grew louder.

Stella tugged the coverlet off her head to her shoulders, keeping her eyes shut tight. She schooled her lungs to take deep breaths. She'd never pretended to be an actress, and when Mama had enrolled her in plays and concerts as a little girl, without fail Stella would be cast as a tree or sunflower. Well, as vegetation, she had learned the art of silence. Please, let it work now.

The door's hinges moaned.

Amid the squiggles across her eyelids, the light spilling in from the hallway cut through the darkness and turned the firework background brick red.

Breathe in.

Breathe out.

The aroma of vanilla tickled her nose. Mr. Hazzard? Was he involved in this too?

Breathe in.

Breathe out.

"She's asleep," he hissed.

"But I felt someone watching me." Dr. Hazzard's voice was hard as steel with a jagged edge. "And I saw the curtain at her window move."

Breathe in.

Breathe out.

The hinges squeaked. "Her window's open, Linda. Probably just a breeze."

Why wouldn't they just go away? Nausea churned in Stella's stomach as bile singed her throat. *Please, God, don't let me be sick.*

Breathe in.

Breathe out.

"Maybe you're right." Dr. Hazzard's tone softened. "But I sensed eyes on me. I'd swear it."

The sick feeling in Stella's middle expanded, and fingers of pain clamped her forehead. Her nerves tangled and throbbed. Why did this infernal migraine have to strike at the worst possible moment and bring its cruelest symptoms in tow?

Stress.

Henry might have been right. About everything.

The door clicked shut, but Stella continued to lie beneath the covers with her eyes closed and her breaths measured. What if Dr. Hazzard had stayed in her room and was lying in wait in the corner? Ready to catch her in the act of innocence, to make her pay for what she'd seen?

The roiling in her stomach calmed.

A door down the hall closed with a hollow snick.

Then, silence.

Stella strained to hear breathing that didn't match the tempo of her own. Nothing. Was she safe?

The clock in the corridor gave off two tinny chimes. Had it only been an hour since Wendell walked down the stairs? Her chest tightened. She should have stopped him. Persuaded him that leaving in the dead of night wasn't safe. If she'd tried harder—

She opened her eyes. Glowworms still crawled across her vision, but she squinted past them to the room's corners. She was alone.

If only this night proved to be a nightmare. But vanilla extract hung like fog in the air, reminding her that this bad dream was as real as the pain in her head.

But Henry was on his way. He might even be in Washington, chugging toward Olalla. For her. Falling tears made the skin around her eyes itch. She'd promised Wendell to leave this wretched place as soon as she could, and she'd make good on that vow as soon as Henry pulled the automobile onto the gravel drive.

She turned over, adjusted the blanket, and tried to sleep. But her mind insisted on replaying Wendell's murder as if it were on a reel at a moving picture show. Except the sound of a gunshot accompanied these images in lieu of the usual silence.

How could she sleep? She slipped out of bed and tiptoed to the window. All lay still and quiet. The moon shone, unimpeded by clouds.

She gripped the curtain. A chilly breeze gusted through the window and cut through her nightgown, but her mind barely registered discomfort. Dr. Hazzard couldn't find out what Stella knew. Once Henry had her safely off the property, she'd beg him to take her straight to the police. Whatever was happening here needed to stop. And she wouldn't go home without knowing the other patients were safe.

What documents had Dr. Hazzard insisted Wendell sign? It just didn't fit. And why ask him to keep his valuables in her safe? As questions flooded, the ache in her temples reached a crescendo.

She crawled into bed and pressed the pillow over her head. No use thinking about it while her brain was a muddled mess. Tomorrow, Henry would come. She'd tell him everything. He would know exactly what to do.

Hopefully nothing would delay his reaching Wilderness Heights. She couldn't stay in this death trap another night.

Chapter Seventeen

Stella clasped her hands behind her back and plodded along the walking trail, passing cabins and breathing in the scent of evergreen. She cast a glance over her shoulder. Mount Rainier stood majestic in the distance, its snowy cap standing in contrast to the shades of green surrounding her. As she pressed forward on her forced march for health, twigs snapped beneath her shoes. The setting sun cast pink and orange streamers across the sky. It was later than she thought. . .than she'd hoped. A band cinched around her lungs, cutting off her oxygen.

Henry hadn't come. Her vision blurred.

Was he so angry with her for the way she'd deceived him that he'd ignored her plea for help? Her shoulders sagged. She deserved it. The way she'd lured him, led him to believe he'd have the final say when all along her plans to check in at Wilderness Heights had been determined.

No. She swiped the tears off her cheeks. He'd only been delayed. Maybe the motorcar had some difficulty. But he'd be here. He had never let her down before.

She recited every cruel word she'd said to him when she insisted he bring her to Washington. Her sharp tone and condescending words burned her cheeks as a weight settled on her chest.

He'd deserted her and for good reason.

Fear frothed and churned like a stormy sea. She turned and started for the main house. Without Jane or Henry—or even Uncle Weston—she was alone. How could she survive this place, Dr. Hazzard, on her own?

Emotion scalded her throat. What if she died alone as Sue had? A sob rose in her chest, but she swallowed it. Crying would do no good. She blinked the stinging tears from her eyes.

Jane must have read Henry's feelings wrong. If he really cared for her, wouldn't he come to take her home? A fleck of purple peeked from a grassy patch beside the trail. She stooped for a better look. A delicate violet turned its face toward the setting sun. An image of Henry giving her a flower at the beach sprang to mind, and her heart constricted. Had it meant nothing to him?

She eased onto the grass and plucked the violet. The petals were perfect, smooth as silk beneath her fingertips. How could it grow in this place? So much fear and death resided here, the blossom had no business showing its face.

I'm alone, and Henry isn't coming.

Hope shriveled within her. She glanced at the flower in her palm and curled her fingers around it, crushing it in her fist. A tear warmed her cheek, then another. She fanned her fingers. The blossom lay mangled in her hand, much like her wishes for perfect health lay in a broken heap at her feet.

Perfect health. She sniffed. What had become of Sue's hopes for perfect health. . .or Wendell's? Now, both were dead.

Her stomach gurgled, begging for food. If only the doctor kept food in the icebox. But Stella had checked when no one was watching. Why bother owning an icebox if you didn't intend to keep food in it? But as many patients as Dr. Hazzard withheld food from, it was no wonder she knew the schemes of the hungry.

Stella lay back on the grass, gazing at the colors displayed by the setting sun. A breeze played with her hair, but she didn't bother to put it back in place. What did it matter anymore? No one on these grounds cared a whit about personal appearance. They only wanted food, and she was quickly joining their ranks.

Should she send another telegram to Henry? But what if Rollie had failed to send the last? Maybe part of her wished he had. If he had discarded it, that meant Henry hadn't willfully neglected it. She clenched her jaw. Wishful thinking on her part. Her mind's method of groping for hope when there was none to be found. Rollie had sent it—that was his job. And telegrams were even more reliable than sending letters through the post office. Mail carriers bragged that not even rain or sleet could stop them. Henry had received her message and chosen to ignore it. Which was exactly what she deserved.

Loneliness expanded within her, squeezing out the hunger in her belly. If only the treatments brought the smallest evidence of improvement, but last night's headache proved their ineffectiveness. She never should have come to this awful place. Henry had warned her, and she'd plunged headlong into her own ways. Now she'd lost him forever.

The sun sank lower on the horizon, and the pink sky deepened to violet. High overhead, stars winked from their courses in the heavens. A Bible passage Mama used to recite when they walked the nature trails filled her mind. "When I consider thy heavens, the work of thy fingers, the moon and the stars, which thou hast ordained; what is man, that thou art mindful of him? and the son of man, that thou visitest him?" Stella's heart swelled.

She wasn't alone. Not really. God, in all His vastness and unbounded love, saw her. Thought about her. Tears trickled from her eyes. In her search for healing and her fruitless attempts to appease Uncle Weston, even in her correspondence with a man she'd never met, she'd neglected the One who had saved her and loved her more than even Mama had. Though she'd never stopped praying to Him, her petitions had become selfish, born more out of habit than true devotion. And every decision she'd made for months—maybe even years—had been dictated by her own wishes. God's plans for her had never touched her mind.

She'd wandered from His loving arms to forge her own path. To contrive a way to make her mark on the world. Now, she lay before Him empty. Broken. Starving in more ways than one. But He'd never demanded some great deed from her. All He desired was obedience.

She closed her eyes. "Forgive me for drifting away. I need You, because I don't know what's best for me. Obviously, I ended up here. And I'm scared. Henry didn't come, and Wendell—" Her voice cracked, interrupting her prayer. "Show me what to do. Keep me safe. And once I'm far away from this place, work out a way for me to make a difference. You know I want to work in the children's home, but if that's not the path You have for me, put me on the right one."

When she opened her eyes, the pressure on her chest eased and peace whispered to the storm within her, calming it until it resembled a sea of glass.

Though she'd chased her own pursuits, God hadn't changed—His love hadn't changed. He'd waited for her at the very spot she'd wandered away and welcomed her back with open arms as the father of the prodigal had his errant son.

Even if Henry stayed in San Francisco, Stella would never be alone.

Chapter Eighteen

That's Peter Rabbit. Can you say 'bunny'?" Henry gestured to a bunny in a blue jacket in the picture book. Daisy prodded a dimpled finger at the furry creature.

He met her gaze but received no response.

"Bunny?" How much should he press? Wouldn't she speak when she had something to say? But according to Rose, the little girl used to communicate with simple words and short sentences before their parents died. He sighed. All in good time.

He leaned back in the chair and Daisy snuggled close. "Once upon a time there were four little rabbits, and their names were—Flopsy, Mopsy, Cotton-tail, and Peter—"

A scream tore through the tranquility. Henry bolted from the chair with Daisy in his arms. He followed the terrified shrieks to the kitchen.

Jane stood there pale as death, with a hand clamped to her chest. A garden snake writhed on the counter in a dusting of flour.

"Get it out! Get it out!" Jane pointed at the squirming creature.

Henry set Daisy down and approached the snake. Something about the coiling, slithering beast set his nerves on edge. Why couldn't it have been a mouse?

With his heart thumping hard against his ribs, he reached for the snake. Where did one grab them in order to maintain the least amount of physical contact? The neck? But other than the head, weren't snakes all neck? Bile made a slow climb up his throat, but he swallowed it.

If only Stella were here. She had never been as afraid of snakes as he had. She'd already have this emissary of Satan out of the house. Her fears centered less around physical things like snakes and rats and tended toward ideas and feelings. Once when they were children, she'd made him promise to stay close to her at the fair. She'd been terrified that he would lose her in the crowd, and she would find herself alone among strangers. He had held her hand tight the whole day. Did she feel alone now, surrounded by unfamiliar faces at Wilderness Heights? Or had she made friends?

Henry shook off the thoughts. She was where she wanted to be. No use worrying about a woman who had managed to get her way yet again.

He grabbed the snake and darted for the door. Still, unease squirmed like a serpent inside him. What if the experience, the treatments, the loneliness, were proving more than she could bear? Were her headaches improving? The very idea of poor digestion causing such things—it didn't add up in his mind.

With a flick of the wrist, Henry tossed the flour-covered snake into the bushes. He rubbed his hand on his trouser leg and stepped into the kitchen.

Jane wiped flour off the counter into a wastebasket, muttering, "How did it get in here? That's what I'd like to know. Snakes don't just crawl into houses and coil their way onto kitchen counters."

A snicker sounded from the direction of the pantry. Jane whirled, fists planted on her hips. "Robby." Though she didn't raise her voice, her tone prickled the hair on Henry's neck. And he wasn't the one in trouble. No telling what effect it had on the boy.

Robby stepped from the pantry, trying to bite back a smile but failing entirely. Laughter erupted, and he doubled over. "You should have seen your face." He slapped his knee. "You were white as a ghost."

Jane's hands clenched. Though there could be no doubt the child was in the wrong, the look on her face showed she was too invested in the situation and her choice of punishment may not fit the crime.

"I'll talk to him." Henry patted Jane's shoulder then motioned for Robby to follow with a jerk of his head. "Let's go for a walk."

Jane pulled a slip of paper from her pocket. "As long as you're out, here's a grocery list. Might as well walk to the market."

Henry stuffed the list in his pocket and ushered Robby outside.

Robby kicked a rock across the pavement. It bounced and rolled until a flowerpot stopped its course. "I'm sorry." His tone was anything but sorry. "I was just trying to have a little fun."

"I understand." Henry strode along the sidewalk. "You've had a rough go of it, and I'm very sorry. But I want you to grow up an honorable man, and that means I have to teach you how to be honorable by being so myself."

"What do you mean?" Robby thrust his hands deep into his pockets.

"Honorable men don't behave in a way that frightens or hurts others. They want to protect the people closest to them." Henry prayed for wisdom. Life lessons were far from easy to share when he had much to be ashamed of himself. When he was guilty of hurting the person he cared about most.

"But I didn't hurt nobody." Robby kept his focus on the ground. "It was only a little garden snake."

"You're right. The snake wouldn't have hurt anybody, but it did frighten Miss Jane."

A smile crept over the boy's face, displaying empty space from the front tooth he'd lost the day before. "It sure did." His words whistled through the fresh gap.

What would Henry do with him? How could he reach a child who thrived on mischief-making? They walked in silence for a moment. The best way to teach a child was by example. But in a short amount of time, Henry had not had many opportunities. He reached into his pocket for the shopping list. When he pulled it out, an envelope came along with it. His letter to Stella, confessing his deceit.

No time like the present. "I'd like to make a deal with you, Robby."

"What's that?"

"I help you become an honorable man, and you help me do the same."

Robby's brow wrinkled. "But I thought you were holerable. Or whatever that word is."

"Honorable." Henry stopped and faced the child. "It means some-one a person can look up to or respect because they do the right thing. You understand?"

The boy nodded slowly. "But you do the right thing."

"Not always." Henry knelt on the sidewalk. "I lied to a friend." He clenched his jaw. "Well, I didn't tell her an outright lie, but I let her believe something that wasn't true and I didn't set her to rights. That's just as bad as lying."

Robby's eyes widened. "What are you gonna do? Tell her?"

"I wanted to tell her the last time I saw her, but she was gone before I had the chance." Henry lifted the envelope for Robby to see. "I wrote her a letter."

"Let's mail it." Robby's eyes brightened, then he bit his lip. "Do you think she'll forgive you?"

How had this scamp managed to voice the heart of Henry's fears so succinctly? Would Stella forgive him? How could she trust him again? She would never see him as respectable or worthy now even if she was able to look past his lowly station. "I don't know."

"You gotta try." Robby grabbed his hand and tugged him to the street corner. A mailbox sat in all its imposing glory. Robby pulled the handle, opening the cavern. "Go ahead. Stick it in there."

Henry sighed. Though he'd rather Stella never knew the truth, he had the children to think of. If he expected Robby to do right, the boy needed to see respectability in action. Henry pushed the letter into the opening. "There. It's done."

Robby let go of the handle and let the flap close with a metallic crash. "You're very holerable."

Henry squeezed Robby's shoulder, and they started toward the market. "I've got a long way to go, and so do you. Just promise me you'll knock off the pranks."

"I'll try." Robby shrugged out of his grip.

Henry glanced heavenward. That was the best he could hope for.

As they neared the market, a street vendor smiled from her booth. Despite the lines around her mouth and eyes, the glow of health brightened her cheeks. Dried bunches of lavender and other herbs dangled from overhead, perfuming the air.

Henry breathed deep. The scent of the lavender soothed his frazzled nerves.

"You look stressed." The woman at the booth tied a ribbon around a sprig of dried yellow flowers. "Is there anything I can help you with?"

Henry began to shake his head, but halted. Stress. What if Stella's migraines were a result of overwrought nerves, not a faulty digestive system? "I don't need anything for myself." He stepped closer to the booth, motioning for Robby to join him.

Robby rolled his eyes but complied.

"I have a friend who suffers from migraine headaches. Is there some herb or tonic that might help her?" His gaze roved the unfamiliar bundles.

"Can you tell me her symptoms?" The woman rose and pulled a wooden crate full of herbs from beneath the tablecloth.

"She's mentioned flashing lights that block her vision. Lots of pain. Sometimes nausea." He searched his brain. There was something else. What was it?

"Does she experience numbness on one side of her body?"

"Yes." Henry snapped his fingers. "The right side, or the left—I don't remember for certain. Does it matter?"

"The side in particular doesn't have significance." She lifted a bundle of small dried flowers with yellow centers and wrinkled white petals. "The earliest recorded migraine headache occurred in Egypt about 1200 BC. They stand apart from more common headaches due to the optical flashes, numbness, and nausea that often accompany the pain." She handed him the bundle. "This is feverfew. Ancient Greeks used it for pain management and fevers, but it is an effective migraine preventative as well. Have your friend crush the leaves and steep them in hot water. A cup of this tea every morning can reduce the frequency of her headache days. It's not a cure, but it may give your friend a bit of relief."

Henry sniffed the dried flowers, nearly choking. Revolting. Stella's refined taste might shy away, but if this foul-smelling herb offered relief, she might gulp it down.

"The tea doesn't taste as strong as the herb smells." The woman's smile lines appeared again.

It was worth a try. Henry nodded. "I'll take one, please." He could give it to Stella as a peace offering when she returned. Despite Dr. Hazzard's glory stories of the miraculously healed Mrs. Barnett, the whole idea of Stella's digestion causing her migraines seemed more and more ludicrous each time he mulled it over.

He met the woman's gaze as she slipped the bundle of feverfew into a cloth bag. "My friend. . .she's at a clinic in Washington, and a doctor is treating her with fasting. This doctor says that all the body's troubles stem from poor digestion."

Robby focused on the ground, bent, and picked something up.

"This wouldn't be Linda Hazzard you're speaking of?" The woman's smile slipped. "Her practices are dangerous. I lived in Washington not long ago. A friend of a friend of mine, Mrs. Elgin Cox, checked into her clinic. She didn't check out alive." Her jaw grew rigid. "Linda Hazzard—I refuse to call that fraud a doctor—she said Mrs. Cox had taken too many medications in her youth and it shrank her intestines, so she was past the point of healing when she arrived. I don't pretend to be a doctor, but I've studied medical books for the last twenty years, and there is no basis for her assertions from a medical standpoint. The woman is a menace, and I'm certain that if not for Linda Hazzard's radical treatments Mrs. Cox would be alive today."

Dread formed a frozen ball in Henry's gut. Were the old Buzzard's treatments something worse than ineffective? Could they be dangerous—life-threatening?

The woman added a bundle of lavender to the bag with Stella's herbs. "If you're concerned for your friend, you'll warn her to get as far from Linda Hazzard and her make-believe medicine as she can before it's too late."

Henry handed her some coins, worry chewing through his brain like termites on wood. "I'll send her a telegram and offer to fetch her."

Robby tugged on his arm. "Come on, Mr. Henry. I found a dime." He held up a dirt-coated coin. "I want to get Miss Jane a flower to say I'm sorry about the snake."

Henry forced a smile. There may be hope for Robby yet. "That's a wonderful idea." He took the bag from the woman's outstretched hand.

"I snuck some lavender in there for you." She patted his hand. "My, but you look tired. Put a sprig under your pillow and you'll sleep like a cat."

"Thank you." Henry crammed the bag into the pocket of his suit jacket. At this rate, his savings would dwindle quickly. But if these herbs helped Stella, they would be well worth it.

She waved to Robby, who ran toward a flower vendor. "Be quick about that telegram. It is true, Mrs. Cox may very well have died of natural causes." She shook her head. "But she might not have. I could have an active imagination, but check on her."

Henry's chest constricted. He'd send a telegram on the way home. If Stella's reply carried even a hint of unrest, he'd get to Olalla as fast as wheels could take him.

Chapter Nineteen

Stella glanced around the cabin. Light peeped in between cracks in the lumber, and the scent of fresh pine somehow intensified the ache in her stomach. Threadbare curtains dressed small windows positioned high on the walls.

"This is your home away from home, Miss Burke." Dr. Hazzard wiped her hands on her skirt. "The perfect place to find healing."

Fighting the urge to roll her eyes, Stella pasted on a smile. "Thank you." She reached into her handbag and pulled out a folded slip of paper. "Would you give this to Rollie for me? I promised Henry I'd keep him updated on my progress."

The doctor took the note and nodded. "Of course." She moved toward the door, slipping the note into her apron pocket. "Your treatment schedule won't change, so be punctual. If you need anything in the meantime, I've hired a new nurse, Gretchen. She can help you."

"Has Sarah gone?" Perhaps Dr. Hazzard had let her go after the incident with Claire. If Margaret Conway got wind of the truth, she'd bring the place down on the doctor's head.

"She has found employment elsewhere." The answer was clipped, inviting no response.

Stella tucked her lip between her teeth.

"I'll leave you now." Dr. Hazzard opened the door, letting sunshine stream in. "Don't forget to walk the trails at every opportunity." With that, she latched the door.

Stella heaved a sigh, her shoulders slumping. If Henry ignored this message as he had the last, she may be tempted to abandon decorum altogether and scream. Not a ladylike response, and Jane would scold her. But she wouldn't mind a good scolding from someone who loved her, unlike Linda Hazzard, whose eyes took on a delighted twinkle at every chance to assert her dominance.

But dwelling on hardships would only invite despair. Stella scanned the room. The small bed covered by a patchwork quilt sagged in the middle, and a simple table with two chairs, a pitcher of water, and cups stood along the wall by the door. A dresser sat in the corner, but there would be no use in unpacking. Not with Henry arriving in two days' time. The icebox was glaringly absent. How had she ever thought herself capable of doing without food for so many days?

A picture on the wall arrested her attention. She cringed. Against an ivory backdrop, a boy sketched in blue gazed at her. Thick curls covered his head, and while he smiled, there was something sinister in his expression. Like the witch from Hansel and Gretel. Who could imagine a woman living in a house made of sweets to be anything but sweet herself? But she was a cannibal. While this little boy bore the look of a cherub, his eyes told her that evil frothed beneath the surface.

She rubbed her temples, slumping into a chair. Was she losing her mind? Seeing frightening images in innocent pictures? She glanced at the sketch again, but the demon child sent another shudder down her spine.

The child in the picture had curls like the little girl in the alley. What was her name? Rose? No. That was her sister's name. Another flower. Lily? Daisy? Stella smiled. Daisy. The little sweetheart had the same curls, but a different temperament entirely from the hobgoblin in the artwork.

The three dirt-smudged faces replayed in her mind. What had become of them? Had their parents returned? Though the boy, Robby, had said they were looked after, there had been no evidence of adult care.

Stella's stomach complained. As she poured herself a cup of water, the pitcher gurgled. With four walls closing in on her and only hunger and the frightening picture for company, she took a sip of water then rested her face in her hands. Sue might have died in this room, in that bed.

Flashes of light paraded across her eyelids.

And her headaches were no better than before. Tears prodded her eyes. Despairing thoughts invaded, reminding her of the stubbornness that had brought her to this point.

She tapped her fists against her temples. No. If she succumbed to despair, this place would be even less bearable. But how could she force her mind to focus on other things when hunger and fear had built such a consuming fire within her? What would Mother have done? She'd been sick for months before breathing her last, but never once had a cross word passed her lips. Mama had always been cheerful, even on her worst days.

Stella closed her eyes. Think. How did Mama thrive in the midst of pain? Others. Mama had always helped others. She'd said that when her mind and hands were busy helping, her own problems would shrink.

But how could Stella help anyone here in the middle of the wilderness? Who could she help? She'd been too late to help Sue. When Henry came for her, she could have him take her to the alley where they'd met Robby, Rose, and Daisy. If their parents hadn't come, she'd take them home and care for them until she could work out arrangements for a children's home with her secret friend. If only she could do something for them now.

She sipped her water until the glass was empty. "I could always pray for them." Prayer seemed like such a small thing. But her mother's verse dashed through her mind again. God had fashioned the heavens with a simple command. He had ordered the seasons and scheduled the tides. Stella's heart swelled to bursting. Prayer was a gift. Any help she could offer the children would be limited, but God. . .He could do anything.

She knelt beside the bed, elbows resting on the quilt, and bowed her head. "Dear Lord, I've been thinking about Robby and Rose and little Daisy. I think they lied to us." Tears sprang to her eyes. "I don't believe their parents are coming back for them. Please take care of them. Don't let them be hurt. Bring someone to take them home, and if it's not too much to ask, let me see them again to know they're all right."

When she lifted her head, sun streamed through the window. Mama had been right about so many things. Stella's heart felt lighter, and her problems faded into the background when she focused on others rather than herself.

Her stomach begged for food as she stood. It wouldn't be long now. Dr. Hazzard would make sure her wayward son took her telegram to the cable office. Henry would take her home, and she would eat to her heart's content. Strawberry ice cream didn't hold the luster it once did. Not enough substance. Broiled steak with parsley butter and a baked potato sounded more to her liking. Her mouth watered. Eggs and toast with sugar and cinnamon. What did it matter? She would happily stop at a pub along the road and eat a bowl of stew.

Whatever she ate first, it must be something she could chew. Something that would settle in her stomach like a rock and remind her what it was to feel satiated. No more orange juice and certainly not lima bean broth.

She opened the cabin door and stepped into the beautiful summer afternoon. Might as well start walking. Other than sleeping, sipping water, and being stared at by that frightening devil baby in the picture, the cabin offered nothing by way of recreation.

Her shoes crunched along the path. Birds chirped from the trees, and a rabbit scuttled into the underbrush lining the property to her right. Movement, a flash of gray, in the woods slowed Stella's steps. Was someone running through the forest?

Another streak of activity. Stella squinted to catch a better glimpse.

Tilda emerged from the woods, met Stella's gaze, and stopped, thrusting her hand behind her back. What did she have? Even if Tilda had found Spanish doubloons, no one at Wilderness Heights would care—except maybe Dr. Hazzard and her family. No, the patients craved only one thing. Food.

Had Tilda found food?

Stella ran toward her, mouth watering.

"What do you have there?" Stella reached for her arm, feeling like a scavenger hunting for its next life-sustaining meal.

Tilda jerked away, and the scent of yeast wafted to Stella's nose. Her stomach begged for a taste.

"You have bread?" Stella licked her lips, which suddenly felt dry.

"Please don't tell Dr. Hazzard." Tilda's voice was strained, her eyes wide. "I was starving. And I'd heard from Doris in the cabin next to mine that the shopkeeper in Olalla has bread she's willing to share."

"I won't give you away. Only let me have a bite." Stella bit her lip, tears smarting behind her eyes.

Tilda motioned with a jerk of her chin for Stella to follow her into the woods.

Stella stepped beneath the tree cover. The temperature cooled in the shade, and the odor of moss and mold nearly squelched the heavenly aroma of fresh bread. Maybe it wasn't fresh, but what did that matter when true hunger rattled her bones?

When Tilda pulled the small roll from behind her back, Stella fought the urge to lunge for it and swallow it whole. If Tilda was willing to share her blessing, that would be a poor way to repay kindness. Stella swallowed away the dryness in her throat.

With trembling fingers, Tilda tore the roll in half and handed one of the segments to Stella. "Here."

Stella snatched the bread from her hand and nibbled the edge, employing every bit of self-restraint she could muster. Once this was gone, who knew when there would be another? She may have to wait for Henry to eat again, so best to savor this morsel. Oh, never had a food so simple tasted so much like manna. She closed her eyes, chewing slowly. "Oh, Tilda. Thank you."

Tilda chewed her entire half of the roll. It protruded like a walnut in a squirrel's cheek. "You're welcome." The lump in her mouth muddled her words. "If you go to the shop tomorrow, we could share another. They wouldn't recognize you, and might be more likely to share."

Stella nodded. "What do you think Dr. Hazzard will do if she catches us?"

"I'd hate to find out." Tilda picked a crumb off her chest and popped it into her mouth. "Probably make us start all over."

"How are you feeling?" Stella followed her example, not letting a single speck fall to the ground untasted. "Has any of this helped you?"

"I think it has." Tilda's eyes brightened. "I used to get headaches every day, but they're less frequent now. Hopefully this indulgence won't set me too far back." She chewed her lip.

"You were truly hungry." Stella squeezed her arm. "It wasn't just a craving. And Dr. Hazzard herself said that feeding cravings is at the heart of the problem."

"Time will tell the real state of things, I suppose." Tilda blew into her hand and breathed in. "I have to go in for my massage in an hour. Do you think she'll smell the bread on my breath?"

"If you drink plenty of water beforehand, I doubt she would."

They strode toward their cabins together. Would eating such a small ration really set them back as Tilda feared? Stella glanced at her friend, who rubbed her willowy hands against her skirt in a nervous fashion. This might be the true test of Dr. Hazzard's methods.

If breaking her fast with half a bread roll brought on a fresh headache, there may be more to Linda Hazzard's belief in digestion than Stella gave it credit for. Nevertheless, she'd been fasting for over a week, and her pain had not dulled in the slightest. Had Tilda really seen improvement, or did she simply wish she had?

Chapter Twenty

Stella stepped into the main house, dreading the internal bath she would receive. Each treatment lasted longer than the previous one. Her first, while unpleasant, had involved only half an hour of suffering. Yesterday's had extended to more than three hours. Why? Were there really so many toxins in her body that had not yet been eliminated?

Fear wrapped clammy fingers around her heart. When Dr. Hazzard examined the contents of her bowels, would she know Stella had eaten solid food? Would there be consequences? She pulled in a breath. *Please, God. Don't let her find out.*

As she walked past the dining room entry, a voice flitted to her ears.

"Please, Dora, you must eat something. Claire would have wanted you to."

Stella peeked her head inside. The Australian woman, Margaret Conway, held a spoon of tomato broth to Dora's lips. The emaciated woman sipped then gagged.

"How are you feeling today, Dora?" Stella stepped beside her and patted her shriveled hand.

Dora sent her a tight smile.

"She's trying," Margaret answered for her. "But I fear I'm not able to get food into her fast enough to make much of a difference." She cut a glance at the doorway and lowered her voice. "She's so weak, she can't chew. So I'm left with nothing more substantial than this tomato broth. I don't know what to do." Worry drew lines across her forehead.

"She'll recover, in time?" How had Dr. Hazzard let Dora grow so weak? Surely if she'd fasted this long, any desire for nourishment would be born of necessity, not craving.

Moisture glittered in Margaret's eyes. "Oh, I hope so. If only I'd known they thought to come to this place, I would have tried my hardest to talk them out of it."

The wall clock chimed. Time for her appointment. Stella moved toward the door then turned to Margaret. "I'll pray for her."

"Thank you."

❦

Stella walked back to the cabin, clutching her stomach. Her legs wobbled with each step, and her middle still swam with the sensation of flowing water. Why had Dr. Hazzard settled on such harsh and demeaning methods of promoting healing?

When she reached her cabin, she stopped. The door stood ajar. She had closed it when she left. Had someone entered uninvited while she was away?

She pressed the door open, and the hinges squeaked. Light crept in through the doorway, illuminating overturned chairs, open drawers, and clothing scattered over the floor. Her pulse throbbed in her ears.

Who had ransacked her cabin, and why?

Dr. Hazzard must be informed. If a burglar was preying on her patients, she'd be indignant. Stella returned to the house as quickly as her legs could carry her.

"Dr. Hazzard!" she called from the foyer.

Footsteps thudded overhead.

Stella hurried to the staircase and met the doctor in her descent.

"What is it, Miss Burke?" Frustration dripped from Dr. Hazzard's every word. "This is a place of healing, and I'll thank you to keep your voice down."

"My cabin." Stella pointed toward the door. "Someone sneaked inside while I was here. They've torn the place apart."

"Nonsense." Dr. Hazzard planted her fists on her hips. "You're imagining things."

"Come, see for yourself." Stella started for the door. "What if I was robbed? The police should be summoned at once."

Anger fueled Stella's trek back to the cabin. She pushed the door open wide and motioned Dr. Hazzard inside. "I'm not imagining anything."

The doctor's shoes clapped on the floorboards and she let out a low whistle. "This is very real." She crossed her arms. Though her brow wrinkled, her demeanor lacked surprise.

Stella studied the woman as she set a chair on its legs. Something was off with her reaction. "Are you going to alert the sheriff?"

"Take an inventory of all that's missing. Bring it to me, and I'll see it gets to the authorities." Dr. Hazzard straightened the haunting picture on the wall.

Sighing, Stella nodded. "Very well. But I'd like to speak with an officer when he arrives."

"That can be arranged." Dr. Hazzard strode out the door then turned on her heel. "Clean this mess up. I don't stand for untidy cabins." With those abrasive words, she left Stella alone.

She didn't stand for untidy cabins? Stella pinched the bridge of her nose. Was the state of disorganization all the woman had taken away from the scene? She hadn't even offered an apology that Stella had been burglarized while under her care.

"The nerve." Stella glanced at the drawing, and the little boy grinned. "As nasty as you are, you know I'm right. I'm a client, and she acted as if I had invited the problem—caused it. Well, I'll show her. I won't clean this place. I didn't make the mess, so the responsibility shouldn't be mine."

As she slumped onto the chair, arms crossed, her mind traveled to Wendell. Her overturned chairs and rumpled clothing paled in comparison to his treatment at Wilderness Heights. Memories of the gunfire and Rollie dragging the body into the woods had never been far from her mind, but with her life in shambles around her, they flooded in like the breaking of a dam. When she spoke with an officer about the break-in, she must tell them of Wendell. His death could not go unpunished.

Had it really been Dr. Hazzard who pulled the trigger? Maybe Stella had dreamed it. But if it had been only a dream that stemmed from an overwrought imagination, where was Wendell? She hadn't seen him since that night.

And she'd heard Dr. Hazzard's voice, warning him to get back in the house. Stella plucked at her lip. Why had she killed him? For wanting to leave the property? For neglecting the rest of his treatment? Trigger-happy lunatic.

Stella glanced around the disheveled cabin. Would her disobedience garner the same punishment? Her chest prickled and tightened. She had to survive until Henry arrived to take her home. Obedience, compliance, may be her only life preserver until then. She snatched a dress off the floor and stood. As she folded it, her mind calculated the hours until she could reasonably expect him.

She'd requested Dr. Hazzard give the message to Rollie to send yesterday morning. Stella had seen the fear in his eyes when his mother was mentioned. He would have sent it the moment she asked. Henry should have received it within hours. Where between San Francisco and Olalla would he be now? Maybe Oregon.

She stuffed the folded dress in her bag. When she reached for another, her open jewelry casket caught her eye. She lifted it, ran her finger along the velvet liner. Gone. All her valuables had been plundered.

None mattered much. They were just things. Her heart skipped a beat, and she felt her ear. Her earrings. The violet amethysts Mama had given her. Unshed tears scalded her nose. No. Of all the things she owned, not Mama's earrings.

She rifled through the jumble on the floor, praying they'd fallen under a pile of stockings and been overlooked by the robber.

No. No, no, no.

Empty-handed, Stella slouched against the bed, burying her face in her hands. Sobs racked her chest, and tears drenched her palms. If they'd taken every stitch of clothing she owned, every other piece of jewelry, she'd have readily given them up. But Mama's earrings? Those tiny amethysts were all Stella had left of her.

Stella dashed moisture from her eyes. This place was breaking her apart bit by bit. Crushing her beneath a weight of hunger and loss. And Dr. Hazzard only cared that the cabin was untidy.

With a sigh, she grabbed her journal and tore out a page. Maybe if she made a comprehensive list, the police could locate her earrings. Clinging to that thin thread of hope, she jotted down her missing items, placing the violet amethysts at the top of the list.

After setting the page on the table, she gathered an armload of dresses, skirts, and stockings and dropped them onto the bed. If she didn't clean up, the consequences could be dire.

Chapter Twenty-One

Stella's head throbbed, and her empty stomach added its alto complaints to the symphony. She pulled the quilt higher and worked to ignore the discomfort. What time was it? When she opened her eyes, fingers of moonlight touched the floor and illuminated the picture above the table.

The child's face came to life, and he laughed. A malicious sound. "You'll never get out of here alive." His voice sounded deeper than any child's she'd ever heard. "I saw what happened to Sue in that bed. You're next." He pointed a chubby finger at her, and fire ignited in his eyes.

Fear coiled around her heart, tightening until Stella's chest threatened to burst. She clamped her hands over her ears. This had to be a dream or some cruel trick. Sue had likely died in this bed. Death's chilling breath blew against her neck. Stella threw off the covers, leaped to the floor, and scrambled onto the chair. It wouldn't take her too.

She drew her knees to her chest and hugged them. The curtain at the window fluttered on a breeze. Had the kiss of death been nothing more than her half-addled brain twisting a bit of reality? Or was it real? She rubbed a hand over her neck. It had felt real.

A glance at the picture showed the boy had returned to his lifeless lines and curves behind the frame. Her breath sawed from her lungs, burning with every inhale.

She'd read stories in her history books with Henry. Tales of men and women delirious with hunger during the Great Famine in Slovakia. They'd seen things that weren't there when their bellies were empty. She pressed a hand to her stomach. The breeze, the child—were they symptoms of starvation? Her ribs were more pronounced than ever beneath her fingers.

The roll she'd shared with Tilda came to mind, leaving her head feeling as if it had been stuffed with cotton. She imagined taking a bite of the roll, worked her jaw as if she were chewing. Her tongue reminded her of the yeasty taste and grainy texture. Sighing, she swallowed nothing but air.

She propped her elbows on the table and rested her head in her hands, avoiding eye contact with the picture. Sleep had fled to a place much more pleasant than this cabin. She struck a match and touched the flame to the wick. No use sleeping now.

Tomorrow she would find that bakery. If the shopkeeper gave her a roll, she didn't have to tell Tilda. If she ate it in the woods before returning to the walking trails, she could eat every morsel. Her mouth watered, but something prodded her chest from the inside. That wouldn't be kind. Tilda had given half of hers away.

Stella massaged her temples. What a selfish monster she'd become. Though she often thought of herself before others, hunger had magnified her self-centered attitude and turned her into a person she didn't like. Her mother's choice to focus on others should remedy that. Stella prayed for the children from the alley. Then prayed for Dora and Tilda. Maybe Henry could find a way to help them escape Wilderness Heights too.

She poured a glass of water and gulped it, wishing it were broth— even that horrid lima bean broth would offer some nutritional benefits. The black sky had faded to gray, and the sun peeked over the hilltop, spewing orange light through the cabin's tiny windows. Stella stood on tiptoe and glimpsed the sky. Blueberry clouds rimmed with strawberry sunlight. Would she ever stop thinking in terms of food?

The clock on the wall informed her that the bakery in Olalla wouldn't be open for several hours. What to do until then? Best to avoid walking the trails and save her strength for the trek into town.

If she sat within these four walls a moment longer, she might lose her mind. Dr. Hazzard's tales of healing people who suffered mental maladies replayed in her ears. Had the people she purported to help had problems before coming to her? She'd said Mrs. Barnett lived with bouts of melancholy. Had she really? Or had enduring the doctor's treatments—starving herself—plied her mind into shapeless putty?

Was the hunger causing Stella to lose her mind? She glanced at the picture. Did the little boy in the frame blink? Tears in her eyes, she looked away. Was she going crazy?

Chapter Twenty-Two

The forest floor was spongy beneath Stella's feet. Her back and shoulders ached from the morning's beating that had masqueraded as a massage. Though Tilda had given her directions to the town and shop, the unfamiliar surroundings closed around Stella, making her second-guess her steps. Was she lost? If she failed to return for her internal bath, would Sam Hazzard bother to come looking for her, or would they leave her to die? Both thoughts horrified in equal measure.

A row of buildings peeked between thinning trees. Olalla. The town was smaller than she had pictured it, more of a village, really. But what did that matter as long as she returned with food? She stepped out of the woods, her eyes latching onto the clapboard building with a sign bearing the name OLALLA MERCANTILE, just as Tilda had described.

An automobile sputtered to a stop outside the shop, and a familiar figure stepped out. Stella froze. Sam Hazzard. If he saw her, he'd know exactly why she was here. He'd tell his wife, and heaven knew the consequences Stella would face. She darted between the trees to watch him enter the mercantile.

Should she turn back or wait until he left to fulfill her craving? No. This was more than a craving. This was hunger. If she'd learned anything from her stay at Wilderness Heights, it was the difference between those two sensations.

Her stomach coiled in on itself, as if realizing how close it was to sustenance. She'd stay. Besides, if the hunger was making her hallucinate, she would rather Henry not find her in such a state when he arrived. It wouldn't be long now. Her heart skipped. Would he be as overjoyed to see her as she would be to see him?

Their last encounter had been rocky, but after she apologized for her behavior, maybe he would come around. Would it be proper to tell him how much she cared for him? She sniffed. What did that matter anymore? Propriety bore no weight in matters of the heart.

But Uncle Weston paid his wages. If he loved her, he may not feel at liberty to say.

Or he might not love her after all. She bit her lip. If she shared her heart with him then discovered he didn't feel the same, she would surely die of shame.

She shook off the gathering gloom that had curled its dark fingers around her. These thoughts were premature. Besides, she'd seen the look in Henry's eye at Dr. Hazzard's office in Seattle. He'd wanted to tell her something then, something personal and heartfelt, but she'd hushed him. He felt more than friendship for her. He must.

A breeze whistled through the trees, making the leaves rustle and alternately glisten and dull. What was Sam doing in the mercantile that should take so long? Purchasing cans of tomato broth and orange juice really couldn't be so time-consuming. After charging exorbitant rates to reside in tiny shacks and feeding her patients either nothing or liquid, how could Dr. Hazzard sleep at night? Maybe that was why she left the lamps burning day and night. Although conning people out of their money wasn't the worst the woman seemed capable of. That crime paled in comparison to murdering Claire, or at the very least harboring her killer. And then there was poor Wendell's cold-blooded killing. He had been accurate all those days ago when he'd said something wasn't right with Dr. Hazzard. And he had mentioned the doctor insisting he sign legal documents and put his valuables in her safe.

Why? To steal them?

What were those papers she had so desperately sought his signature on?

Stella shuddered. Dr. Hazzard had never suggested safeguarding Stella's jewelry, but now it was gone too. Had the doctor opted to take them without Stella's permission and bypass the hassle of asking? Or had her devoted husband and fearful son completed the job on her behalf?

Sam exited the shop, a briefcase in hand, and climbed into the motorcar. No tomato broth. He turned in the seat and planted his feet on the ground once more, eyes fixed on the tree line where she hid.

As she ducked farther into the foliage, her heart climbed into her throat. Had he seen her? She held her breath, though he couldn't possibly hear her from his position near the store.

He spat on the ground then returned to his seat inside the vehicle. Sputtering, the car wheeled down a lane that must lead to Wilderness Heights, kicking up dust in its wake.

Stella released a puff of oxygen. She would wait a moment longer, in case he returned. Birds flitted overhead and squirrels argued on a tree branch. One held a nut, and the other stood empty-handed. Never had she possessed so much in common with woodland creatures, but the intrinsic desire for food made her sympathize with the poor little squirrel who had none.

Once the road dust settled, Stella stepped out of the woods and strode toward the mercantile. She pressed open the wooden door, the effort making her bruised, tired muscles scream. A bell jangled.

"Can I help—" The plump, smiling woman behind the counter pulled in a sharp breath, studying Stella from her feet to her crown. She shook her head, clicking her tongue.

The same sound Jane made when displeasure set in. Homesickness choked the greeting from Stella's throat, and she blinked once then again to quell the tingle in her eyes.

"You're hungry." A statement, not a question.

Stella glanced down. Her dress may as well have been hanging off the shapeless form of a clothespin doll. How frightening she must appear. She ran a hand over her cheek. So hollow and gaunt. She nodded to the shopkeeper and fished in her pocket for the few coins she had brought from San Francisco. A mercy the Hazzards hadn't found them. "I have money."

The woman offered a tight nod. "What would you like?"

Stella scanned the bounty behind the glass display case, mouth watering. Her stomach punctuated the silence with a cry of either pain or delight at the prospect of food. She laid her money on the counter. "Would this be enough for two rolls?"

"Of course." The shopkeeper didn't bother looking at the coins. It may not have been the right amount, but she was kind enough to make the sacrifice.

"Then I'd like two, please."

"How long has it been since you last ate?"

Stella eyed the shopkeeper as she dropped steaming rolls into a paper bag. How close was this woman to Sam Hazzard or Dr. Hazzard herself for that matter? Could she be trusted not to tell either of them Stella had hiked to her mercantile for food? She licked her dry, cracked lips. "I ate a little something yesterday. Or the day before." Stella shook her head and massaged her temple. "I don't quite remember."

"You're from Starvation Heights, I take it?" She handed Stella the bag.

Stella tilted her chin. Was that what the townspeople called the place? "You mean Wilderness Heights." If word somehow trickled to the Hazzards that Stella had come to Olalla, the punishment for speaking ill of the sanatorium would far outweigh the consequences of eating a bit of food. And Sam had lingered so long then left with only a briefcase, not a month's worth of supplies. He must have some connection to the store's proprietor. The paper bag crinkled beneath her fingers, and she fought the urge to devour the rolls without a thought for manners or etiquette.

"Yes. Yes, of course." The woman's gaze dropped to the floor then traveled back to Stella. "Can I ask you something?"

Stella nodded slowly and took a step back. The shopkeeper's prying eyes left her with the sensation of beetles crawling on her skin.

"Why do you stay? Are her methods really helping?"

Chewing the inside of her cheek, Stella tumbled the question through her mind. Simple questions typically merited simple answers, but this case was so far removed from ordinary. She opened her mouth to speak but snapped it closed. Could she trust this woman with the dark truth? The fact that no one left Wilderness Heights without Dr. Hazzard's permission?

Wendell. She ought to go to the police and tell them of his death.

"Where is the sheriff's office?"

The woman's eyes widened at the abrupt change in topic. "Just down the street three doors." She scoffed, shaking her head. "But you've likely missed him."

"Where has he gone?" The warm bread screamed for Stella to take a bite. No. Better to wait.

"He goes into Seattle on Tuesdays. And the deputy has been out of town caring for his ailing mother since last month." The woman wiped work-worn hands on her apron. "This is a sleepy town. Not much happens here. If you'd like me to give him a message for—"

"No." The word sounded cold as it landed in the space between them. Though the woman had been nothing but kind, doubt feasted on Stella's mind. How close was this woman to the Hazzards? Until Stella knew for certain, there was no way she could trust her. "Thank you." She moved to the door. "Have a nice day."

With a clink of the bell above the door, she stepped into the sunshine, moving at a half run, half walk to the tree line. *I will let the authorities know of your death, Wendell. Of your murder.*

Henry should arrive this afternoon, tomorrow at the latest. He would bring her into town to speak with the police.

Once beneath the cover of leafy boughs and pine branches, she rammed her hand into the paper bag and pulled out a roll. The soft bread warmed her fingers. How fresh it was.

She held it under her nose, savoring it for a moment, but another audible complaint from her stomach threw self-control out the window. Without so much as a real taste, the first bite landed in her stomach barely chewed. Stella chastised herself. To eat this roll without savoring it was like throwing diamonds into a pigsty. She schooled her mouth into temperance as she tasted, chewed, and swallowed the next morsel.

With half the roll consumed, Stella stowed the remaining portion. Best to save some for later. If Henry didn't make it to Wilderness Heights until tomorrow, it would be wise to hold on to the rest for breakfast.

Did the people of Olalla really call Dr. Hazzard's sanatorium Starvation Heights? Unease slithered down Stella's spine. How much did the townspeople know about what happened behind those closed doors? Her mind jumped to the story the boy had told of walking skeletons. If anything, the people of Olalla had seen firsthand the results of the treatments Dr. Hazzard touted as medical but that Wendell had more accurately described as Chinese water torture. If the townspeople knew the truth, why had they done nothing? Said nothing? If the sheriff had seen the skeletons, why had he not stopped by the clinic and checked on the poor souls who wandered the walking trails?

Stella shook off the despair that pressed on her shoulders.

Time to bring Tilda the other roll.

She gazed into the bag. Her chest warmed. Along with her half roll, two others lay untouched. She glanced over her shoulder toward the shop. Maybe she'd judged the storekeeper too harshly. If she sided with Dr. Hazzard, she wouldn't have gone out of her way to help the patients break their fasts with so much indulgence.

The way back to the sanatorium didn't feel as endless as the trip to the shop. When Stella stepped through the trees onto the trail that led to Tilda's cabin, she tucked the bag of contraband beneath her arm. She knocked on the door.

"Come in." Tilda's faint voice sounded weak.

Stella pushed open the door, stepped inside, then closed it tightly behind her. The curtains at the tiny windows were drawn, and gloom shrouded the room. "Are you quite all right, Tilda? I brought you a roll. It should help you get your strength back." She kept her voice a whisper. If poor Tilda suffered another migraine, Stella wouldn't be the one to make matters worse. She knew the excruciating pain too well.

Her friend groaned from her position on the bed and planted a hand over her eyes. "Keep it. I never should have eaten that bread." Tears hung thick in her soft voice.

"You think the bread did this?" How could she believe such lies after falling into the clutches of several headaches while strictly adhering to the fast?

"What else could it be?" Tilda rolled onto her side, pulling the pillow over her head. "Dr. Hazzard said she would tell me when my body was rested enough for digestion. I didn't trust her, and now look at me. Will I have to start over? I don't think I can." Cracks formed in her voice.

"It won't come to that." Stella knelt beside her, rubbing her arm. "Everything will turn out well in the end, I'm sure of it."

Was she? If Henry didn't arrive and Linda Hazzard found out she'd broken her fast, would anything ever be all right again?

Chapter Twenty-Three

Stella stashed the rolls in her jewelry casket. The burglars had already emptied it, so if they returned, what reason would they find to look again? Though she'd given her itemized list of missing valuables to Dr. Hazzard, the woman's chilly, noncommittal demeanor left Stella less than certain the matter would be handed over to the authorities. Why did the doctor insist on covering and overlooking every crime that occurred under her roof?

The skin on Stella's neck tingled. What if the doctor was at the heart of everything? Wendell's blood dripped from Dr. Hazzard's hands. No doubts remained on that score. But the other deaths? The robbery? They may share common threads.

The woman—Claire—her neck had been peppered with bruises, but Dr. Hazzard didn't seem concerned or even surprised. She'd wanted to wait until after dinner to call the funeral parlor. Why?

Stella slipped her jewelry casket into a dresser drawer.

Then there was Sue Chandler. The doctor had said medication in childhood had directly caused her death, but what sense did that make? Even if tonics had made her health fragile, they wouldn't have killed her, would they? If Sue had never come to Wilderness Heights—Starvation Heights felt more fitting—would she still be alive?

And Dr. Hazzard's use of the handsaw on poor Sue. A lump knotted Stella's throat. No amount of verbal finagling could justify cutting her into pieces. Even if the undertaker had planned to cremate her.

And now Stella's cabin had been burglarized and her valuables stolen. She eased onto the bed. The jewelry. That was the only thing missing. While she hadn't brought her family's most precious pieces, what she had brought was worth at least five hundred dollars. But the amethyst earrings were priceless for sentimental reasons.

Her brain churned through the scant facts of each of the crimes. Wendell had said that the doctor asked to put his items of value in safekeeping. Then she'd tried forcing him to sign legal papers. Had she wanted to hold on to his belongings with the hope of keeping some for herself? Would the papers requiring his signature have given Dr. Hazzard some claim on Wendell's wealth?

It seemed too much like fiction to be true. What sort of woman would go to so much trouble for money? But Rollie had blackmailed her, threatening to reveal her secrets if she didn't pay him. How much did he know? Stella might know only a small portion of what had transpired on these grounds.

And what of Sue and Claire? Dr. Hazzard hadn't grown rich after their deaths. Had she? Or had she insisted they sign the same paperwork she had thrust upon Wendell? Could all of this be a scheme to fill her bank accounts to bursting?

Stella let her head droop into her hands. Her brain struggled to process the possibilities. There was no proof. She sighed. But the pieces seemed to fit.

"Argh!" She flopped back onto the pillow. "How could I have been so deceived?" The promise of perfect health mocked her. Dr. Linda Hazzard didn't give the slightest care for her health. Money was the force that drove her forward.

Stella pushed off the bed and moved to a chair. If someone ever made her a promise that sounded too wonderful to be true, she'd never believe them again. Why were people so cruel?

She checked the wall clock. Time for her massage, and the doctor expected punctuality.

As she trudged to the main house, the breeze pulled wisps of hair from her braid and blew them in her face. The shopkeeper had asked why she stayed. Because she had no friends close by with the means to take her far away. She knew no one in Olalla. And if she went to one of the townspeople for help, how could she be certain they wouldn't bring her back to face the Hazzards' wrath?

Until someone who knew her and cared for her arrived, how could she feel safe? It wasn't as if she could run into the woods and live off the land. She knew nothing of survival on rugged terrain.

She strode into the house. A hush permeated the foyer, and her footsteps echoed through the space. Where had everyone gone? As she neared the stairwell, the office door beside the dining room caught her eye. Dr. Hazzard usually kept it locked, but it stood ajar.

Stella strained at the stairs, listening for signs the doctor or her family was nearby. Nothing.

She grasped the doorknob.

The hinges groaned. Light spilled through a window behind the desk. Papers stood in a neat stack before the desk chair. Stella tiptoed closer to examine the sheets. The first contained notes from a medical journal by a man named Dr. Tanner. She perused the words. This doctor touted fasting as strongly as Dr. Hazzard with one exception. He didn't feel internal baths were necessary for healing. Brilliant man. Stella rolled her eyes.

She turned the page over. Her hand flew to her throat. Squinting, she leaned in for a closer look. Surely she'd read wrong. LAST WILL AND TESTAMENT stood out in bold letters across the top of the paper. Was this what the doctor had urged Wendell to sign? She scanned the lines, and fear clamped its talons around her heart.

Her name. Stella Burke.

Someone had written her name in the blank. She tried replacing the documents in order, but she fumbled the pile. Papers fluttered to the floor.

She scrambled to retrieve them. How would she ever put them back as she had found them? Would Dr. Hazzard notice if they were out of order? With the pile arranged as best she could, Stella set it down and started for the door.

A glance in the wastebasket halted her steps.

That looked like her handwriting on one of the crumpled pages. She reached into the trash and smoothed the wrinkles.

Her message to Henry.

She couldn't breathe. Had someone sucked the air out of the room? Eyes burning, she swallowed a sob. He wasn't coming. Probably didn't know how desperately she needed him.

A creak from somewhere in the main part of the house sent her pulse rushing in her ears. She had no business in this room. With her lip clamped between her teeth, she hid the message Dr. Hazzard had discarded in her sleeve.

Footsteps thumped on the stairs. "Miss Burke?" The doctor's voice filtered from above.

Stella slinked out the door, clicking it closed behind her.

"Miss Burke?" Sternness wove through the fiber of Linda Hazzard's voice.

Punishment for tardiness must be less than for snooping. Stella started up the steps. The doctor emerged from the room Stella had slept in upon arrival. Hands on hips, she glowered at Stella. "What have I told you about punctuality?" Dr. Hazzard ground the question through clenched teeth.

Stella's hands balled into fists. The nerve of this woman to cover up Claire's death, to murder Wendell in cold blood—and then to dare to confront her for arriving past her scheduled appointment. And Stella hadn't been late; Dr. Hazzard had.

As she swallowed the ball of fire forming in her throat, Stella forced a contrite expression. Henry wasn't coming, and until she found a way to escape, playing along might be her only means of staying alive.

Dr. Hazzard lifted her nose, pulling in a breath. "Do I smell bread?"

Nausea rushed through Stella's middle, and she prayed she wouldn't spew her roll all over the doctor's shoes. "Is the cook baking?" Such a weak response, but she couldn't very well admit to breaking her fast.

Dr. Hazzard's eyes narrowed. "Come along. We're running late enough as it is."

Chapter Twenty-Four

Stella sat at the table in her cabin, head in one hand, fighting to hold her eyes open. Pain surged through her temples, and her fingers traced the outline of her ribs over her nightgown. The curved bones protruded as if preparing to take leave of her body. The ache in her stomach had become a constant companion.

If she had never experienced true hunger before, this must be it. What else could the unbearable gnawing within her be called? She longed to return to the shop in Olalla and beg for another roll. With her money spent, pleading was her only option. But if Dr. Hazzard found out, there'd be the devil to pay.

She pressed her fist to her middle. The devil would have to stand aside if she came within fifty yards of any kind of food—yes, even that vile lima bean broth. She'd gladly gulp a bowl if it was offered. At the thought of Satan himself, she glanced at the picture on the wall. The wicked child smirked at her pain. "If I ever get out of here, I'll take great pleasure in breaking you into fragments on my way out the door."

The painted lips appeared to spread in a macabre smile.

"You laugh now. But your days are numbered." She scrubbed a hand over her face. Had days without food stolen her senses and left her talking to paintings?

The wall clock chimed. The time for her internal bath drew closer. She groaned. It had been three weeks, and not the slightest variation in the frequency of her migraines. Though they still proved a daily occurrence, maybe they were less severe. Or perhaps the ache in her stomach superseded the one in her head.

She lifted the note she'd penned off the table, tracing Jane's name with her index finger. Although Henry had not received either of her messages, Stella couldn't give up. Since he wasn't able to help her, the responsibility to find another way off the property fell on her shoulders. But she wouldn't trust Rollie with another telegram. The snake had proved he couldn't be trusted. And if Henry refused to make the drive, Jane could take the train. But Jane was so much older than Henry, and if Dr. Hazzard made her departure difficult, how much better to have a man like Henry at her side? Stella sighed. Whatever happened, God could work it out. Maybe the doctor wouldn't give her trouble. She might let Stella leave, no questions asked.

Stella cringed.

That's what she'd believed before Wendell had tried to leave. And no mention had been made of him by Dr. Hazzard or anyone else since that dreadful night.

She couldn't bring the message to her appointment. If Dr. Hazzard saw it, she would put the pieces together, and if she ascertained Stella's knowledge of the three dead patients—

That couldn't happen. She must hide the note here and pray some kind soul would deliver it to the telegraph office. If only she could catch Margaret Conway alone. Such a sympathetic woman, and her care for Dora went beyond that of a faithful servant. She loved Miss Williamson, wanted the best for her. Too bad Dora believed Wilderness Heights was her best chance at health. Why wouldn't she agree to leave? Dora was as thin as the wire in an incandescent bulb, and only since Margaret had taken to spoon-feeding her had she begun to look remotely human.

Please, God, let me cross paths with Margaret. She'll help me send the wire. I know it.

She returned the letter to the table then snatched it to her chest. If Sam or Rollie searched her cabin again while she was at the main house for treatment, they couldn't find her plea for help. They'd give it to Dr. Hazzard, and she'd be in the same quandary as if the doctor found it in her possession. Where could she hide it? All three Hazzards already gave her suspicious glares when she entered the house, so she could leave no clue to fuel their distrust.

Heart thumping, she scoured the small space for a hiding spot. Where would they not look? Surely they'd go through her bags again. She pulled open drawers in the bureau, and when she found nothing, her eyes caught on the framed picture on the wall. That horrible drawing had been here since the day she moved in, so the Hazzards may not give it another thought. She lifted it off the wall, and dust coated her fingers. The demonic cherub smiled at her as if he knew the dark secrets she guarded for the sake of life and limb. She flipped the frame. After inducing sleepless nights with his narrowed eyes on her, hiding her message was the least this goblin baby could do.

The paper backing peeled easily. Stella turned the picture over and kissed the child's cheek. "Thank you, you scary demon. But this doesn't mean we're friends." She secreted her folded note behind the paper and hung the frame back on the nail.

With any luck they'd have the same aversion to the picture and steer clear.

She hastened to slip off her nightgown then pulled a dress over her head. The fabric swallowed Stella whole, falling in saggy folds around her ankles. How much weight had she lost? One glance in the mirror above the washbasin reflected her haggard features. She touched her cheek. Even her skin felt frail. If she couldn't find Margaret Conway or someone else to take her message to the telegraph office, she'd hike into town and carry it herself. Maybe beg for a slice of bread in the process.

Her gaze darted to the clock. Ten minutes until her appointment. She slipped into her shoes and raced out the door.

Breathing hard, she took the trail as quickly as her weakened legs would carry her. She threw the door open and strode into the house. The place was silent as a catacomb. Why did the doctor and her family seem to scatter like bugs under a light during the day? Were they nocturnal?

She started for the stairs, but stopped as she passed the dining room. Margaret Conway and Dora Williamson sat alone at a table. Margaret spooned broth into Dora's mouth. "You must eat something." She lifted the spoon and smiled. "You're getting better every day."

"I miss Claire." Dora's voice quavered.

"Me too. But she'd want you to build up your strength." Margaret's eyes glimmered. "You know she crawled into town to send word to me. She knew you were in trouble."

Sunlight filtering through the window caught a tear as it slipped down Dora's sunken cheek.

"She would want me to take you home."

"But my treatments aren't over. I'm not cured." Dora rested a bony hand over Margaret's.

Stella stepped into the room, and both women trained eyes on her. "Go with her, Dora. I've seen things. Awful things. I want to go home too, but my friend did not come for me. Margaret cares for you. Please, take the opportunity and go as far from this place as you can."

Margaret stood. "What have you seen?" Her hand clamped the chair back until her knuckles turned white.

Would she tell Dr. Hazzard Stella's secret?

Stella shook her head.

"You have to tell me." Margaret strode to Stella and grasped her hand.

"Why?" Stella snatched it away. How could she trust this woman? Though she'd claimed her arrival was to remove Dora from Dr. Hazzard's care, neither of the women had left. Dora stubbornly insisted on staying, but why didn't Margaret make her see reason or forcefully drag her off the property?

"I need all the information I can obtain about the happenings at this house," Margaret whispered. "I'm working with a lawyer in Seattle to build a legal case against Dr. Hazzard." She bit her lip and cast a glance at the empty doorway. "Claire Williamson died here not long ago. Circumstances lead me to believe she may not have died of natural causes. I want her death avenged."

Stella licked dry lips. The sincerity in Margaret's eyes softened her distrust. Dr. Hazzard deserved punishment for the deaths of men and women under her care. This might be Stella's opportunity to bring justice for Wendell and Sue, but she couldn't testify from her secluded cabin. And Dr. Hazzard would shoot her and have Rollie drag her into the woods before letting her speak out in court. There was only one way to ensure her own safety and Dr. Hazzard's conviction. "Come to my cabin tonight. If you help me get away from here, I'll tell the lawyer everything I know."

Margaret nodded slowly and swallowed hard. A smile touched the corners of her lips. "I will see you tonight."

Footsteps sounded on the stairs, and Stella turned to find Dr. Hazzard striding toward them.

A stiff smile turned her mouth, and she raised a brow. "Ready for your internal bath, Miss Burke?"

❧

Stella peeked out the curtain into the darkness. Where was Margaret? Had she told Dr. Hazzard Stella was hiding something, that she knew more than she ought?

She dropped the curtain and stepped to the table. Her Bible lay open, and she sat down before it. Reading might keep her mind from floundering through frightening thoughts until Margaret arrived as she had promised.

Stella had left off with the children of Israel at the banks of the Red Sea. She could almost hear the clatter of the Egyptian horses and chariots as their slave masters pursued. Then the words of Moses to the frightened Israelites froze her finger on a line of Scripture. "Fear ye not, stand still, and see the salvation of the Lord." The salvation of the Lord. Stella had read the account enough times before to know that His salvation had defied nature. For He controlled nature. God had more than vanquished the enemies of His people, but they hadn't needed to lift a hand to help. All they had to do was stand back and watch His mighty power.

God, show me Your might. Please, let Margaret deliver my message and bring Jane to help me. Dora and I aren't the only ones here. None of us are safe. Deliver us. Help me to stand still, because it isn't easy. I don't want to fight this battle on my own.

A knock sounded at the door, and Stella stood and opened it. Margaret bustled in, glancing over her shoulder.

"I don't think I was followed." She glanced around the cabin.

"I wish I had more suitable refreshment to offer you, but I do have water." Stella motioned to a pitcher on the table.

Margaret shook her head. "No, thank you." Determination glinted in her green eyes. "Please tell me everything. When did you arrive? Please, it's very important."

"Three weeks ago." Stella grabbed the painting off the wall. "Before I share details, I need you to do something for me."

"Anything."

Stella slipped her message from behind the paper sheeting and held it to Margaret. "See that this message is sent to Jane Wallace. The directions are written at the top. Until I'm safely away, I'm afraid—"

"You've nothing to fear from me." Margaret took the paper and tucked it into her handbag. "I understand your concern. But please know I'm not on Linda Hazzard's side. I don't trust that woman. When I arrived to tend to Dora and Cl—" She sucked in a breath. "Dr. Hazzard was wearing one of Claire's dresses. And I've since seen her parading about in Dora's earrings and her fox stole." She lowered her voice as if the demon child in the painting would carry her secrets to Linda Hazzard if he overheard them. "Hazzard convinced Claire to sign legal documents that named her Claire's sole heir when she died. I think she's luring wealthy people here to take advantage of them. You're not safe, and I won't pry information from you before you're ready to share, but would you answer one question for me? And I ask it only for myself, not the lawyers."

Stella nodded. Something in Margaret's eyes loosened the taut nerves between her shoulders.

"Did you know Claire Williamson?" Tears shimmered in her eyes. "I really must know how she was before—"

"I didn't know her." Stella sank onto the bed. Dr. Hazzard and Sarah Anderson had called the dead woman Claire on her first day here. Certainly it must be the same woman Margaret begged word of. "What did she look like?"

"She looked much like Dora. Same brown hair." Margaret held a hankie to her eyes. "She didn't want to come here. Dora convinced her."

Stella closed her eyes. Poor Margaret. Poor Dora, to hold the guilt of bringing a sister to the place where she'd be killed. "I believe I saw Claire my first night here."

Margaret's brow puckered. "But you just said you didn't know her."

"I didn't, but I came across a sight I wasn't supposed to see." She buried her face in her hands. "But I can't unsee it now. I walked past a water closet, and Dr. Hazzard and a nurse named Sarah—she doesn't work here anymore—were standing over—" She rubbed her temples. The throbbing was starting up again.

"What were they standing over?" Margaret held the handkerchief over her mouth.

"It wasn't a what." Stella chewed her lip. "It was a who. They called her Claire. Dr. Hazzard told Sarah to call Butterworth's. But I saw her, lying on an ironing board above the bathtub before she was taken away. She was even thinner than Dora, if you can imagine."

Margaret shook her head. "But she looked like Dora? The same hair color?"

Why was this woman so obsessed with the color of Claire's hair? Why did something so petty matter now? Stella nodded.

"I knew it." Margaret's jaw hardened.

"I don't understand." Stella poured a glass of water to remedy the dryness in her mouth.

Margaret paced from the door to the bed. "When I went to Butterworth's to view Claire's body, the. . .person. . .they showed me looked nothing like her. After seeing Dora's condition, I didn't expect her to be plump and healthy as she once was, but her hair color was wrong, and the shape of her face. I knew it couldn't be her." She spun to face Stella. "Why all the secrets? Why show me the wrong body?"

Stella's hand clutched her throat and her mind took her back to the washroom where Claire's body had lain.

"What? You remember something?" Margaret knelt beside the bed and rested her hands on Stella's shoulders.

"Her neck. There were bruises around her neck."

Margaret's jaw slacked. "You think she was murdered?"

"I can't be certain."

"Dr. Hazzard will pay." Margaret raised a fist in the air. "I don't want to hate her, but every bone in my body does." She rose and moved toward the door. "I'll see your message safely to the telegraph office first thing tomorrow. When you're free, I will find you. Will you tell me everything then?"

"Of course. Everything." Stella swallowed past the growing knot in her throat.

When the woman shut the cabin door behind her, Stella sank back onto the bed. Help was on the way. And Linda Hazzard would answer for her crimes. Stella sat straight as a board, pulling in a breath. That smell.

Vanilla.

Her heart rose into her throat. Sam Hazzard. Did the doctor's husband know Margaret had come to her cabin? Had he overheard their conversation, deciphered their plans?

But he couldn't hear through the cabin walls. Certainly not.

She glanced at the painting of the baby. The child's eyes read her doubt, and his lips smirked at her discomfort. Stella blew out the lantern and crawled into bed, clothes and all.

She listened to her ragged breathing in the silence. *Please, God. Help me to stand still and see Your salvation.*

Chapter Twenty-Five

A scream ripped through the air, sending Henry out of bed like a shot. Not bothering to grab his robe, he stumbled out the door toward sounds of wailing. Dawn's gray light bathed the corridor, helping him gain his bearings.

Sobs filtered from the cracked open door of Rose and Daisy's room. He dashed inside. Rose sat on the bed, her back to the wall and knees gripped to her chest, terror scrawled on her little face. Daisy huddled in the corner, tears in her eyes. Her thumb in her mouth muffled her wails.

"What's all this?" Henry scooped Daisy into his arms then settled on the bed beside Rose. "Did you have a bad dream?"

Rose shook her head, dashing her tears with fisted hands. "There's a monster."

Daisy took her thumb out of her mouth long enough to wrap her arms around his neck in a death grip.

"There are no such things as monsters." He held out his arm, and Rose scrambled beside him and burrowed against his chest. "Did you dream it?"

Rose shook her head. "I saw it." She pointed to the corner beside her chest of drawers. "When I screamed it hid under my bed. Told me not to tell you."

Henry chewed the inside of his lip. A little too specific for a dream. The whole affair reeked of Robby. The boy had been almost too docile lately. And his failure to give details regarding the papier-mâché project he'd been laboring over added a fresh layer of

178

mystery. "Is he still under the bed?"

Rustling of the quilt and a low groan confirmed the little sinner's location. Rose nodded, eyes wide.

Henry untangled Daisy's arms from his neck and set her on the bed. Her lip quivered, and fat tears dangled from her lower lashes. She held out her chubby arms to him. "Just a moment, Daisy." He planted a kiss on her clammy forehead. Would she ever speak?

Henry knelt beside the bed and lifted the covers. There, between the floor and springs, lay a miniature goblin. The papier-mâché mask he wore resembled a misshapen clown. Its bulbous nose painted red, the dark eyes sunken, and a mouth so twisted by evil that it would frighten a grown man. But behind that devious grin hid a mischievous boy who'd better enjoy his last moments of freedom. Punishment must be swift and just. Despite their conversation and Robby's assurances that he wanted to protect his sisters, not torment them, they found themselves in the same predicaments far too often.

"Robby, get out from under there." Henry lifted the blanket higher.

The boy squirmed away from him. "I don't want to."

"You scared your sisters half to death. They thought you were a monster." He glanced at the two little girls huddled on the bed, still crying softly.

"So I did pretty good, huh?" The grin in Robby's voice made Henry bite back a smile. Robby had worked hard on the mask, and as far as frightening things went, he'd outdone himself. And he was just a boy. This was just another one of his pranks. But he'd terrified his sisters, and he had to be made to see that sort of behavior would not be tolerated.

"Robby, I know you're only looking for a bit of fun, but you need to show Rose and Daisy that it's just you under the mask. They won't rest easy until you do." And they'd never agree to go to sleep in this room again. Not after a creature from Hades had paraded around their beds.

Jane bustled into the room, the concern on her face eclipsing the fear in the little girls' eyes. "What's going on in here?" Her clipped tone and the tear whispering down her cheek brought Henry off his knees.

"Robby frightened his sisters, and now he won't come out from under the bed." Henry wiped his hands on his pajama pants.

Jane planted her fists on her hips. "Robby, what are your middle and last names?"

"John Warner." The defiance in his voice shrank to contrition as he addressed Jane.

"Robert John Warner, get out from under that bed this instant and apologize to your sisters. We haven't time for your pranks today."

The boy scooted from under the bed. In the daylight, the mask was even more grotesque than when Henry had seen it from the shadows of the bed.

Rose and Daisy screamed.

"Take the mask off." Jane wagged a finger.

Robby grabbed the giant nose and pulled the mask over his head. He cast a fearful look at Jane. "I'm sorry, I—"

"You should be sorry. But don't apologize to me. Look at Rose and Daisy. They'll be afraid to go to sleep tonight. It's them you must apologize to." Jane motioned to his sisters.

Robby stepped beside the bed. "It's just me. I'm sorry I scared you."

Rose's tears slowed. "You're mean."

"I said I was sorry." Robby crossed his arms.

"Now, be off with you." Jane shooed Robby toward the hall. "Get dressed. You've an extra list of chores today as penance for frightening your sisters."

Robby skipped out the door, a smile on his lips as if the chores were an easy price to pay for the juicy bit of excitement he'd had.

Henry scrubbed a hand over his face. What would he do with that boy? What would he do without Jane and her commanding ways? He lifted Daisy off the bed. "See, girls, monsters aren't real. You're safe here."

Rose glared at Robby's retreating back. "He wasn't sorry enough. He scared Daisy." As if Rose herself hadn't been the one screaming blue murder at the sight of the masked marauder.

"Never you mind that, my dear." Jane tucked a blond curl behind Rose's ear. "Now get dressed and come downstairs."

"Are you all right?" Henry followed Jane out of the bedroom. "When you came in, you looked like you'd seen a real monster."

Jane pulled a folded paper from her pocket. "I went to work early this morning, as Mr. Weston had some mending for me to do, and I planned to finish early. This came while I was there. It's from Stella."

Henry swallowed past the desert in his mouth. After three weeks, she'd finally sent word. "Did her telegram concern you?" He schooled his expression into what he hoped was detached interest and set Daisy on the floor.

She ran into the bedroom and grabbed a dolly by the arm.

"There's something not right about it." She handed him the page. "It's very cryptic."

"Telegrams usually are." He unfolded it and scanned the contents.

I need you urgently Stop Take the first train Stop Tell Henry about the sand dunes Stop

Sand dunes. His gut twisted. "She's in trouble."

"What does she mean by sand dunes?" Jane wrung her hands.

"It's something that happened when we were children." Henry hurried to his room with Jane close behind. "We were at the beach one day, playing, climbing the dunes." He pulled clothes from his closet and laid them on the bed. "One moment everything was fine, and the next, the sand gave way and started to bury her. I called for help, but the governess was too far away to hear. I managed to pull her to safety. No one ever knew. She begged me not to tell for fear we wouldn't be allowed to play at the beach anymore. We never went near the dunes after that."

Jane pulled in a trembling breath. "She must be in danger, or she wouldn't have mentioned it."

"Never mind the train. If you stay with the children, I'll go to her." In her distress, Stella must have forgiven him for deceiving her. Why else would she have sent him such a pointed plea for help? But why hadn't she answered the telegram he'd sent two weeks ago? He shook his head. That made no difference now.

"I was hoping you'd offer." Jane dabbed her eyes with a handkerchief. "Do you need money for the train?" She reached into her pocket.

"With a stop in every town along the way, I don't have time to take the train." He pulled a carpetbag from under the bed and stuffed clothes haphazardly into it. "I need an automobile. It'll take half as long if I drive straight through."

"But where can you get one? I haven't the money for that."

Henry raked his fingers through his hair. One option sprang to mind, though it was less than legal. "Don't worry your head about it. The less you know the better when the police come around."

Henry hid behind the garage at the Burke estate. Using Stella's car to drive to Olalla wasn't exactly stealing. No, he hadn't been given permission, but Stella was two weeks from turning twenty-five. Technically, the car belonged to her—or would very soon—and he was driving it to Wilderness Heights where she was staying. In the end, she'd drop the charges of theft that Weston would surely wield against him.

He peeked through the window. The new chauffeur placed a wrench in the toolbox. He wiped the workbench with a cloth and puttered about the space. If only Henry could lure him out of the shed long enough to crank the engine and beat a hasty retreat. But how? What would entice the man away from his work? Nature would call eventually, sending the driver on a trip to the privy, but precious minutes were ticking by. No time to waste.

Henry glanced down at his plain clothes. White shirt. Black pants. He'd never pass as a house servant and convince the chauffeur the master had called for him. An idea struck. He grabbed a handful of dirt and smeared it across his face then decorated his shirt with another. Then he tore his sleeve and dirtied his trousers. Hopefully he looked pitiful enough to be convincing.

He stumbled into the garage with a theatrical limp. "Help me." He grabbed the driver's shoulders. "I've been robbed, and I need a place to hide."

The driver's heavy black mustache tipped down in disgust. He smacked Henry's hands away. "Well, you can't stay here."

"Please. I need help." Henry injected desperation into his tone. "If they find me, they'll kill me."

The driver's eyes softened. "Let me speak to Hartsell. He may be able to keep you in the kitchen until you're out of danger." He brushed dust from his uniform.

"Thank you." Henry's heart rate sped as he watched the man stride toward the house. This was it.

He gave the handle a solid crank, and the engine roared to life. Then he hopped behind the wheel, put the motorcar in gear, and started down the driveway.

"Stop!" The chauffeur ran from the back of the estate and chased him down the pebbled drive. "Stop! Thief!"

Henry turned onto the main road, pressing his foot on the pedal until it touched the floor. What sort of trouble had Stella found herself in? He blinked away images of her hurting in a hospital. It couldn't be as bad as all that. Could it?

Dear God, let me get to her in time.

Chapter Twenty-Six

Stella brushed her hair then twisted it into a lumpy braid. Had Margaret sent her message to Jane? Would she tell Henry? If he still cared about her, even as a friend, he'd grasp the urgency in her words. He and Jane may already be on their way. She shook her head and tamped down her rising optimism. After two prior disappointments, wishing for him to take her home seemed too grand a thought to entertain. Somehow, hope seemed a crueler taskmaster than Dr. Hazzard, for it buoyed her spirits then sent them plunging beneath the icy waters of despair—whereas she had come to expect detachment, even mean-spiritedness from Dr. Hazzard and had never been disappointed in the treatment she received from the woman.

A knock at the cabin door returned Stella to reality. Probably Dr. Hazzard making her morning rounds. Stella opened the door. The doctor stood just outside on the dusty path. Morning draped a mist over the landscape, intensifying the tangy aroma of pine sap. This place could be truly beautiful if death didn't lurk behind every rock and tree.

"How are you this morning, Miss Burke?" Dr. Hazzard asked in her usual brusque manner as she brushed past Stella into the cabin.

Did Stella dare request food again? She'd kept her hunger to herself for over a week, and the gnawing in her middle had increased with each passing day. Her ribs showed through her skin, much like the photographs she'd seen of children in impoverished countries. Beneath the bruises on her back, the bones of her spine could be counted. Surely the toxins must have made their escape.

"I'm truly hungry, Dr. Hazzard." She sank onto the chair. "Could I please have some lima bean broth?" Maybe requesting the most repulsive food on earth would convince the doctor this went far beyond craving and gluttony. In truth, the thought of lima bean broth did not evoke disgust as it once had.

Dr. Hazzard took the seat beside her. "Let me see your tongue." She tilted her head to catch a glimpse of Stella's mouth.

Obedient, Stella opened her mouth and stuck out her tongue. What did the doctor expect to learn from an examination of her tongue?

Dr. Hazzard's expression remained stoic as she studied Stella's tongue for a long moment. "I've seen enough. It's unclean." Her jaw hardened. "Which means you are unclean. Lima bean broth is a long way off."

How could that be? She'd been fasting for nineteen days. Her strength had faded, and exhaustion dogged her every step on the walking trails. Many more days without nourishment, and she may not be able to walk at all.

"I have something I wish to speak with you about." Dr. Hazzard clasped her hands in her lap. "You haven't shown the improvement I'd hoped."

The meaning behind the doctor's words sucked the air from her lungs. Was she dying? Like Sue? Stella clasped her hand to her chest and willed back the tears.

"I've called a lawyer. Life is such a fragile thing, and it's best to have your house in order should something happen to you." Dr. Hazzard smoothed a wisp of dark hair that dared to defy her tortoiseshell combs. The light spilling through the window glinted off a jeweled earring.

Stella's stomach dropped. The pear-shaped amethysts arranged to resemble a violet's petals interrupted her heart's steady rhythm. Why, the woman was wearing Mama's earrings! The very ones missing from the cabin after it had been ransacked. Stella's blood boiled. How dare Dr. Hazzard rob her? Then flaunt it before her without a care?

"I've asked the attorney to visit after your massage this afternoon. He's drawn up all the necessary paperwork. You need only sign," Dr. Hazzard continued, as if she were guilty of nothing more than caring for her patients' best interests.

"And what exactly would I be signing my name to?" Stella clenched her hands in her lap. If this woman believed her to be as weak of mind as she was in body, she'd learn the bitter taste of disappointment before the day was spent.

"Just general last wishes." Dr. Hazzard waved a hand in the air as if making final arrangements was as natural as breathing.

"But I've not given the lawyer my wishes." Stella folded her arms over her chest. "Whose wishes would these be? Yours?"

The doctor's eyes narrowed to slits. "Of course they'd be yours, my dear." The syrupy sweetness in her voice turned Stella's already aching stomach.

"I'm not signing any papers until I've made my wishes known." Stella stood. Though her frail body did not match her stern words, she would not be trampled on.

"There's no need to get upset." Dr. Hazzard wiped her hands on her skirt. "It's not an easy topic to discuss. Especially when one considers the despair you've sunken into."

More mind games? "What do you mean? I'm not in despair."

"There's no use denying it." The doctor motioned for her to sit, and Stella's wobbly legs urged her to comply. "When we first started the regime, you had hope the treatments would help. Over time, that belief has dwindled. Now you've no confidence in fasting, and it shows in your countenance. I've known people who lost hope. And it usually leads to—"

Was Dr. Hazzard insinuating what Stella suspected? The unspoken words hung in the air like fog.

"Leads to what?" Stella chewed the inside of her cheek.

"I knew a woman once. A bright young thing. She had everything to live for. A husband who adored her and a baby on the way." Dr. Hazzard's eyes took on a faraway glaze. "Then one day, life changed. Her husband died, and she lost the child she was carrying. She was alone, and loneliness overwhelmed her. Hope vanished. I found her. She had hanged herself with a scarf—much like this one on your bed." She gestured to the scrap of lavender fabric. "Ghastly business. But not surprising. For when one loses hope, the will to live soon follows."

Stella shuddered. How had the doctor known she struggled with loneliness? And if she really believed Stella tottered on the brink of despair, why elicit thoughts of suicide? Shouldn't taking one's life be the last topic to mention to a person in a precarious state of mind? And to practically give instruction on how to accomplish such a task. Was Linda Hazzard planting the seed in her mind, hoping it would germinate once the last will and testament was signed? Stella drew a quivering breath and studied Dr. Hazzard's eyes. Something evil lurked in their inky depths. This woman was wickedness incarnate.

"I'll thank you not to mention such things again." Stella massaged the back of her neck. Bones greeted her fingers where healthy flesh used to be. "It unsettles me."

"But it's something to think about."

"It most certainly is not. What a morbid topic. I'd rather speak of internal baths, though I despise them more than anything in the world." Her voice carried a sharper edge than she'd intended. It wouldn't do to anger this woman, disturbed as she was.

"Just trying to help, Miss Burke." Dr. Hazzard stood. Her probing gaze tied Stella's nerves in knots. "See that you're on time for your treatments today." She bustled out of the cabin.

Alone again.

If only Jane were here. Or Henry. Someone to talk to. She glanced at the picture on the wall. Anyone besides that mischievous imp.

A bird's song from outside the window drew her from the turmoil in her mind. She walked to the glass pane where a nest sat in the crook of a tree branch. The bluebird with a rusty orange breast chirped as if this place held not the slightest hint of fear. Probably enjoying the freedom to come and go as he pleased. Mama's Bible recitations sprang to mind. A verse about sparrows trusting their Creator to care for them. About God seeing the little birds, knowing when they fell. Then Mama's words rang clear. "You, my darling, are more precious to God than the sparrow. And since He takes such good care of them, you can be certain He will do the same for you. He loves all His children equally. You will never be forgotten or alone."

Stella's eyes burned. Her chest ached to have Mama back. She was so wise, and Stella needed that wisdom now. Needed to feel Mama's arms around her one last time. But she was gone.

He loves all His children equally.

The words plucked a chord in her heart. If God viewed all men as equal, perhaps He didn't care so very much that she and Henry traveled in different circles. Her stomach fluttered. Ever since Jane had reminded Stella of the matrimonial duty assigned her at birth, she had viewed an attachment to him beneath her. Believed she would be doing him a favor if she admitted to caring for him, as if she were better than he.

Shame seared her cheeks. What a fool she'd been. An arrogant fool. She had fancied herself so very great and Henry so low. But on what grounds? She blinked back the burning in her eyes, but the tears refused to be staunched.

If anything, her high opinion of herself proved her a poor match for him. She recalled the many times his solid thinking had prevented her from falling into traps set by her own selfish desires. She'd never been one to look at all the facts before making decisions, and more than once she'd paid the price, but Henry's counsel had often grounded her before her escapades developed serious consequences.

Why hadn't she trusted his suspicion of Linda Hazzard and Wilderness Heights? He'd warned her, but she'd demanded her own way like a petulant child. What must he think of her? Well, whatever negative thoughts swirled within his mind, she deserved every single one of them. She crossed her arms and leaned against the window sash.

God, help me see when I'm acting only for myself and stop me. I don't want to be this way, but it's a struggle.

How would Henry feel when she told him about the man she'd been corresponding with since Papa died? Would Henry allow her to assist in operating the children's home when—

When would she learn not to get ahead of herself? She'd skipped forward and borrowed trouble from a day that may never come. Even if she found a way to escape Wilderness Heights, Henry may object to a lifetime with her. Who could blame him?

But no matter how he viewed her, one fact remained. In God's sight they were equals. Not even Uncle Weston could deny it. Or Jane.

Her heart warmed at the memory of the compassion in Henry's

eyes when he looked at her. Would he gaze at her the same way when he saw how thin and pale she'd become? Stella glanced in the mirror. Only traces of the woman who had arrived at Wilderness Heights remained. But Henry wouldn't care. She'd never been a beauty, but that hadn't altered his steadfastness.

A tear tickled her cheek. She brushed it away. If she died here, her revelation would make no difference.

And the prospect of death had gnashed its snarling fangs when Dr. Hazzard mentioned the paperwork she wished for Stella to sign. Never had Stella felt more vulnerable, more weak.

She eased onto the rickety bed.

Wendell had been correct in all the fears he'd related that night. The doctor had tried cheating him out of his money in the same way she wanted to funnel Stella's wealth into her own coffers. And the earrings. A sob escaped her lips. She might never get them back.

She must escape this place before something sinister befell her. If she signed the papers to avoid Dr. Hazzard's suspicion, she'd be worth more dead than alive. But if she refused to sign—

The memory of a gunshot ripping the silence and Wendell's lifeless body crumpling to the ground sent her heart beating at breakneck speed. Though escape could prove deadly, she couldn't wait for Jane or Henry to arrive before running from this place.

What if Margaret hadn't kept her promise to wire the message? Every day that Stella waited compounded the peril she faced.

She must make her escape. Tonight. Once darkness fell. Wendell had lived in the main house when he'd attempted to leave. His tread on the stairs must have given him away. Leaving from a secluded cabin had to be safer.

She bit her lip until the copper taste of blood touched her tongue.

Vanilla extract had scented the breeze when Margaret left last night. The hair on Stella's neck prickled. Sam Hazzard had been walking among the cabins. What other explanation was there for his signature aroma? Did he patrol the grounds every night? Would he catch her in her flight to the tree line?

She squared her shoulders. A risk she'd have to take. Staying here may postpone her death but not prevent it. And if she must die, let it be in an attempt to gain freedom.

If God watched the sparrows as He promised, if He cared for her as fiercely as Mama said, He would help her know what to do, where to run.

Stella knelt to pray, but no words came. The fear mangling her brain stalled them in her throat. Should she ask for safety? For a way of escape? A miracle? Did she possess the strength to run? Even if her legs were sturdy enough to carry her into the woods, what then? She could lose her way and die in the forest instead of the cabin, but either way, she'd die alone.

Despite the wordlessness of her prayer, peace wrapped her in a warm embrace. She wasn't alone. He was with her.

Chapter Twenty-Seven

S tella stepped through the tall oak doors into Dr. Hazzard's study, her body still swirling from her treatment. No matter how firm the lawyer's convincing, Stella would not sign her fortune away to a quack. Yes, Henry had been right about that too. Dr. Hazzard embodied the very definition of the word charlatan. Were the stories of Mrs. Barnett and Edward Anderson true, or were they simply lies contrived to bolster a patient's confidence in the damaging methods of a fraud?

She met Dr. Hazzard's cool gaze and offered a nod of acknowledgment. It wouldn't do to upset her now. A guise of ignorance might be her best option under the circumstances.

"Miss Burke, this is my attorney, Mr. John Arthur." The doctor motioned to a bald bespectacled man behind the desk. "He's here to discuss your final wishes."

Stella eased into the offered wingback chair. "I'm not sure I'm ready to speak of such things." She folded her hands in her lap in her best attempt to appear demure.

Mr. Arthur adjusted his spectacles and cleared his throat. "These matters are never easy." He studied her from head to toe with no reaction.

How many walking skeletons had this man seen in this very room and yet done nothing to put an end to the madness? Was he in collusion with Dr. Hazzard? Maybe he received a portion of the inheritance when her patients died. Stella's stomach roiled, and this time hunger was not the culprit.

"I will be well again." Stella forced a smile. "Surely these arrangements are premature."

"Just hear the man out." Dr. Hazzard's steely timbre proved her patient facade was wearing thin. She took the chair beside Stella.

As Mr. Arthur leaned back in his seat, he stroked his mustache. "I've got the paperwork compiled. It will be as quick and painless as signing your name. You needn't think about it again for many years to come."

"May I read the document first and consider it? Uncle Weston usually advises me on such matters. I would wish to write him for advice before signing anything." She smoothed her baggy skirt, cringing at the feel of her knobby knees beneath her palms.

"Really, Miss Burke," Dr. Hazzard said. "The sooner you arrange your affairs, the better. One never knows when something terrible will happen."

Stella tried to swallow, but the dryness in her throat hindered her. Her heart trembled instead of beating. Though the doctor's tone was tender, the words strongly hinted at a threat. "I'll be as quick as I can in reviewing the paperwork. You have my word on that. I'll read it this evening after my walk, and if all is well, I will sign tomorrow."

"But what if something should happen to you tonight? All your possessions would go to the state by default." Dr. Hazzard leaned forward. Vexation tinted her words.

"Why should anything happen tonight? Aside from the fact I could eat my own arm were there flesh on it, I feel quite well. I'm in no danger before morning. Besides, I haven't a cent to my name for another two weeks. There's no rush to sign any documents. Uncle Weston controls all the capital until my birthday." Unless a wild animal attacked her in the woods as she escaped. Stella hardened her jaw. No amount of cajoling would persuade her to change her mind. And if Dr. Hazzard understood the true state of things, it may afford her time to make her escape.

Dr. Hazzard sighed between clenched teeth. "Very well. This can wait until morning." She motioned to Mr. Arthur, and he handed Stella the documents.

Stella rose, thanked the attorney, and left the room. She'd take the paperwork with her tonight. Prove that Dr. Hazzard planned to absorb her fortune upon Stella's death. She would not remain at Wilderness Heights long enough to determine whether Linda Hazzard planned for her death to be natural or assisted.

No. Come nightfall, Stella would make her escape.

And Tilda must accompany her. But was she strong enough to survive the trek into Olalla? Stella hiked toward her friend's cabin. Though the afternoon sky boasted patches of blue, storm clouds gathered in the west. It had rained nearly every day since her arrival. Stella quickened her pace. California's sunny skies and sandy beaches would seem all the sweeter after her absence.

She rapped on Tilda's door.

"Come in." Why did her voice sound so weak?

Stella pressed open the door and stepped inside. Tilda sat beside the table in her nightgown, her stringy black hair loose around her shoulders. Were her cheeks more sunken than the last time? Stella's chest tightened. If Tilda didn't get out of this place soon, she'd suffer the same fate as Sue Chandler.

"How nice to see you." Her friend offered a feeble smile.

Stella crouched beside her, grasping her bony hand. "You're unwell. I must get you away from this place."

Tilda slipped her hand from Stella's with a shake of her head. "If I'm unwell, it's all my own doing."

"How can you say that? You're wasting away here. A stiff breeze would blow you clear to the coast." As Stella rose, lightning pricked the perimeter of her eyesight. No, no, no. Not now.

"I shouldn't have eaten that bread." Tilda scrubbed her hands over her cheeks. "Such a setback. Why can't I be strong like you?"

"I'm not strong." Stella swallowed past the tingling in her throat. "I used to think I was, but I need help. I'm afraid, Tilda. Afraid of what will happen to me if I stay and terrified of what Dr. Hazzard will do to me if I try to leave."

"Leave? You must feel much better if you're prepared to go home."

Stella shook her head. "I feel worse now than when I arrived. I only suffered migraines at home. Now starvation has been added to my list of troubles."

"Fasting and starvation are two different things." Tilda's voice firmed. She'd bought into Dr. Hazzard's rhetoric, but surely the truth would hold a more persuasive power.

"They're not different in the way Linda Hazzard uses them." Stella knelt beside her friend. "How many people do you know personally who have found perfect health since you arrived?"

Tilda crossed her arms, her elbows jutting at sharp angles beneath the fabric of her nightdress. "There's Mrs. Barnett and Edward Anderson. And I heard about—"

"No." Stella squeezed her arm. "Dr. Hazzard told us about those patients. With your own eyes, who have you seen who has benefited from fasting and being beaten daily?"

With a slight lift of her chin, Tilda met Stella's gaze. "I feel better." Coming from one of the walking skeletons Henry had warned her about, the claim was rich.

"You can't mean that." Pain throbbed in Stella's forehead as the dancing lights swallowed her vision. She rubbed her eyes.

"Another headache?" Tilda's voice softened as she rested a hand on Stella's shoulder. "Lie down for a few minutes."

"Fasting hasn't helped." Stella allowed her friend to help her to the bed.

"You haven't given it enough time." Tilda covered her with a quilt. "The best things don't happen in a moment."

"If I give it much more time, I'll die here."

"Nonsense. Why—"

Stella grabbed her hand. "People have died here, Tilda. It isn't safe. Has Dr. Hazzard asked you to sign legal documents yet?"

Tilda eased her hand back. "Yes. I signed them last week. It's wise to plan for contingencies."

If she'd already signed over her belongings to Linda Hazzard, Tilda was more of an asset dead than living. Stella's headache peaked while crawling numbness spread up her arm and through her left cheek. Unless Tilda left Wilderness Heights, she would die here. With her fortune bequeathed to the so-called doctor, there was no hope of—

"You must come with me." She reached for Tilda but caught only air.

"With you? Where?" Though Stella couldn't see her friend past the pain in her eyes, her voice carried from across the room.

"I'm going home."

"And Dr. Hazzard thinks you're ready?"

"I haven't a mind to care what that old battle-ax thinks." Stella flexed her palm, coaxing life into her deadened fingers.

"You must go without me." Chair legs scraped the floor. "I've no plans to leave until the doctor deems me able."

Stella covered her eyes with her hand. Dr. Hazzard's stories had turned Tilda into a mindless puppet. If Tilda wouldn't come of her own volition, the police would have to drag her off the property. One way or another, Stella would see her friend safely away, though Tilda would probably despise her for it.

※

Exhaustion tugged at Henry's eyelids. Determined to keep them open, he worked his jaw. But the gentle, methodic thump, thump of the wheels against the road sent his head drooping toward his chest.

He sniffed, rubbed his eyes, then squinted at the gray ribbon stretching toward Washington State and Stella. She would have received his confession letter by now, but she'd still included him in her message to Jane. Either she'd forgiven him or she found herself in so much trouble that her bitterness paled in comparison. *Please, God, let it be the former.*

What kind of danger was she in? The old Buzzard's treatments wouldn't have made his list of relaxing weekend activities, but they didn't sound like a means of torturing spies into sharing state secrets either. It had to be more than general discomfort, or she wouldn't have referenced that day at the sand dunes.

Memories of that event still crept into his nightmares. Though the sun had been shining and all appeared well with the world, he'd almost lost Stella. The sand had pulled her down so quickly he'd barely had time to think before grabbing her arm. He'd nearly fallen into the sinking trap himself.

Only by the grace of God had he found sure footing to pull her up. Whatever she suffered, he prayed for a way to help her once again.

The sun hung low in the west, bright as a tangerine, its rays staining the sky in shades of pink. Though he'd made good time, four hundred miles—eleven more hours—still separated him from Stella. A sign that read WELCOME TO MEDFORD streaked past the window. The thought of Stella spending another night at Wilderness Heights with a woman as heartless as Dr. Hazzard weighted his foot on the starter.

Her final letter to the man he'd masqueraded as sprang to mind for the hundredth time since he'd received it. Now that she knew the truth of his deception, was there any chance she'd still work with him? Of course, it would take several years before he saved enough money to make a go of a children's home. He straightened behind the wheel to fight a twinge in his lower back. Though Stella would soon have the resources to fund the entire operation, he'd never allow it, even if she offered. What sort of man took advantage of a woman and allowed her to foot the bill for his dream when he could raise the money in time?

But if she'd merely mentioned him in the telegram out of necessity, none of these questions would matter a whit. She may be the same selfish woman who'd conned him into that first trip to Olalla then sent for him the moment she needed a ride back to her posh life. He smacked the steering wheel. No, there was so much more to her than that. He'd seen it. When they were young with the rescued kittens. Then again that day with Ethel and the children. Stella wasn't wholly selfish, and while she'd mentioned her battle with living an unfulfilled life in that last letter, she had also noted that her current situation was the only life she'd ever known.

How could he expect her to behave in a way she'd never seen demonstrated by her father and certainly not by her uncle? And though her mother had died so long ago, the impression she'd left on Stella had made an impact. Mrs. Burke had been a kind and generous woman, and while her years of influence on her daughter were short, she was the reason Stella showed compassion to the needy.

He shook his head. Why give Stella so much thought? She'd rejected him the last time they were together, stopped him before he could declare his feelings for her. And his deception had jeopardized their friendship. Why, he wouldn't blame her if she waved goodbye forever after he brought the car to a stop at the front door of her estate.

Darkness fell, and he switched on the headlamps. He rolled his neck until it popped. Worry chewed at his brain. What had made her send word to Jane?

Jack's story of walking skeletons elbowed its way to the front of his thoughts. Surely it was fantasy. But what if Stella had seen them? Perhaps there was something to the boy's tale, but there must be more to it than decomposed men and women digging free from the graveyard he claimed existed at Wilderness Heights. A shudder tickled Henry's spine.

Hold tight, Stella. I'm coming for you.

Chapter Twenty-Eight

S tella blew out the candle, bathing the cabin in darkness. Still, she sensed the eyes of the child in the painting on her. She pressed her ear to the door and strained to hear footsteps on the other side. If Sam Hazzard caught her—

She couldn't think about that now. The legal documents she'd stuffed in her bodice dug into her skin, brittle reminders of the danger breathing down her neck. No wonder Dr. Hazzard, no, Buzzard—Henry's nickname felt more appropriate—had been desperate for her to sign beside the X. Her signature not only would endow the old Buzzard with Stella's entire fortune should she die, but also granted the charlatan power of attorney. She'd gain full access to Stella's bank accounts as well as the right to make all legal decisions on Stella's behalf. Although Stella wouldn't inherit until her birthday, the power of attorney might supersede Uncle Weston's legal guardianship. Had the Buzzard done the same with Sue Chandler? Certainly, she'd tried with poor Wendell.

One glance at the clock informed Stella it was fifteen minutes past one. She peeked out the window toward the main house. Dark. Everyone must be asleep.

Clasping her shawl with one hand, she gripped the knob. The door groaned on its hinges, and the cool night air crept in, sending a shiver across her arms.

As she stepped outside, the darkness swallowed her. How would she ever find her way into town without a lantern? She turned to step back into the house and grab the light, then halted. No. If Sam patrolled the grounds, the flame would alert him to her plans.

Lord, help me find my way out of here.

The tree line stood out in black against the night sky. The scrap of moon provided faint light, but not enough to be of service. And not enough to give away her location to prying eyes. Might as well focus on that small positive instead of the fact she may never see daylight again.

She padded toward the trees. If her sense of direction could be trusted, the little shop where she'd bought the rolls of bread lay just beyond the woods. If only Tilda had agreed to come along. The darkness wouldn't seem so formidable if loneliness didn't accompany it. And after all Tilda's suffering, how could she believe the Buzzard's treatments held value? And blame herself for their failure due to one break in her fast?

Once Stella gained her freedom, she'd return with the police and have Tilda removed despite her arguments. How could she be so blind to the truth?

A twig snapped beneath her foot. She froze, waiting for Sam to barrel toward her and drag her back to the cabin. He wouldn't dare kill her. With the documents still unsigned, she was worth more to them alive than dead. But what of Wendell? This was much the same scenario. Sam may not hesitate to silence her as well.

A hush blanketed the landscape, and Stella stepped into the woods. The tree cover provided an additional layer of safety. Mold and pine sap teased her nose as she plodded on. Her legs screamed with each step. How would she ever make it to Olalla?

"Miss Bu-urke." A singsong voice chilled her to the bone.

Sam Hazzard.

Her heart thwacked against her ribs, and she pressed her back to a tree trunk. *No, God, please. No.*

She clamped a hand over her mouth. If he heard her ragged breathing, he'd close in on her. A tear slipped down her cheek and over her hand.

"I know you're out here." His tone carried a sinister sweetness. "It's not safe. Let me take you back to your cabin." Footsteps crunched through the underbrush. Were they getting closer?

Vanilla floated on a breeze, turning her stomach. Would she never escape this horrid death trap? How foolish she'd been to ignore Henry's concern.

Dried pine needles crackled too close for comfort, and her breath stalled in her lungs.

"There's no use hiding," Sam continued, his voice nearer with each word.

With her heart fluttering instead of beating, Stella prayed for deliverance. Rustling in the trees some distance away sent Sam's feet scraping along the forest floor.

Was he turning around?

"Ready or not, here I come." His footsteps faded, and Stella let a pent-up breath escape slowly.

She strained for any sound that might signal his location, but silence prevailed once more, though the scent of vanilla still fogged the air. Resting her fingers on her bodice, she touched the papers that would bring the police to the old Buzzard's door. Would anyone believe Stella if she couldn't prove her accusations? Would they believe her at all? As she recited the words she planned to tell the police, they sounded like the ravings of a lunatic to her own ears, and she'd seen the truth firsthand. If she lost the attorney's papers, she might as well run away without a glance over her shoulder.

But what of Tilda? She'd die here if Stella didn't find someone to drag her out of the cabin and away from the horse doctor she believed held the keys to perfect health.

Perfect health. Stella's stomach knotted. It had sounded too wonderful to be true, and it was. She'd never place herself in such circumstances again. And when she returned home—

A hand clamped around her arm, and a scream ripped from her lips.

"I told you it was no use," Sam whispered in her ear. "Your treatment isn't finished, Miss Burke. Wouldn't want those toxins to kill you."

Stella's first instinct told her to fight, but her legs trembled beneath her, barely holding her upright. Fighting would get her nowhere.

"Why the rush to get away?" He dragged her toward the cabins, sending a surge of pain through her arm. "You know disobedience will get you into trouble."

The image of Wendell's body flashed. She knew the price of noncompliance all too well. But the cost of following orders had proved just as high for Sue.

The papers hidden in her clothing crinkled. No. He couldn't find out she planned to take her story to the police. She pressed her free hand to her chest to quiet the rustle. "I wasn't trying to escape." Would he have Linda Hazzard fill her full of buckshot if she admitted her plan?

Sam stopped, and she wrenched her arm free. "You expect me to believe that?"

"Your wife said that walking helps flush out the toxins." She kept her hand clamped over the papers in her dress. "I couldn't sleep. So I walked."

He gripped her elbow and led her out of the woods, the fragile moonlight shining full on his features. "Why did you hide from me?"

"For all I knew, I was alone. Then you come traipsing through the woods like a criminal running from the authorities. You frightened me."

Sam lifted a brow. He studied her, clenching and unclenching his jaw.

He didn't believe her. Lying had never been her strong suit. Normally, that wouldn't bother her.

Slowly, he shook his head. "Tilda thought you might say something like that."

His words stole the air from Stella's lungs. Tilda? Tears pricked her eyes. Though the woman had bought the fanciful dreams Dr. Hazzard was selling, Stella never imagined her friend would give away her plans.

"Surprised, aren't you?" A smile stained Sam's voice. "She was worried you wouldn't finish your treatments."

Did Linda Hazzard have her patients under some sort of spell?

As he tugged her to her cabin, Stella's mind raced. He didn't believe her, so what would be her consequences for trying to escape?

"Get inside." He thrust her through the doorway and slammed the door.

She leaned against the wood, listening to his scuffling and grunting on the other side. A heavy thump reverberated through the pine boards. Was he trapping her inside? She pounded her fist against the door.

"Don't bother," Sam called. "I've barred the door, but don't worry. I'll send Rollie tomorrow afternoon. He'll escort you to the main house for your treatments then see you back safely."

Stella trailed her palm over the rough surface and rested her forehead against it. She was little more than a prisoner, and the husband of a madwoman held the key.

With her hope of escape snatched away, Stella crumpled to the floor. Tears burned her eyes, and sobs choked her. She drew her knees to her chest and hugged them.

The darkness inside the cabin mirrored the hopeless black pit burgeoning within. Would she die in this room? Gloom weighted her shoulders and forced the breath from her lungs. If God really cared for her more than the sparrows as Mama had said, as His Word said, why hadn't He allowed her to break free? Now she was more trapped than ever.

Stand still, and see the salvation of the Lord.

The words whispered through her soul as a moonbeam cast its blue glow through the window. How could standing still prove such a hard task when those two little words carried so much simplicity? Even in her weakened condition, her muscles ached for action and her brain calculated ways to gain freedom.

Stand still.

She buried her face against her knees and sighed. *God, help me to wait on You. It's just so difficult to be still when I want to break down the door.* A chuckle escaped her throat. How foolish that must sound on the lips of a woman as fragile as a newborn babe. *I know I'm weak. But You're strong. I need help trusting that Your way is best, because I'm not particularly good at not getting my way.* Guilt squeezed her chest. She'd treated Henry abominably when he hadn't bent to her wishes. *Please let me see Henry one more time so I can tell him how sorry I am.*

She stood and felt her way to the bed. As she eased onto the thin mattress, the springs squeaked. She pulled the legal documents from her bodice and slipped them under the pillow. Her nightgown's silky fabric brushed her fingers. Might as well get comfortable.

She wouldn't be allowed outside until her treatments tomorrow afternoon.

After wriggling out of her dress, she changed into her nightgown. The cool purple fabric skimmed a delicious chill over her arms. The scent of home still clung to the material, and she lifted the collar to her nose and breathed in.

Moisture dampened her cheeks. Would she ever see home and the people she loved again? And the man she'd corresponded with for years hadn't sent a single letter since her arrival. He'd abandoned her.

She drew the quilt to her chin. Her chest felt hollowed out, but instead of plunging into its inky depths, she prayed.

Why was trusting so hard?

Chapter Twenty-Nine

The morning sun cast golden light over the tall pines as Henry pulled the address from his pocket—the one Stella had enclosed in the last letter she'd written for the man he'd pretended to be. Water spots marred the ink, blurring the street name. He tightened his grip on the steering wheel. The last thing he needed was a setback.

A sign that read WELCOME TO OLALLA, WASHINGTON—POPULATION 407 flashed past. Quaint storefronts lined the town's main street. He pulled up to a general store and hopped out of the automobile on legs that wobbled from disuse.

He pushed the door open, and a man behind the counter greeted him. "Good morning." A German accent colored the words.

"Morning." Henry strode to the counter. "Could you give me directions to Dr. Hazzard's clinic?"

"To Starvation Heights? Sure." The man rubbed his bearded chin.

A sick sensation curled in Henry's gut. "What did you call it?" He rubbed the back of his neck. What had Stella fallen into?

"Starvation Heights." The proprietor poked his thumbs through his belt loops. "Always wondered what sort of hoity-toity fools would check into a place like that. Or stay long enough to look as ghastly as they do."

"You've seen the patients?" Henry raked a hand through his hair.

"Yah. Not long ago, a woman stopped by the shop. My wife gave her a bit of bread. Looked like she hadn't seen food in months, or so Betsy told me." He shook his head. "They could leave anytime, so why choose to stay?"

Why indeed? Stella, headstrong as she was, would never stay in such a place willingly. She'd march out, giving Linda Hazzard an earful as the door swung shut behind her. If the quack doctor's methods weren't working, or worse, if they were killing her, why not walk out? But Stella's message had been urgent. Maybe she was too frightened to leave—or too weak.

What if Dr. Hazzard's patients weren't able to leave? Perhaps Stella had found herself in trouble when she asked to check out. If the old Buzzard insisted she stay, or worse, held her prisoner—

His breath hitched. "I need the directions immediately. My friend is there, and she sent word for help."

The shopkeeper checked the clock. "If you wait twenty minutes, the doctor's husband will be in. Sam could take you. He's a regular around this place."

"I don't have twenty minutes to wait." Henry splayed his fingers across the counter, his heart rate speeding like a car at the Grand Prix. "Please. I need to go now."

The shopkeeper scribbled the route to Wilderness Heights on a notepad, tore off the sheet, and handed it to Henry. "It's not far."

Paper in hand, Henry darted for the door.

"Hope your friend's all right," the man called after him.

Henry's feet pounded across the gravel toward the automobile. With a jerk of the crank, the motor sputtered to life, and he jumped behind the wheel. Heart slamming against his ribs, he followed the hand-drawn map. *God, please, let Stella be okay.*

Starvation Heights. The name rippled through his chest, leaving a dark swirl of dread. Did Linda Hazzard really betray her patients' confidence and starve them? The idea seemed too shocking to be true.

But the little boy from the bank—Jack—his talk of walking skeletons begging for bread. He'd said his aunt had seen them, that she ran a shop in Olalla. Could the proprietor's wife, Betsy, be the boy's aunt? And she'd given food to a woman recently. Might it have been Stella?

His gut twisted. What would he find when he finally laid eyes on her? Would he even recognize her, or would she be too altered?

He cut a sharp left turn, and a rambling white house came into view. Cabins dotted the hills behind the structure. At this distance, they looked like the little houses Robby fashioned from twigs when he wasn't terrorizing his sisters.

Angry clouds gathered overhead, signaling an impending storm.

As he ground to a stop, pebbles crunched beneath the tires and thunder grumbled in the distance. A few stray drops fell, splattering the windscreen. He leapt from the automobile, dashed up the porch, and pushed open the front door. The foyer showed no signs of life. His boots thudded against the wood floors with each step. She was close. He swallowed the knot in his throat. She had to be. Unless he was too late.

No time to think about that now.

"Stella!" His voice hit the sterile white walls and fell dead to the floor. Had Dr. Hazzard left the premises?

A door overhead slammed, jolting Henry's nerves. As heavy footsteps creaked down the stairs, he strode to meet whoever was coming to greet him. If only it were that old Buzzard. He'd had two days on the road to fashion the words he wished to spit at her, and they were both stern and eloquent. If he was allowed to think such a thing of his abilities. His hands clenched.

A dark-haired man stood before him, brows raised. "What's all the hollering about? Dr. Hazzard is treating a patient, and she'd thank you to keep your voice down."

"I don't care what Dr. Hazzard would thank me to do." Henry squared his shoulders. Vanilla clung to the man like an overcoat. Probably the Buzzard's husband, Sam. He looked like the man who'd driven Stella away from the office in Seattle. "Miss Burke sent for me. I'd like to see her."

"I'm afraid that's not possible." Sam Hazzard's lips slanted in an unsettling smile.

"What did you do to her?" Had he arrived too late? Determined not to exhibit the unrest warring within, Henry flexed his jaw.

Sam raised his hands in surrender. "I've done nothing to harm her." He crossed his arms. "Miss Burke doesn't wish to see you. She's not taking visitors." Thunder cracked, and rain pelted the windows.

Lies.

Did he take Henry for a fool? If this man believed a weak excuse would shoo Henry away, he'd better brace for disappointment.

Heat seared the back of Henry's neck. "Her message indicated she was in danger. Either you tell me where to find her, or I will rip this place apart searching."

"Miss Burke is indisposed." The man's tone hardened. "This is a place of healing. And I suggest you respect our methods or I'll summon the police."

"Sam," a shrill voice called from upstairs.

"Coming." Sam's voice shifted from commanding to submissive. He started to turn then took a step nearer Henry. "This conversation is over." His finger jabbed Henry's chest. "Go back where you came from."

Sam tromped up the stairs, and Henry paced to the front door and back. How could he be expected to leave without seeing Stella? She was in some sort of trouble, and until he discovered what it was, going home wasn't an option. He raked a hand through his hair.

But the man had flatly refused to allow Henry a visit with Stella. If Sam wouldn't take him to her, Henry would find her himself. He strode toward the doorway on his left until an accented voice stopped him midstep.

"She's not in the house."

Henry turned to the origin of the voice, and a slight, gray-haired woman pinned him with an urgent look. "Where is she? I must find her."

"You're Henry? From the telegram?" Her brow wrinkled.

This woman knew about Stella's message? He nodded. Who was she? How did she know Stella? No time to share life stories. Once he and Stella were safely away, perhaps.

"She's in a cabin behind the house. Take the path on the right, and she's in the third."

Henry gave her shoulder a squeeze. "Thank you."

He yanked open the door and ran down the porch steps. The sheeting rain soaked him to the bone. His pulse throbbed in his temples as he pressed toward the path on the right. Puddles splashed with each footfall. If Sam Hazzard caught sight of him—well, no doubt he would disapprove, maybe worse—but his threat to call the police could be a blessing. The authorities might be summoned to this place before the day was done. Lightning rent a jagged streak across the darkened sky.

At the door to the third cabin, he stopped short. Rainwater dripped into his eyes, and he dashed the drops away with a fist. A bar positioned over the door held her captive. Why?

He grabbed hold of the beam, grunting under the weight, and shoved it to the side. Then he pulled open the door, eyes closed. *God, don't let me find her dead.*

"Henry?" The sound of his name on Stella's lips snapped his eyes open. He stepped inside the tiny cabin, and his breath caught. She'd grown so thin, just a shell of herself. Could this really be his Stella?

Then the unfamiliar woman smiled. His chest warmed. He would always recognize that beautiful smile. The purple collar of her nightgown peeked from under the shawl she held tight around her shoulders with bony fingers.

"Stella, I'm sorry, I—"

"You came." Her eyes glistened, and she reached a hand to him.

"Of course I did." He took a step toward her and grasped her hand, so fragile in his own. Her skin was cool and slick as glass. "You have to forgive me."

Confusion scrawled lines across her brow. "Why?" The longer he looked at her, glimmers of her old spunk showed him she was still there. Only her exterior was altered. Her heart remained unchanged.

If she knew of his deceit, accusations would replace the questions in her eyes. His heart skipped. Had she not received his letter? He opened his mouth to confess, but concern for her safety and the urge to run from the Hazzards snapped his lips closed.

Later.

"I'll tell you when we're safely away from Starvation Heights. If Sam Hazzard discovers I'm out here, he'll have my hide." He gave Stella's hand a gentle tug, but she remained immobile.

Did she still put stock in this crazy notion of fasting? Urgency sent static waves through his nerves. There wasn't time to convince her, so he'd simply throw her over his shoulder and make her see reason after they'd sped away.

He glanced at Stella, and the fear in her eyes froze the blood in his veins. He followed her gaze to the object of her terror.

His stomach dropped.

His eyes clashed with Sam's. Rain trickled from the end of the man's nose. A clap of thunder shook the cabin. Henry balled his fist, prepared to fight for Stella's freedom, but the doctor's husband lifted a shovel. Lightning brightened the cabin for a fraction of a second, glinting off the shovel's blade.

Sam brought it down hard. Pain seared red-hot in Henry's head.

Stella screamed.

The world faded to black.

Chapter Thirty

Stella dropped to her knees beside Henry. Blood trickled from a gash in his forehead. No. How could Sam be so cruel? She brushed a finger near the wound then met Sam Hazzard's gaze. "You're a monster. When I leave this place, I'll tell the police what you've done."

A smirk tilted his lips. "I could pay a visit to the sheriff myself." Sam rested the shovel's handle on his shoulder. "This fella was here to kidnap you. Pretty serious crime."

"He'd never do any such thing." Of all the asinine accusations. Stella let out a huff through her nose, scooting closer to Henry. She pressed a kiss to his cheek. He had come to rescue her. That was all that mattered. Sam might hold them hostage here, but Henry wouldn't be down for long. Together they would find a way to break out of the cabin and then—

Sam tossed the shovel through the open door and gripped Henry's hands.

"What are you doing?" Stella clung to Henry's shirt, unwilling to let him go. She had waited too long to see him, and there were still so many things she had to tell him. But maybe Sam would have Dr. Hazzard inspect the wound on Henry's head. No. He needed a real doctor. She grasped Henry's leg with all her strength. She couldn't let Sam take him away. Better to let an actor from a traveling medicine show tend the gash than the old Buzzard who probably found her medical license along with the customary coupon in her box of Cracker Jack.

"Let go. I'm taking care of a problem." The cool, detached cadence of Sam's voice froze Stella's muscles.

What could he mean? A ball of dread exploded in her middle.

Sam dragged Henry across the threshold. Stella screamed, grabbing at his feet, but her weak muscles foiled her attempts, and they slid through her fingers. "No. Please. Where are you taking him?" Her voice cracked in her throat.

"Somewhere so's he won't bother us again." Sam dropped Henry onto the dirt path. Lightning illuminated the sky, casting ghoulish shadows across his features.

"Don't. He didn't mean any harm!" But the slam of the door overpowered her words. The thud of the beam Sam propped over the door echoed like thunder in Stella's chest.

What did Sam plan to do with Henry? Stella dashed to the small window and stood on tiptoes.

Gripping Henry's hands, Sam tugged him toward the main house. Henry's shoes left skid marks in the mud, which were quickly filled by rain. Though part of her wished Sam Hazzard was intending to have his wife bind the jagged wound on Henry's temple, logic told a different story. Neither one of them cared whether Henry lived or died.

Tears burned her cheeks. She'd never see Henry again. *Please, God, don't let him die.*

❧

"Just dump him in, Rollie."

The words fell distant and hollow, fighting to be heard over the roar of pain in Henry's ears.

"You sure. . .we could always. . .and that should do the trick." An unfamiliar voice faded in and out.

The pair of voices battled a duel, making little sense in the muddled fog of his mind.

What was happening? Why were they arguing?

"Shut up and get out of my way." The sounds grew nearer.

Henry fought to open his eyelids, but they were so heavy.

Stella. He'd seen her. . .for the briefest moment. She was alive. Still alive. He tried swallowing past the desert in his throat.

Something gripped his arms and legs. He wriggled to free himself, but either the hold on his limbs was too strong, or his muscles were too weak.

Focusing his energy, he forced his eyelids into submission. Why couldn't he see? Pinholes of light filtered through something over his face. Rough fabric scratched his cheeks. Black swirls lapped at the corners of his vision, and his head felt as if it had been filled with helium.

No. Don't sleep.

He had to stay awake. Stella needed him. She may be alive now, but more time spent under Linda Hazzard's care would certainly spell her doom.

When he opened his mouth to shout for help, the sound died in his throat.

"Ready?" a male voice said.

A pause, then Henry's body lifted from where he'd lain. His heartbeat drummed in his temples.

"One. . ."

Whoever held his shoulders jerked and emitted a grunt.

"Two. . . Three."

On the final count, the pressure on his extremities vanished. Suspended in the air, he struggled to find something solid, but when he went to flail his hands, ropes bit into the skin on his wrists.

Splash!

Chilled water engulfed him, stealing his breath. His feet clambered for footing, but found nothing firm. He struggled to refill his lungs as he sank beneath the surface. The water seeped through the material covering his face. The shock of the water returned his drifting senses, and he fought the ropes, kicking his feet to keep from dropping like a stone to the bottom.

His bonds held fast.

Fear clawed his chest. *God, help me. Stella. . .Stella.* What would Linda Hazzard do to her?

Henry contorted his hands. If only he could see what he was doing.

His fingers brushed twine. With a swift tug, the string gave way, and the fabric covering his face floated upward. He shook the burlap sack away with a head jerk that granted him a murky view of the rope at his wrists.

His lungs burned, and the drive to inhale screamed in his chest. How much longer could he survive without air?

Kicking for the surface, Henry worked his wrists. His skin tore with each effort at liberty. Blood curled in the water from the struggle.

Just a little more.

Bubbles sputtered from his mouth. He kicked harder. His calves burned. He fought the involuntary urge to inhale. It was no use. The surface might as well be miles above him. The last gush of air left his lips in a swollen gurgle.

Water pressed in around him. So this was how his life would end. Darkness edged the corners of his vision.

Stella's image played in his brain like a moving picture show.

Their rambles in the meadow, hunting violets for her mother.

His shoulders relaxed. Leaves and other bits of debris drifted lazily in the brackish water surrounding him.

The kittens they'd fed with an eyedropper. What sorry little bundles of fur they had been before he and Stella rescued them.

A strange sense of peace wrapped him tight. His legs stilled their paddling, and his eyelids drifted closed.

That day at the sand dunes.

His eyes snapped open. Red from his wrists floated past his vision.

Fight.

He couldn't give up on Stella, not when she needed him. If he couldn't find a way to save her, what hope did she have of escaping the Buzzard's talons alive?

Working the bloody ropes, he prayed while his feet managed weak kicks.

His hand slipped free, and he swam for the surface.

A dark blanket began to descend over his vision once again. *No. God, no. Let me survive this.*

How much farther? He had to be close.

His face broke the surface. He gasped, filling his lungs with life-giving oxygen.

Rain poured around him, plunking the water and creating bubbly splashes. In a few strokes, he reached the shore. He fell onto his back, and his stomach roiled. When he rolled over, lake water and bile spewed from his mouth. Coughing, he swiped his hand over his lips. The gashes on his wrists left a metallic taste on his tongue.

The ropes had chewed nearly to the bone. A humid breeze clawed at his tattered flesh, and he clenched his teeth against the sting.

Where was he? A glance around the lake didn't offer familiar landmarks or points of reference. He stood, fighting the quaver in his legs. Where had Sam Hazzard gone?

And how would Henry get to Stella before her time was up?

He scanned the landscape.

Mount Rainier stood behind him, and masts from what looked like a schooner flapped to his left. The mountain was situated in the same general direction to Stella's cabin. He glanced at the dreary hills to his right.

She had to be somewhere east of him. He scrambled up a low rise to a road littered with pebbles, each breath that sawed through his lungs adding fresh fire to the urgency boiling at his core.

No vehicles or signs of life inhabited the gravel road, which meant Sam Hazzard had long since returned home. How could he get to Stella before the Hazzards—

The faint sound of an automobile engine scuttled, and he turned toward the sound. With arms waving over his head, he flagged the driver. A Model T drew to a stop beside him, and the eyes of the man behind the wheel widened in surprise. His mustache twitched. "I say. You look like you could use a hand, my boy."

Henry climbed into the motorcar, relief offering a temporary balm to his troubled mind. "I must get to Starvation Heights."

Chapter Thirty-One

Stella paced the cabin. Where had Sam Hazzard taken Henry? The cold glint in his eye had prickled her nerves. Whatever the man had done with him, it couldn't be good.

After Sam dragged Henry out of sight, she had pounded on the door with the last shred of her strength, but to no avail. What if Henry needed her? Her shoulders slumped. What good could she do him in her weakened state?

She dashed tears from her eyes. What if Sam killed Henry? Breath left her lungs in a painful gush. He would never know of her change of heart—how very much she cared for him.

With her pulse rushing in her ears, she stepped to the window. Could she squeeze out of it? It was so small. She mentally measured the pane then glanced at her spindly form in the mirror. Over the last weeks, she had shrunk, but was she thin enough to fit?

And even if she managed to climb through the window, what help could she offer Henry? She hadn't the first notion where Sam had taken him. And even if she could find Henry, the Hazzards might afford them nothing more than the favor of allowing them to die together.

I could run to Olalla for the police.

Sam's automobile hadn't returned, and she would have a clear shot to the tree line.

She clenched her jaw and pulled a chair to the window. Its legs scraped the wood floor. When she stepped onto the seat, she made eye contact with the sinister cherub hanging on the wall. "If I never see you again, it will be too soon." She tried to lift the sash, but it stuck on something.

Why must everything be so difficult? As if the stars in their courses worked against her.

After repositioning her fingers, she tried again. The window groaned, raising slightly. Raindrops dampened the sill as she pushed with all her might. Bit by bit, it opened, and triumph coursed through Stella's veins.

She poked her head through but froze when she saw the muddy ground below. Falling face-first into a puddle wouldn't be the best option. She worked first one leg then the other through the opening until she perched on the sill, half inside and half outside the cabin.

Wood dug into her hips on each side. Although it was a tight fit, she just might make it. Wriggling her legs, she squeezed through the window. Unable to see her feet, she swung them around, hoping to find someplace solid to plant them.

Now her hips were free.

She rotated until her arms held the window ledge. From this position, she could drop to the ground and make a dash for the woods. She slid down, grasping the sill.

Almost there.

Hands clamped around her waist, and a scream climbed from her throat.

"You're scrappier than I thought." Sam's voice carried a smile, and the vanilla on his breath soured her stomach. How had she not heard him approach? He pulled her from the window and planted her legs on mushy earth.

She met his wicked gaze. Movement behind him flagged Stella's notice. Dr. Hazzard marched toward them, one hand keeping her skirt from skimming the puddles. The nearer she drew, the more pronounced the rage in her eyes.

"Where do you think you're going, Miss Burke?" All the syrup and honey from their meeting with the attorney had vanished from the Buzzard's voice.

Stella straightened her shoulders. Both this woman and her husband were insane. That was the only explanation for their behavior, and she would put an end to it or die trying. "What have you done with Henry?"

Fury flashed in Dr. Hazzard's eyes, and she clamped a hand on Stella's arm. "Never mind him. He's a problem that's been eliminated." The cold nature of her words made it sound as if he was little more than a toxin to be eradicated from the body.

Stella tried jerking her arm from the woman's iron grip, but no amount of wrenching would break her free.

"Now it's time we eliminated the problem you've become." Dr. Hazzard's jaw clenched.

"But I haven't signed your precious papers." Stella clung to her last thread of hope. The one reason Dr. Hazzard couldn't kill her. Yet. "Admit it. You still need me. Otherwise, what was all this for? The beatings, the starvation. If I don't sign that will, you walk away from this empty-handed."

Dr. Hazzard chuckled. "You still think I need your signature? My, but you are naive." She shook her head. "You signed the check-in paperwork, and your signature wasn't difficult to duplicate. And it won't be difficult to post-date the death certificate."

Stella's heart stuttered. If the one thing that made her indispensable had been erased, the Hazzards must see her as nothing more than a threat to their livelihood. She screamed until her throat grew raw, and fought Dr. Hazzard's grip, but the exertion only tired her.

"Where is the motorcar?" Dr. Hazzard lifted a brow to her husband.

"Rollie's bringing the Butterworth's vehicle around." Sam motioned with a thumb toward the road. "He shouldn't be much longer."

Butterworth's? Weren't they the people sent to take care of Claire and Sue? But that couldn't be right. Those women had been dead when Butterworth's was summoned. . . . The full force of Dr. Hazzard's intentions stole Stella's breath and sent a rash of goose bumps over her skin.

Stella met Dr. Hazzard's fiery gaze. This woman planned to kill her. And she had probably already killed Henry. *God. When are You going to save me?*

A motor sputtered toward them. If only the sound signaled Henry's return. But the self-satisfied smirk on Sam's lips told her that possibility had died earlier in the day. Tears sprang to Stella's eyes. The vehicle screeched to a stop on the soupy road, and yellow words contrasted against the dark green background.

Butterworth's Funeral Parlor.

Stella's stomach hit the ground. She struggled against Dr. Hazzard's claws. "Let. Me. Go." She stomped on the woman's foot, and her grip loosened. With her arm free, Stella ran toward the woods, stumbling in the mud.

Tree branches slapped her face, but she brushed them aside and pressed on. Her heart pounded and her breath came in jagged gasps. Her foot caught on a tree root, and she fell headlong to the forest floor.

"Just give up." Rollie's voice sent her scrambling to her feet. She started to run, but he picked her up and draped her over his shoulder like a sack of flour.

"Let me go!" She pounded her fists against his back and kicked, but he plodded toward the Butterworth's automobile as if she were a noncompliant child instead of a woman fighting for her life.

When Rollie turned, Stella glimpsed a wooden box lying on the ground behind the motorcar. A coffin. A scream jarred her lungs but escaped her lips as a raspy whimper. Her captor hefted her around and dumped her in the casket.

"Please, no." She moved to sit up, flashes of light curling at the corners of her eyes. Not again. Not when she needed all her faculties to fight for her life. Sam held her shoulders against the bottom. Splinters scraped her skin through her nightgown.

"If you could keep quiet, we wouldn't have to do this the hard way." Dr. Hazzard uncorked a bottle, held a rag to the rim, and tilted the vial of clear liquid. "Hold this over her nose and mouth." She handed it to her husband.

"You'll never get away with this." Stella squirmed beneath Sam's hold and screamed for help.

Sam clamped the rag over her nose, and Stella turned her head from side to side, avoiding the sweet fumes on the cloth. He couldn't do this. Where was God in the midst of this? Had He left her to fend for herself?

The sickening scent crept into her nose, and despite her struggle, she inhaled.

Gray dots formed in her vision, and her body ceased to obey her commands.

"Thank you, love. That did it." Sam removed the cloth and bunched it in the coffin beside Stella. He rose and stood beside his wife. The pair gazed down on her.

Stella's eyelids fluttered as she fought the sleep that threatened to overcome her.

"Finish the job, Rollie. I don't have to tell you how important this is to your future." The old Buzzard's voice hardened to flint. "If only you didn't fritter away the money I give you." She cast a final unfeeling glance at Stella then walked away.

Sam reached for something on the ground then stood with a wooden cover in his hands. He fit it over the coffin, bathing Stella in darkness except for the tenacious light that pushed through the cracks between boards.

In the enclosed space, the odor of ether swelled and tickled her nose. The sensation of being lifted then dropped left only a faint imprint on her floating brain.

Where were they taking her? Her eyelids grew heavy, but she forced them open.

How could she escape their clutches when everything about her screamed frailty? The fumes scratched her throat.

Was Henry alive? She sniffed. He couldn't be, not when she considered the look of triumph Sam Hazzard wore. If only she could see Henry one more time. She'd left so many words unsaid, and there would be no chance to apologize for both viewing him and treating him as beneath her.

Why had God allowed this? He knew Linda Hazzard for who she was.

Stella's head swam. Her thoughts undulated one on top of another.

But Henry had tried to warn her, and she had chosen not to listen. What if God had given him that unsettled feeling?

This was all her fault. Still, God knew her weaknesses. He loved her. He saw her.

Dear Lord, Your children stood still and saw Your salvation. I can't be any more still than I am now. Without You, there is no hope. Do something mighty. Tears scalded her eyes. *And this may be too much to ask, but let Henry be all right. He tried to save me. Please don't let him die, or I'll never forgive myself.*

Chapter Thirty-Two

Henry thanked the driver and hopped out of the motorcar a hundred yards from the turnoff to Starvation Heights. Any rattle of the wheels or thrum of the engine could give away his plan to the old Buzzard and her husband. The pair were not to be trifled with. After Sam had tried drowning him, Henry lost all doubt the man would so much as blink at the thought of killing Stella with the same disregard for human life.

Henry ran into a stand of trees along the road, clothes clinging to his skin, blood staining his sleeves. On his left, Starvation Heights stood. How did a place filled with evil give off such an unassuming air? As he approached the drive leading to the house, the clatter of an automobile stilled his steps. He pushed aside a leafy branch to get a better view.

Were Sam and Linda Hazzard fleeing the consequences of their criminal activities? Surely starvation and murder wouldn't go unpunished if brought before judge and jury.

The brightly painted words on the sides of the motorcar caught his eye.

Butterworth's Funeral Parlor.

Henry's gut contorted. They must have been called to collect a body. But whose? Stella's? Heaven forbid. When the vehicle turned the corner, a plain pine box rattled in the back.

His heart stalled. A scrap of purple fabric peeked from beneath the lid. The same pale shade as the nightgown Stella had been wearing when Sam bashed his head with the shovel.

221

Was she—

His heart wilted, and emotion scalded his throat.

No. The thought was too awful to entertain. He had to follow them. Get Stella out of their clutches before it was too late. But how? He'd never keep pace on foot.

Henry glanced toward the house. His motorcar—Weston's—still sat on the gravel drive. He dashed to it, cranked the handle, and leaped behind the steering wheel.

Linda Hazzard ran onto the front porch, waving and shouting for him to stop like a drill sergeant breaking in new recruits. But Henry pulled away from the house and sped to the road. He would have liked to run her over, but he hadn't the time. The funeral home's vehicle had turned left, and though it had disappeared, fresh tire tracks in the mud would serve as a guide.

He followed the tracks while sending prayers heavenward.

If she wasn't dead, why put her in a casket? The only possible answer nagged his brain. They had killed her. She was already dead.

But it couldn't be. Stella had so much to live for. So much she wanted to do and so many lives to touch with her generosity. Perhaps the Hazzards used the funeral home equipment to secret her away. Yes. That had to be it. He'd cling to the tenuous hope no matter how improbable it might be.

His heart swelled into his throat. What if he opened the coffin and discovered he was too late?

≈

Stella groaned. The ache in her head bore different qualities than her usual migraines. This time it felt as if someone had stuffed her skull with cotton and set it on fire. She reached to rub her temples, but rough wood grazed the back of her hand, limiting her movements.

Where was she? Gentle rocking lulled her into a sense of safety.

She swallowed past what felt like steel wool in her throat. Light shone before her eyes in dim stripes. The scent of fresh-cut lumber resurrected bits of memory. The cabin. Henry. Oh, how her head throbbed. Snippets of her run into the woods, her fall, flashed in her mind. Why had she run?

Dr. Hazzard with the cloth. "Eliminate! Eliminate!" Stella winced as she replayed the pounding of the doctor's fists against her back. She sucked in a sharp breath.

"It's time we eliminated the problem you've become." The words echoed in her brain, adding strength to the pounding behind her eyes.

The coffin. Her heart climbed into her throat.

A creak and the steady movement stopped. The slam of a door.

She tried to scream, but her voice lay dormant in her lungs. Though she rammed her fists against the lid of the casket, her attempt at making her presence known sounded weak to her own ears. How would anyone find her?

And Henry. Was he alive or dead? She choked on a sob.

"You got the hole ready?" She'd never heard that voice before.

"That's what you told me to do." Rollie's tone dripped with its usual sarcasm.

A hole? Stella's heart clawed at her rib cage. They wouldn't—they couldn't—

The coffin lifted and jostled. She scratched the wood holding her prisoner. Splinters stabbed under her fingernails and warmth trickled down her wrists and dripped onto her cheek.

She dug into the depths of her soul and screamed Henry's name. But could he hear her? Would anyone hear?

～

The tracks turned left onto a dirt path. Trees pressed in on either side as Henry wound into the heart of a forest. He poked his head out of the open window and scanned for any sign of the Butterworth's vehicle. The rain had slowed to a drizzle.

Was he headed the right direction? The path looked deserted. If this proved to be nothing more than a hunter's trail, precious time would be wasted. Time that could make the difference between Stella living or dying. If that old Buzzard and her murderous husband hadn't killed her already. Maybe if he had been honest with Stella about the letters, about his feelings for her, things could have been different. She might have looked past his lowly position, defied her uncle, and shared happiness with him. Maybe she never would have heard of Linda

Hazzard and her so-called clinic in the wilderness.

A scream ripped the air, sending birds flapping from the trees. The syllables of his name hung suspended. Stella. That had to be her. His pulse sped as he pressed hard on the starter. This was the right path. Stella was alive. Determination buzzed through his veins. He drove over a dip, and the motorcar lurched, sending up a spray of mud, but he didn't slow his pace. She was running out of time, and he must find her.

Hold on a bit longer, Stella. I'm coming.

❧

Somehow the claustrophobic pine box magnified the sound of shovels cutting damp earth above her. Stella shouted until her throat ached, alternating between Henry's name and primal shrieks. How would anyone hear her when she lay in a box underground? The sickening thump of dirt hitting the coffin ushered a fresh wave of terror. She clawed her wood prison, not caring about the tiny slivers sending pain-filled warnings to her brain.

Thump.

Thump.

With each shovelful of dirt her chances of rescue shrank. She would die out here, and no one would find her. Fear sucked the oxygen from the space, and dirt seeped through the cracks, raining into her eyes and mouth.

She had feared dying alone in a cabin at Wilderness Heights, but with Rollie Burfield and some strange man burying her alive, her former fears sounded more like a happy dream. What she wouldn't give to be back in her cabin. Margaret Conway might have taken her away once she convinced Dora that Dr. Hazzard meant to harm her as she had Claire. Why hadn't she waited?

Because there were no guarantees Dora would ever be convinced.

And where was God in all this? Mama had said over and over that He cared, but where was the evidence of that?

The verse played through her mind to the steady beat of dirt hitting wood. "What is man, that thou art mindful of him? and the son of man, that thou visitest him?"

Stella was no better or worse than any other person, yet still, God thought of her. He was the same always. In her quest to break free of Dr. Hazzard, had she shifted her focus from God's power again? He had commanded His children to stand still on the banks of the Red Sea, and they had seen a miracle that day. The same God who had parted the waters held her in the hollow of His hand. If God hadn't changed, then the fault lay on her shoulders. Had she truly stood still or waited long enough to see God's delivering power? No. She had seized every glimmer of opportunity, and her headstrong will had brought her to this point.

The sounds of shoveling muffled into silence. How far underground was she?

Now, trapped in a coffin beneath the dirt, she lay in a position with no other choice but to trust. Her breathing grew shallow. God saw her. He loved her. He hadn't left, even though loneliness crushed her chest and the earth swallowed her whole.

God, I'm standing still. I have nowhere to look but to You. Help me.

Chapter Thirty-Three

The green automobile with yellow letters appeared in the clearing ahead. Henry killed the motor and stepped from the vehicle. Two men with shovels scooped dirt from a pile. The older man whistled in a tone-deaf manner.

Stella's scream had faded into memory, followed by sickening silence. Had they killed her then buried her in the middle of the forest?

He blinked away the sting in his eyes. Thoughts like that would only slow him down. If Stella still breathed, she needed him to keep a cool head.

Henry padded closer on the balls of his feet. The element of surprise might be his only weapon. As he approached, he scanned the scene. Both men were strangers, probably Butterworth's employees. Were they in on Linda Hazzard's scheme somehow? A pile of shovels in the back of the Butterworth's auto drew his attention. He wasn't completely unarmed.

Once at the vehicle, he gripped a shovel. How could he hope to disarm both men? He crouched near the front of the motorcar, waiting for the moment to strike.

"Where's the water jug?" The younger man swiped a sleeve across his brow, leaving a dirty streak.

The older man paused his whistled tune. "In the back." He scooped another shovelful of dirt and resumed the mournful melody.

The young man strode toward Henry, and he gripped the shovel's handle. This was it. When the gravedigger rounded the automobile,

226

Henry stood and raised the shovel. The stranger's eyes widened and he opened his mouth, but Henry brought the blade down hard before he could alert his accomplice. The man crumpled to the ground, blood trickling from a cut on his forehead.

Henry darted a glance at the other digger. So engrossed in the steady rhythm of his work and the tune on his lips, he didn't lift his head at the thud of his comrade hitting the ground.

The man lifted a hand toward Henry, not bothering to cast a look his way. "Bring the jug here when you're done with it," he hollered from his spot at the edge of the grave.

Henry stepped beside the man, shovel ready to swing.

The digger glanced up, meeting his gaze. "Who are you?" His eyes widened and his nostrils flared.

Henry swung, but the man dodged the blow and countered with one of his own. His shovel's tapered blade connected with Henry's head, filling his mouth with grit, but the force wasn't strong enough to topple him.

Henry fought back with another blow, and while metal struck skull, his opponent remained upright. Sweat dripped into Henry's eyes, but he didn't bother to wipe it away. He rammed the shovel into the gravedigger's gut, and the man let out an oof.

The digger growled, tossed his shovel aside, and lunged at Henry, barreling into his middle. The momentum sent Henry sprawling flat on his back and knocked the air from his lungs.

While he gasped for oxygen, the man loomed over him and landed a solid punch to Henry's jaw. Stars exploded across Henry's vision.

Why had the Hazzards employed such a behemoth? If only this one had been as easily bested as the young man by the motorcar. Another blow to the nose, and Henry tasted blood. He spat on the dirt.

He cut a glance to the freshly turned earth. Stella might still be alive, but every minute stole a bit more of her air supply. *God, help me.* If Henry didn't reach her soon, she'd surely die.

He couldn't let that happen while he still breathed.

With a primal growl, Henry fought back. Springing to his feet then swinging his fists, he connected with the man's jaw. The stranger took a wobbly step backward. The shovel the younger man had discarded stood propped in a pile of dirt. If only Henry could reach it—

He closed in on the gravedigger and landed another strike with his left hand.

The man stumbled then fell to the ground.

Henry grappled for the shovel.

Scrambling, the man pushed up on his hands and knees.

Shovel clenched in his palms, Henry raised it above his head.

The man stood, clenched his fists, and dove headfirst for Henry.

Henry brought the shovel down on the back of his head, and the gravedigger collapsed.

Ragged breaths burned Henry's chest, but he didn't have time to catch his bearings. How long could Stella hold her breath? What if they'd already killed her? He fought the terror building in his chest like storm clouds.

He drove the shovel into the dirt. With each scoop, he prayed.

Stella couldn't be dead. Wouldn't he feel something if she were no longer counted among the living? Some profound sense of loss? Urgency drove him forward. Something trickled from his nose, and he swiped it away with a fist. The back of his hand came away red.

The shovel hit wood. His heart rose into his throat, and he dropped to the ground, reaching his arms into the hole. A brush of his hand over the lid removed stray dirt.

He closed his eyes and breathed a prayer. What would he find inside? The prospect of Stella's lifeless form tempted him to wait a moment longer. But if she was alive—

He pulled on the lid. Something held it fast. With his heart throbbing in his throat, he pawed at the dirt surrounding the casket, ignoring the pain in his shredded wrists. When he'd cleared enough space, he jumped into the grave and tugged on the lid. Wood creaked as the board lifted. Stella lay thin and frail. Dirt peppered her face and nightgown. Her eyes were closed, and she didn't stir. Up close, the hollows in her cheeks reminded him of a skeleton. How could the Buzzard have been so cruel to someone as full of life as Stella?

"Stella." He stroked her cheek with his thumb. "Wake up. Please wake up."

Nothing.

Other than the emaciated state of her body, no marking spoke of a brutal attack. Had she run out of air? Suffocated? Tears bit his eyes. His throat thickened. He was too late.

He gathered her close, dusting the earth from her cheeks. Face buried against her hair, he whispered in her ear. "I wanted to tell you I was sorry—I am sorry." His voice tripped over a sob. "For so many things. I lied to you. Pretended to be someone I wasn't, and if you would have found out, it would have hurt you. I never meant for that to happen. I had hoped you would believe me when I said I'd do anything to keep from causing you pain. Because I love you."

His muscles stilled. Faint breaths leaked against his neck. She was alive. His nerves hummed. She needed a doctor. He lifted her out of the coffin and climbed out of the grave. She was fragile as spun glass and felt nearly weightless in his arms.

He passed the two gravediggers on his trek to the motorcar. Both lay motionless. He'd get Stella to a hospital and send the police to arrest these men for attempting to kill her.

When he opened the back door, Stella stirred. A low groan. Her eyelids fluttered. Then she squinted to focus on him. A weak smile tugged one corner of her lips. "Henry."

Though her voice was thick and scratchy, never had his name sounded more melodious. "My darling." He laid her on the bench seat. "You're alive. I wasn't sure. I—"

"I love you," she rasped, and her words stopped him cold. He couldn't have heard her correctly. Pleasing her uncle meant everything to her, and such a declaration would bring his wrath on her head. "Aren't you going to say anything?" Her eyes clouded, and her tongue trailed over cracked lips.

His chest tightened. She still didn't know the truth, and if she did, her feelings for him might change. "You're overwrought." He brushed her hair out of her eyes. "I'm taking you to a hospital. Once we've got you on the mend and you've had a chat with the police, I'll get you home."

A tear slipped from the corner of her eye and dropped onto the leather seat. He resisted the urge to kiss her forehead. Once she learned about the letters he'd written, about the part he'd feigned, she'd never want to see him again.

But for now, she was safe, and that was all that mattered.

Chapter Thirty-Four

Stella plucked at the white sheet. The hospital bed felt like heaven after three long weeks at Wilderness Heights, but a weight had settled on her chest and no amount of counting her blessings or thinking of others would lift it. She'd told Henry she loved him, and he hadn't said anything. Her throat prickled.

Of course, she'd grown up with her every whim fulfilled. But Henry was an independent man with a mind and wishes of his own. She couldn't expect him to fall at her feet just because she'd spilled her heart. She squared her shoulders. He didn't feel the same, and she ought to respect it. Still, the sting of rejection jabbed between her ribs with every breath.

How would she face him again, knowing she'd shared a part of herself with him, and he'd tossed it aside like yesterday's garbage? But she had to face him eventually. How else would she get home? She could buy a train ticket to be sure, but that would take twice as long. And in the state she was in, she needed Jane's arms around her and her soothing voice to assure her that all would be well in the end. Even though Jane would disapprove of Stella's feelings for Henry, she'd understand and help her through the heartache.

If only it would have worked out. Her plans to grow the business after her birthday would keep the company running, hopefully with even more profit. Her employees would have no complaints. In fact, they would thrive once her ideas were enacted. Then she could have married Henry without fear of failing the men and women who counted on her to make wise financial decisions. But Henry didn't want to marry her. He didn't love her at all. If she hadn't convinced him to bring her here under false pretenses, maybe he could have found a way to care for her. But as the matter stood, not even her fortune could entice him to pretend he cared.

Most men would pledge their lives to her inheritance. Not Henry. Grief squeezed Stella's heart. He was a good man. The best. Not even the promise of wealth could tempt him to be anything less than honorable.

Rustling in the doorway summoned her away from the gloom in her mind. A man in a tweed suit strode in, and Margaret Conway followed. The Australian woman rushed to her bedside and took her hand. "When your young man alerted the police about Wilderness Heights, I came straightaway. This is Detective Martin. You can tell him everything. Dr. Hazzard must pay for all the harm she's done."

Stella nodded and glanced at Detective Martin. His jaw was rigid as he sank into a chair beside her bed. He crossed one leg over the other and leaned back as if he had all the time on earth to discuss Starvation Heights and the woman who had wanted her dead.

When Stella glanced up, Henry leaned against the doorframe. Bandages bound his wrists. She turned her eyes on the detective, avoiding Henry's gaze. She would've liked to ask Henry to wait in the hallway or the visitors' lounge, but after he had risked his life to save her, that wouldn't be fair.

"Now, Miss Burke." The detective pulled a notepad from his pocket. "Why don't you start at the beginning?"

❧

As he drove toward San Francisco, Henry replayed Stella's interview with Detective Martin, and his gut twisted. Poor Stella had seen unspeakable things. And she'd insisted on staying in Seattle until her friend Tilda was safely away from Starvation Heights. How Stella could harbor so much concern for the woman who had shared her plan of escape with Sam Hazzard eluded him. Though he'd seen sparks of empathy and selflessness in Stella before the ordeal, he'd never dreamed the depth of character she possessed.

He swallowed, but it did nothing to alleviate the lump in his throat. She loved him. Or at least, she loved the person she thought him to be, honest and brave. He had to tell her about the letters, but the right moment hadn't presented itself. After all she had suffered, admitting his falsehood would only add to her burden. Her soft snores from the back seat tore at him. She'd been through so much, and he couldn't withhold his secret forever. How he detested the thought of making matters worse.

He passed a mile marker. In half an hour they'd be home. His grip tightened on the wheel. To be more accurate, Stella would be home. He'd be sent to jail for stealing Weston's automobile. His conscience smote him. He'd done what he had to do for Stella, but what would happen to Robby, Rose, and Daisy if he went to prison for auto theft?

They would be sent back to the children's home, even though they hated it. Would they find another chance to run? Go back to stealing bread? Perhaps Jane would see to their welfare. But with Stella home, her job would return to its normal demands.

"I need to apologize." Stella's voice from the back seat jarred his nerves. She'd slept most of the trip, and the silence had been both a blessing and a curse. On one hand, he'd longed to tell her that he hoped she meant what she had said at the gravesite. On the other, the silence had offered him time to think about the wounds his deceit would inflict. Okay, so maybe the quiet had only been a curse.

He glanced at her reflection in the windscreen. Was she crying? "Why would you possibly need my forgiveness?" He was the one owing her an apology.

"I told you that I would respect your feelings about Dr. Hazzard's treatments. And if you felt uncomfortable, I wouldn't stay." Her voice cracked. "But I had no intention of following through with my promise. I wanted to be healed so badly that I treated you with contempt. I'm sorry."

The road along the seaside gave way to the familiar shops and storefronts of San Francisco. Henry let the words of her apology sink in. Her treatment of him had left a sting, but he had never lived with the pain that was Stella's constant companion. He turned onto a street lined with lavish estates. "You're forgiven. I would never hold anything against you."

Stella sighed, a sound that rattled Henry to the depths of his soul. "I've caused so much trouble. If I had listened to you, things could be as they always were. But even though I'll be home, I have this premonition that nothing will be the same again." She sniffed. "That we— That you won't want anything to do with me now."

"Stella, no matter what happens, and despite the hurtful truth I must tell you, please know that I have no regrets in coming for you when you needed me." Confessions seemed to be the order of the day, and he must share his own. He pulled into the drive at the Burke estate, killed the motor, and turned to face her. Her tears strangled the air from his lungs. "I have to confess. . ." He reached for her bandaged hand, ignoring the impropriety of his actions. "I beg your forgiveness. I have deceived you for—"

"I've called the police. They're looking for you." Weston stomped toward the parked automobile. "How dare you steal my motorcar? I intend to press charges for your crime, you—" His gaze cut to Stella, and his jaw slacked. The fire in his eyes sputtered to a faint flicker. "My dear, you look dreadful. I had believed you were getting treatments for your headaches. What did they do to you?" He opened the door and held out his hand. "I'll have Jane make you comfortable."

Stella slipped her hand from Henry's grasp then stepped out of the automobile into her uncle's embrace. "Uncle Weston, please don't punish Henry. I don't know what happened, but I know that everything he did was for me."

Weston wrapped his arms around her and met Henry's gaze over her head. A mix of emotions warred behind his dark eyes. "I'll drop the charges." He rubbed her back. "For you, my dear." His voice was soft and tender.

Maybe Henry had read their relationship all wrong. While Weston cared for money and position more than he ought, how could Henry have believed the man cared nothing for his niece? The compassion he showed her told Henry a different story than the one he'd convinced himself was true.

Henry climbed out of the motorcar. "I should go." He thrust his hands into his pockets. His fingers brushed the cloth bag of herbs, and he pulled it out. In his haste to get her home, he'd forgotten them.

"This is for you." He extended the offering to Stella.

She took it from him, brow puckered. "What is this?" She held it to her nose and breathed in. "It smells awful."

"I ran across an herbalist a week ago. Asked her if there was a cure for your migraines." He met Stella's dark eyes, teeming with emotion. "There's no cure. But she said this herb—it's called feverfew—might help if you steeped it in hot water like tea every morning."

Tears glittered in Stella's eyes. "Thank you." The words were so faint he barely heard them.

Weston nodded his thanks, his own eyes glistening.

Henry kicked a rock on the ground, turned, and walked away. For the last time.

Chapter Thirty-Five

Stella glanced at her reflection in the gilded mirror above her dressing table as Jane wrestled with her hair. In the week since she'd arrived home, the hollows in her cheeks had begun to fill. Henry's tea leaves had been a godsend. Since her first cup, only one headache had blossomed into a pain that sent her to bed early. A huge improvement from daily debilitation.

She met Jane's gaze in the mirror, forced a smile, then focused on the bottle of perfume in front of her.

How she missed seeing Henry every day. Something had happened between him and Uncle Weston, although her uncle wouldn't say what.

At least Henry had promised to accompany her to the trial in Washington State, but when that event would take place, she hadn't the slightest idea. The prosecutors were still working to gather enough evidence to convict Dr. Hazzard, and they didn't want to begin a trial without reasonable certainty they could receive a guilty verdict.

The two men who had buried her alive had fled the premises and were nowhere to be found by the time the police had arrived. She was fairly certain one had been Rollie Burfield, but since she hadn't seen his face, the district attorney didn't believe her recognition of his voice provided solid enough evidence to accuse Rollie of a crime. He claimed the knot on the back of his head was the result of a bar fight, and the authorities hadn't contradicted him.

"You're looking much better today, dearie." Jane fastened a jeweled comb in Stella's hair. "The bloom in your cheeks is returning." Her shoulders sagged. "I just wish I hadn't been in such support of Dr. Hazzard. Every night I wonder. . .if only I'd tried to stop you—"

Stella turned on the stool and took Jane's hands. "Never mind that. I'm home, and that's all that matters."

Jane nodded. "I thank you for saying it. It's good to have you home. The place wasn't the same without you."

Stella smiled. "I missed you too."

Jane's eyes glinted with mischief.

"You're up to something. What is it?"

"I've got a letter for you." Jane's delighted grin warmed Stella's chest. She handed her an envelope.

Familiar pointed handwriting decorated the front. Stella took the letter, and her heart wilted. After considering the matter further, she'd given up the notion that her mystery friend had abandoned her. No doubt his letters had been intercepted by Dr. Hazzard or Sam. But she couldn't pick up writing again as if nothing had changed. A part of her used to think they might have a future together. Not anymore. Not as long as Henry breathed. But despite his talk of forgiveness, she hadn't seen him since he brought her home. Part of that must be thanks to Uncle Weston's temper, but Henry was a grown man with a mind of his own. If he wanted to talk to her, why not send a letter or a telegram? He must not wish to continue their friendship now that his employment had been terminated. But that wasn't like him.

Stella forced a smile. "Don't look so excited, Jane. It will come to nothing." She set the message on her dressing table.

"You should at least read it." Jane prodded her with a hairpin.

Stella slipped a single sheet from the envelope and unfolded it. Nothing he could write would change her mind or persuade her they could be more than friends. Or business partners if he agreed with her ideas for the children's home.

She scanned the words.

My dearest Stella,

Meet me at Rodeo Beach tomorrow at 10:00 a.m. I'd like to talk about the children's home. Your ideas are splendid. In a way, I've started helping children already. They were sort of thrown my way by the hand of Providence. I'll bring them along. They could use a beach outing.

I look forward to seeing you at long last with no more secrets between us.

Yours very truly

Stella folded the page and fit it back into the envelope. Jane's gaze nearly burned a hole in her skin. Stella jutted her chin. "He wants to discuss a business matter."

"Is that so?" Jane wrangled a wayward strand into place, a smile twitching her lips.

Stella closed the message into a drawer as her brain struggled to sort her varied feelings. The dream of making a difference in the lives of others flowed deep in her veins. Running a clothing manufacturer wasn't enough despite the fact she played a minor part in the lives of her employees. The longing to touch individuals on a soul level far outshined the simple task of signing paychecks. But what if this man had more than a business partnership in mind? Though he'd never used the word love in his letters, his endearments and his tone had made her feel cherished. Like she mattered to him in a way she'd never mattered to anyone before. If the feelings he harbored for her traveled beyond friendship or business, how would she tell him she didn't feel for him in that way? Would their uneven emotions clip the wings of their plans before they took flight?

"I don't think I should meet him." Stella smoothed her skirt.

"Are you running away from a difficult conversation?" Jane added a few jeweled pins to Stella's hair in strategic places.

"Perhaps."

"If you run away, you could be missing a golden opportunity." She patted a stray curl. "Sometimes you've got to stand still and face what comes head-on. And trust that God will guide you."

Stand still.

That command seemed to fit so many of life's situations. When she'd finally given the outcome at Starvation Heights to God, he'd brought Henry to her rescue just as her circumstances were at their bleakest. Now, standing still required she meet the man she had written to for so long and tell him in person that she wished to help him make a home for needy children but nothing more. Running from her problems was just as much against God's desire for her to stand still and see His handiwork as making weak attempts to fight for her own way.

"Will you go with me?" She squeezed Jane's hand. "I don't think I can do this alone."

Jane offered a sad smile. "I wish I could, but some things in life must be handled without an audience."

Stella chewed her lip. *God, help me to know what to say.*

⁂

"You're sure this is a good idea?" Henry fumbled with his necktie while he stood in front of the mirror. Another failed attempt. He untangled the knot and started over.

"I'm more than sure." Jane handed Daisy to him then motioned him closer.

With Daisy settled on his hip, Jane set his tie to rights and smoothed his collar.

"You look dashing. She'll not refuse you."

"But I lied to her." He caught Rose by the shoulder as she passed and wiped jam off her cheek with his thumb. "She'll never forgive me."

"I think she may be able to look past it this once." Jane snatched Robby's shoes from the middle of the rug. "Will that boy never learn to put things where they belong? Miss Stella will have her hands full with this one. Robby!" She strode out of the room, waving the pair of shoes.

Even if Stella looked past his deception and agreed to go forward as partners in the children's home, would Henry be satisfied with nothing more than a business relationship? He swallowed past the dryness in his throat. Not hardly. He'd marry her today if she'd take him.

Daisy glanced at him with wide blue eyes. "Sad?" Her chubby hand stroked his cheek.

At the sound of her tiny voice, tears sprang to his eyes. She'd finally spoken, and her word had been meant to comfort him. He hugged her tight. "I am a little sad. But I let myself down, and I'm paying the price for it now."

Daisy kissed his cheek. "Wuv you."

His heart swelled to bursting. "I love you too, little one." He glanced at the wall clock. Time to start for the beach. "Are you ready to meet Miss Stella again?"

Daisy nodded, though her eyes registered no recognition of the name.

Was he ready to see her again with so much guilt hanging between them?

Chapter Thirty-Six

The salty breeze tugged a wispy curl from Stella's braid and blustered it into her eyes. She tucked the stray strand behind her ear, keeping her focus on the path leading to the shore. Waves crashed against the rocks behind her. Any moment now, she would see him— her mysterious letter writer. Her eyelids drifted shut as she prayed for wisdom. Hurting him was the last thing she wanted to do, but aside from helping with his charity work—

Children's shouts and giggles rode a gust from somewhere over the rise. Stella's breath hitched. His idea to bring the children had been inspired. At least if emotions ran high, the little ones would serve as a distraction.

A boy wearing a gray suit and cap jogged down the hill, tugging a golden-haired girl behind him. As they neared, recognition stirred within her. Robby and Rose. The children she'd met that day in the alley. Her eyes pricked with unshed tears.

The mystery benefactor had said God brought these children to him. Her vision blurred as they ran to her and little Rose threw her arms around Stella's waist. She'd given God so little credit for answering her prayers, but He'd been working all along. Even though she hadn't seen or felt it happening. Stella hugged Rose close.

"How are you, my dear? I've prayed for you."

Rose muttered something against Stella's dress. Robby stooped, picked up a sand crab, and flashed a mischievous grin.

"I don't know what you're planning, young man, but I don't like the look of it." Stella tried to inject sternness into her quavering voice, but failed miserably. Still, Robby had the decency to blush three shades of red. "Where is your sister? Daisy?"

Robby pointed to the top of the hill. Dune grass fluttered, and a man's head came into view. The brim of his hat shielded his face, but the broad shoulders and confident gait stilled the breath in Stella's lungs.

She licked dry lips. It couldn't be. Her vision misted.

But with each step the man took toward her, Stella's heart beat faster. It was him. Henry.

With her hand pressed over her mouth, she tried biting back sobs to no avail.

Henry stopped a few yards away, whispered something to Daisy, and set her on the ground. She grasped his fingers in her little hand, and they walked the rest of the way together until they stood directly in front of her.

Stella thumbed tears from her eyes and patted Rose's head, then the girl moved away to join her brother on the beach. Robby whooped and hollered, chasing a flock of gulls who then congregated farther down the beach, likely plotting their revenge.

"Stella." Henry's voice brought fresh tears. He crammed his hands into his pockets. "I'm sorry I lied to you. Pretended to be something—someone I'm not. As much as I love your passion for the children's home, I have to say, it's not what I want." He swallowed hard and met her gaze. Then he took her hand. "I mean, it is what I want. But I wish. . ."

The words of his letters filtered through her mind and lifted her heart to new heights. Of course he'd written them. How could she have been so blind to think otherwise? Henry had always been her dearest friend, caring for her with a depth and constancy no one else showed. Her heart swelled. He wanted more than friendship.

"I don't bring anything to the table." His voice lowered along with his gaze. "I've no wealth to offer you, nothing you don't already have. But I'd give you my whole heart, for what it's worth."

Stella squeezed his hand. "Henry, look at me."

Their eyes met, and the raw emotion in his gaze sent her pulse thrashing.

"It is I who should apologize. All this time, you wrote me, knowing how desperately I needed a friend. But I was blind and arrogant. I thought you were beneath me." She cringed at the ugly truth. How had she ever believed something so terribly wrong? "But as I examined my heart and my motives, I found that my character was lacking, not yours. I'm selfish, but I don't want to remain this way. I want to put others first. . .just as you do. Truthfully, you are a far deal too good for me. You're the best friend I've ever known, and I don't deserve you—"

Henry pulled her close and brushed his thumb against her cheek. "You keep talking of friendship." He searched her eyes, and her stomach fluttered. "Please tell me I have a chance at more. I've loved you since we were children. And though we are so very different, I can't keep quiet about it for another moment. You said in Washington that you loved me. I pray you meant that in a deeper way than friendship."

"I do love you. As so much more than a friend. I didn't know just how much for a long while. But Henry Clayton, you mean the world to me." Time slowed and Stella rose on her toes. Her lips brushed Henry's in a gentle kiss. His arms tightened around her, and warmth coursed through her veins. Loved. In his embrace, she felt deeply loved. And not for money or other superficial things, but for herself. Because Henry knew her flaws and loved her for them, not despite them.

A gentle tug on her skirt broke Stella from Henry's kiss. She glanced down at little Daisy, who stood with one arm raised. "Up," she said around the thumb in her mouth.

"Come here, my love." Stella scooped her up and held her close. Then she cast a glance at Henry. "I know we intend to be more than business partners." She tried and failed to hide a smile. "But I'd like to use the estate for the children's home. I'll be twenty-five next week, and it will be mine to do with as I please. Wouldn't it be a good place for the children to run and play?"

"But your uncle?" Henry twined an arm around her waist.

"Leave him to me." Stella rested her head on his shoulder and surveyed the glistening waves. Rose had Robby half buried beneath the sand with only his head and arms showing.

"Are you sure you're up to it?" Henry kissed her cheek. "The children can be a handful, and I know you're unwell."

"The tea you brought has helped a great deal. It's not a cure, but I've seen improvement. I did keep a journal while I was in Washington. Your notion that the headaches are tied to stress holds a lot of truth." She looked into his eyes, and Daisy's head flopped against her shoulder.

"The children won't lower your stress. And Robby will most likely compound it."

A scream from the beach flagged their attention. Robby erupted from the sand and chased Rose with something in his fingers. Probably that sand crab. Stella smiled. "I think much of my stress stemmed from frustration. I wanted to do something meaningful with my life but couldn't find a way to make a difference. You've given me the world. Just knowing that I'm doing what I was made to do. . .and having the opportunity to work alongside you, I already feel lighter."

"Does that mean you'll marry me?" He whispered the words low in her ear, and she bit back a smile.

"I admit I did you wrong." She arched a brow. "But that doesn't mean you don't have to give me a proper proposal. Get down on one knee."

Henry grinned, his boyhood charm still very much alive. "I don't have a ring yet. Jane didn't give me time to prepare when she planned all this."

Stella tilted her head. "Jane? But I thought—"

"She's had a change of heart too." Henry brushed windblown curls from her face.

"I don't need a ring, you know." Stella rested her head atop Daisy's. She could hold this precious child forever.

"Are you sure?" He tossed her a lopsided smile.

"You said that all you brought to the table was your whole heart." Emotion burned her throat. "My dear Henry, that's more than enough."

"Well, then." He dropped to one knee and took her free hand. "Stella Burke, I'm poor and ordinary, and you could do worlds better than me. But I love you. So much that I don't know quite how to put it into words. If you'll have me, I'll try my whole life long to make you happy. Would you marry me?"

Tears trailed hot down Stella's cheeks, and the breeze whipped past and dried them. "What do you mean you didn't have time to prepare?" She squeezed his hand. "You've never been so eloquent."

"I've had many years to build this moment in my mind. I never dreamed I'd have the opportunity to share my heart. . .with you." He glanced at the ground. She followed his gaze. A violet grew near a patch of dune grass. He plucked it and held it out to her. "I'm still waiting for your answer."

"Well, of course I'll marry you." She took the flower and lifted it to her nose.

Henry stood and kissed her.

Though heartache, grief, and fear clouded her past, the future seemed to be tinted purple. The color of home and family.

Epilogue

February 1912

S tella held Henry's hand as the jury returned to the courtroom after their deliberations. Dr. Linda Hazzard sat behind the defense table, her cool demeanor no different from what it had always been. Not giving off an inkling that she felt the slightest sting of regret for her cruelty.

"Don't look at her, darling. She's an evil woman." Henry lifted Stella's hand to his lips.

The wood-paneled walls smelled of pine, conjuring memories of the cabin. Stella steeled her nerves. How she'd love leaving this place far behind.

Margaret Conway and Dora Williamson were noticeably absent. Though Dora had improved much over the past year, the trial had dredged up memories of her sister and sapped her strength. Besides, even if Dr. Hazzard was convicted of murder, no amount of retribution could bring back Claire Williamson.

Stella scanned the faces on the prosecution's side where she sat with Henry. Tilda. No longer a walking corpse, she looked much improved. She glanced at Stella and sent her an apologetic smile, eyes glistening.

"Have you reached a verdict?" the judge asked from behind the bench.

The foreman stood. "We have, Your Honor."

Stella's grip on Henry's hand tightened. Though the prosecutor had presented a solid case against the charlatan, even proving that Linda Hazzard had forged Claire Williamson's name on legal documents and stolen most of her money and valuables, a murder conviction was by no means certain.

The foreman read from a sheet of paper. "We the jury in the case of the State of Washington versus Linda Burfield Hazzard find Mrs. Hazzard guilty"—he paused—"of manslaughter."

The courtroom erupted with whispered indignation.

Manslaughter. Wasn't that a much lesser charge than murder? Stella caught Henry's eye, and he shook his head. His lowered brows confirmed this was not what they'd hoped for.

The judge banged his gavel. "Order. Order in the court."

A hush settled over the room.

"I hereby sentence Linda Burfield Hazzard to two to twenty years' hard labor at the Washington State Penitentiary." He struck his gavel again and left for his chambers.

Two to twenty years? Somehow even the maximum didn't feel like enough for all the anguish Linda Hazzard had caused. When Stella had related her memory of Wendell Church's death, the Hazzards had flatly denied murdering him. Sam had claimed they thought Wendell was a prowler. Said if they'd have known he was a patient, Linda never would have pulled the trigger. Poppycock.

And with Sue's body cremated, police were unable to determine if the cause of death was murder or a fatal ailment as the old Buzzard claimed.

As the prison guard fastened shackles on Linda Burfield Hazzard's wrists, the woman locked eyes with Stella. A cold chill snaked down Stella's spine. So much hate resided in those black pits.

Henry wrapped an arm around her. "Let's go home." He kissed her temple.

"But this isn't how the story is supposed to end." Stella chewed the inside of her cheek. "Where is the justice? This doesn't atone for Claire or Sue or Wendell. It's not fair."

"I know." He pursed his lips. "But God sees. He knows exactly what happened at Starvation Heights, though I have a feeling we don't know the half of it. Let Him take care of the old Buzzard."

Stella allowed Henry to lead her from the courtroom. The tiny diamond in her wedding ring glittered in the sunshine. He was right.

Judgment didn't belong to the state of Washington; God was more than capable of meting out the appropriate punishment.

She took her seat in the automobile, and once Henry eased behind the wheel, she scooted closer to him.

"I've got something for you." He handed her a brown paper package.

She raised a brow. "What's this?" Two odd lumps bulged beneath her fingers.

"Open it and find out."

Unable to fathom what the packet contained, she tore the paper. Her breath hitched. Mama's earrings. She shook the clusters of amethysts into her gloved hand. "Oh, Henry." She met his gaze. "How did you get them back?"

"I asked one of the investigating officers if he'd keep an eye out for them."

She threw her arms around his neck. "Thank you. I thought they were gone forever."

Henry planted both hands on the steering wheel. "You ready to get home to the children?"

"Of course." She linked her arm with his. "I'm looking forward to the little girl arriving next week."

"Me too. Can you imagine losing both parents in two weeks' time?" Henry steered onto the main road. "Poor little mite."

Stella rested a hand on her belly. Should she tell him her secret? They'd vowed to keep nothing hidden after he confessed to writing the letters. "We'll have another arrival in the near future." She rested her head against his shoulder.

"Have you gotten word from Mrs. Bates?" He stared ahead, oblivious to her implications. Such a man.

"No." She bit her lip to contain her smile. "It won't be for several months. We'll have time to prepare."

Henry mashed on the brake. Thank goodness the road was deserted. "You don't mean. . . ?" His eyes met hers, and a grin tilted his mouth.

Stella could only laugh with joy and nod.

"Oh, my darling." He pulled her close and kissed her. "We've been blessed."

They had been blessed. Hope welled within her. Through her most trying time, God had grown her, shown her where she was wrong, then given her bounty beyond her wildest imaginations. Dr. Hazzard's cold glare flashed through her thoughts, but Stella shoved it away. Nothing the woman had done could rob her of this moment. She wouldn't allow it. Besides, Henry was right. God would take care of Linda Burfield Hazzard. It was just another opportunity to stand still and see His hand at work.

Author's Note

Stories like this one give me the chills and, in the words of Anne Shirley, make me "deliciously scared." Somehow, they're more frightening than the old Nickelodeon show Are You Afraid of the Dark? and every Stephen King novel ever written. For me, the element of truth puts the tale of Linda Burfield Hazzard in a league of its own. When the last credit of a psychological thriller movie fades away, I can flick off the light and fall asleep, knowing the story I watched was the product of some screenwriter's imagination.

Not so with Linda Burfield Hazzard.

And though she should have received a much harsher sentence for her crimes, she was released from the state penitentiary in Walla Walla after two years when the governor of Washington granted her a full pardon. Then she and Sam Hazzard, an alcoholic who found his solace in guzzling vanilla extract, moved to New Zealand where she opened a practice. While there, she worked under the titles of dietician, physician, and osteopath. She published another book and made enough money to move back to Olalla and open her dream sanatorium in 1920.

Fortunately, the state of Washington had pulled her medical license, so instead of advertising as a clinic, Hazzard referred to it as a "school of health." Since Dr. Hazzard preferred conducting her own investigations after her patients passed, she built a basement under the new structure that served as an autopsy room. Linda Hazzard continued her starvation techniques, so this room was never empty long.

In 1935, the sanatorium burned to the ground.

Three years later, Linda Burfield Hazzard began to feel unwell. Since critics of her practices dogged her at every turn, she decided to show them just how miraculous fasting could be and started a fast of her own. She died before attaining perfect health. Though it is unknown how many patients she starved to death, twelve is a cautious number. Thirteen if we include Linda Hazzard herself.

Apart from Linda Burfield Hazzard, many of the characters in this story really existed or were based on real people.

Claire and Dora Williamson sought treatment for multiple ailments from Linda Hazzard, and they were assured perfect health if they underwent what Hazzard called her "most beautiful treatment." By the time Claire realized the danger she and her sister were in, she was too weak to walk into Olalla for help. She crawled from Wilderness Heights toward town, clasping a message for Margaret Conway. A little boy found her between the health spa and Olalla and delivered the message to the telegraph office for her. She died soon after.

While visiting family in Australia, Margaret received the telegram. Claire's cryptic message convinced her all was not well in Olalla, and Margaret took the first boat bound for the United States. When she arrived at Wilderness Heights, she was told Claire was dead. She stopped at the Butterworth Funeral Home to view the body, but the person the mortician told her was Claire looked nothing like her.

Dora was so emaciated that she barely looked human. Although Margaret worked to convince her to leave, Dora was determined to stay until her health returned. So Margaret stayed with her and oversaw her care. She tried feeding Dora regular meals, but her charge was weak and had lost the ability to chew solid food. The liquid diet continued until Dora relearned how to eat properly.

Sam Hazzard and Rollie Burfield worked for Linda Hazzard throughout the years. Though Sam was already married when he married Linda and was brought up on charges of bigamy, he remained sporadically faithful to his second wife and helped make her dreams for a fasting clinic a reality.

Her son Rollie, a failed actor, relied on his mother for money. He never amounted to much himself.

Wendell Church's character was based on one of Linda Hazzard's victims, Eugene Stanley Wakelin. He died of a bullet wound to the head on the Hazzards' property. While it couldn't be proved that Linda Hazzard pulled the trigger, it was generally believed she murdered him.

Rumors swirled around Olalla that Linda Hazzard and Butterworth's were in collusion. It was reported that they buried or cremated the bodies of Dr. Hazzard's victims before family members were notified, thus keeping the truth of Hazzard's barbarism from coming to light. None of this could be proven, but the grapevine grew wild with speculation.

If you're interested in trying Linda Hazzard's methods for yourself (I don't recommend it), her book Fasting for the Cure of Disease can be found in natural health stores. It's also available for download on Amazon.